Coming Up Next

PENNY SMITH

HARPER PERENNIAL

London, New York, Toronto, Sydney and New Delhi

Harper Perennial
An imprint of HarperCollins*Publishers*
77–85 Fulham Palace Road, Hammersmith
London W6 8JB

www.harperperennial.co.uk
Visit our authors' blog at www.fifthestate.co.uk

First published by Harper Perennial in 2008
1

A catalogue record for this book is available from the British Library

ISBN 978-0-00-726889-4

Set in Minion

Printed and bound in Great Britain by Clays Ltd, St Ives plc

Mixed Sources

Product group from well-managed
forests and other controlled sources
www.fsc.org Cert no. SW-COC-1806
© 1996 Forest Stewardship Council

FSC is a non-profit international organisation established to promote the
responsible management of the world's forests. Products carrying the FSC
label are independently certified to assure consumers that they come
from forests that are managed to meet the social, economic and
ecological needs of present and future generations.

Find out more about HarperCollins and the environment at
www.harpercollins.co.uk/green

For Mum and Dad, and Mrs Windsor

CHAPTER ONE

In hindsight, the holiday had probably not been a good idea. Two weeks earlier, Katie Fisher had presented the Friday-morning programme, said, 'Thanks for watching,' to a nation in nightwear, and gone to collect her suitcase from the newsroom. Then, an unusual occurrence: she had been called in by the editor. He was normally too busy shouting at his minions to notice the presenters coming and going.

She had stepped breezily into his office and waited for him to say something. It was such a long time coming that, mentally, she started to take his clothes off. Yes, she thought. Unattractive underpants with his skinny little legs hanging out the bottom like spotty Twiglets. Possibly a fat pudenda, lightly sprinkled with ginger hairs. So, I have to make one choice to save the life of my brother. Lick the Twiglets. Or cut off my hand. No, too easy. Lick the Twiglets or …

'Sorry?' she asked.

'I said,' he put his fingers together, 'that the annual research had thrown up some interesting information.'

'Oh?'

'Yes.'

'What?'

'Well ...' He paused.

She got the impression he was enjoying this.

'They seem to be having a few problems with your, erm, allegedly quirky sense of humour.'

'What's that supposed to mean?'

'The viewers – and therefore the advertisers – appear to find your brand of humour unappetizing. Unappealing. Unfunny. Irritating.'

Katie had never been good at concealing what she thought. The viewers could always tell exactly how she felt about the celebrity she was interviewing, or the story she was telling. So Simon could see that she hadn't been expecting what he'd just told her. And, yes, he was enjoying it. He didn't like Katie. She had made it quite obvious that she thought he was repulsive, despite his considerable efforts when he had arrived at the breakfast-television station.

'So, what do you want me to do about the fact that viewers have a problem?'

'Nothing, really. I mean, it's you, isn't it? You're the queen of the lame joke. The princess of puns. Top banana of the never-ending once-upon-a-story. The managing editor suggested I told you, in line with procedure. That's all.'

In line with procedure? What was he talking about? 'Well, thank you,' she had said, after a pause, with a tight smile. 'Thanks very much. In that case I'll have a lovely holiday, shall I? Good. See you in a couple of weeks, then. And I'll go via the humour-bypass surgeon and see if I can check in for a quick one. I've got BUPA, after all.'

On the plane, though, she had spent the entire flight worrying.

No matter which way she cut it, with a vodka and tonic or the next passenger's roll and cheese ('Are you sure you don't mind? Just that I haven't eaten since five this morning ...'), it didn't look good.

The advertisers ruled the airwaves. They wanted mothers with children – they *craved* mothers with children. If they didn't get their mothers with children they were like King Kong after a back-sac-and-crack wax. They were hurt and angry. They wanted to be soothed. Unlike King Kong, they were more articulate. They'd be demanding changes. And while nobody editing or managing a show would fire the presenters just because the advertisers said so, they'd certainly have a quick look at them.

At thirty-five thousand feet, Katie couldn't stop wondering if her career was coming off the rails. Four years of four a.m. starts and going to bed at eight p.m. Four years of relationships crashing on the rocks of her bedtime. And possibly, if she was honest, her bed. She had never used the excuse that she had a headache. There had been no need. The faint snoring usually gave away her terminal tiredness. She would be ready, waiting, willing and able in her rubber nurse's outfit, with a Rabbit vibrator primed and ready to go, but if the foreplay lasted longer than five minutes, the Rabbit was the only thing still buzzing.

She wasn't old, she thought. Strictly, yes, she was middle-aged, if you considered middle age to be halfway through life, but she didn't look old. How she felt was a different matter: more Volvo than Ferrari, more bedsocks than stockings.

Had her jokes gone off?

Or had they only just noticed the smell?

She groaned out loud. Which seemed to upset the man in the aisle seat. She was feeling bloody-minded and did it again, with gusto.

He gave her a look, but no more.

That was the wonderful thing about travelling with the British: in general, they didn't like to make a fuss.

If they sacked her, would she go quietly?

Right, she thought. I'll think about this for half an hour and then I'll enjoy my holiday. Do what Dad says: 'Don't worry about the things you can do something about. Just do something about them. Don't worry about the things you can't do anything about, because you can't do anything about them.'

Having made that decision, she proceeded to get more and more depressed about it. She thought about all the worst things that could happen. They gathered around her, looking worse and worse and worse.

Eventually she checked her watch, flagged down a passing stewardess and ordered the equivalent of an elephant tranquillizer in vodka.

The hangover had lasted two days. But most of the holiday had been wonderful. She had gone to Barbados to stay with some friends in a beautiful house on the west coast. She had rarely seen daylight. Barely eaten a meal.

She had kissed assorted men, none of whom she'd be able now to pick out in a police line-up, and only put on a pound. She could hazily remember an odd incident with a banana. Had she eaten it? Who *was* that bloke? And then she had answered the call on her mobile from her agent.

Jim Break had been brusque and to the point. 'Hi, Katie. I'm not going to beat around the bush. They're not renewing your contract. I understand you spoke to Simon before your holiday ...'

Katie, eight hours away by plane, five hours behind in time, had been about to drink her first coffee of the day. She put down her cup with a shaky hand. So it had happened. Her lovely job – her lovely, well-paid job, which she had worked so hard to get – was an ex-job.

'Katie?'

'I'm still here,' she said.

'We'll have a longer talk when you're back from Barbados,' he said, 'but I do need you to make a decision now, about whether you want to go back on air for the weeks you'd be owed, if you got paid to the end of your contract, or take it as holiday. You don't have to tell me right now, but by the close of today. As in, within the next ... what time is it now? ... three hours. Remind me what time it is there.'

'Ten in the morning.'

'Right. So, if you ring me before lunch?'

'What do you think I should do?'

'Entirely up to you. There are upsides and downsides to whichever option you choose. But they'll announce it on Monday with the name of your successor.'

He could hear her breathing.

'Keera, I assume?' she finally said.

'Yes. Listen, I'll call you later when you've had time to think. Ring me if you need to talk it over.'

She had phoned him ten minutes before the deadline and spent her last few days in Barbados in a haze of rum punch.

The flight home had been a blur. She had avoided eye contact with everyone, apart from the stewardess with the drinks trolley.

Her mouth felt as if she'd been sucking on the lint from a tumble-dryer, and her eyes were as pink as soft-set raspberry jelly when she let herself back into her flat in Chelsea. She put down her bag, opened it and then, on autopilot, began to unpack everything into the laundry basket.

She ought to get on with whatever needed to be done about the job. Was there anything she could do on a Sunday?

She went to the fridge, opened it. Yes, it definitely needed tidying. She put the beers on the left, moved the vodka and white wine to the right. She wiped the mayonnaise bottle and ate the pickled dill cucumbers so that she could throw away the jar. Then she took all the tins out of their cupboard and stacked them according to the size of the vegetables within. She retuned the radio.

She could procrastinate no longer. She pressed play on her answerphone.

It was Jim. 'Call me when you get in. You don't need to go to bed early on Sunday night.' Followed by The Boss. 'Just a brief message, Katie. I'll explain when you ring me. You won't be needed for the show on Monday.'

She stood in the kitchen, staring out of the window at a pair of ladybirds in the first throes of love. I should have gone caravanning in Shropshire to save the five thousand quid I'll be needing for the bloody mortgage, she thought. I should have seen this coming. I should have done something. I should have … Should I have cleaned the windows so that I don't constantly have wildlife fornicating on them?

Bugger Dad's advice on worrying. What the hell was she going to do to pay the mortgage?

CHAPTER TWO

Katie Fisher had been bequeathed two outstanding attributes by her parents: wavy auburn hair (mother) and the ability to talk on any given subject for any amount of time (father). Both had stood her in good stead.

She had done her journalism training the hard way. After college, she had slept with the deputy editor of the local weekly newspaper – he had resembled a tapeworm in a stripy jumper. She had moved fairly quickly to a local daily paper, partly because of the tapeworm's refusal to accept that hanging about with his hook out was not going to rekindle their 'romance'.

A few years later, she had decided it was time to move on. She had performed various lewd acts on a man who had claimed he could get her into radio. Then she had discovered he meant hospital radio. After that, she checked the labels: if they did not display the four cherries in a row, she didn't display her ample charms.

Her move into television had come at some cost to her sofa. But, then, the sofa was what she aspired to. The sofa of *Hello*

Britain! The cost to her own, in reupholstering and stain removal, was a small price to pay for her dream job. She had a beautiful penthouse flat in Chelsea with views over the river, a silver Audi TT and an enormous mortgage. When she had taken it on, she had experienced a moment of panic. But what was the worst that could happen?

She had smiled at that. Her brother had once asked the same thing when they had decided to hit tennis balls for the dog from her bedroom window instead of taking him for a walk. The neighbours had had rather a lot to say on the subject of wrecked greenhouses, and the dog had had to wear a cone round his neck for months to stop him gnawing at the stitches.

She had signed the mortgage document with a flourish, and her years at *Hello Britain!* had ensured that she'd paid off a fair chunk. Nevertheless ...

She lay on the leather sofa and pondered her future. And thought about the reaction of her friends, most of whom would be obviously upset for her, but probably secretly thrilled. Who had said something about it taking a strong man not to see the rise of a friend without thinking it should have been them up there – and not to gloat as that friend fell?

Whoever.

She needed to speak to someone.

Andi. She was in the business yet not. Andi was a producer at Greybeard Television, which made some of the best-known programmes on the box, mostly dramas and serials with style.

'Andi? It's me. I've been sacked.'

'God. Why?'

'Not being funny. Or something. Probably not *just* not being funny. It was sort of intimated before I went on holiday, and when I was on holiday the sharpened axe fell on my sunburned neck. I was given the option of working out the month left on my contract or taking it as holiday. I chose to work it out. Then they came back and said they'd decided otherwise. So I don't even get the chance to say goodbye.'

'Or slag them off?' asked Andi.

'As if I'd commit career suicide like that. My replacement is the wicked witch of the north, Keera Bloody Keethley. I bet she's been putting on that fake poor-Katie face she does so well. It's amazing she can manoeuvre her toothbrush of a morning, she's holding so many knives to plunge into people's backs.'

'You always said you liked her.'

'*Quite* liked her.'

Katie pulled out three eyelashes in a clump. It was a habit that left her with occasional bald spots, but was curiously satisfying. Not top of her list – like tidying. Not up there with sneezing either. But a bloody close third. She selected one and chewed it.

'Katie?'

'Yes – sorry. Just thinking about all those bastards who are going to be *sooooo* happy about this. Colin the news editor for one. He's never liked me – not since I threatened to report him for fondling the barmaid at the Queen's Head and Artichoke. Do you know how hard I worked for that bloody job? All those wankers I had to shag? Not to mention all that training. Law, frigging public administration, shorthand. Talking of which, do you remember Don – with the really short arms and small hands?'

'I don't know. Erm. Local radio?'

'No. Don. The editor of the *Evening News*.'

'Sorry. There have been rather a lot.'

'Thanks for reminding me.'

Don had been short, balding, with a few teeth missing at the back, and a round, hard stomach – from endless business lunches and copious quantities of ale – which he was fond of patting as he said, 'All bought and paid for.'

'Don,' Katie had said, 'you was robbed. Surely you could have got a bigger one for all that money.' She had given him a smile and raised her eyebrows.

That had been all he had needed to leap on her after a drunken lunch just down the road from the newspaper offices. He'd given her a peach of a job, doing fashion and motoring. Noses out of joint all round because of the freebies.

'Anyway. He was the one I nicknamed Mr Horse.'

'Oh, right. The one who liked you to get togged up in jodhpurs and whip him while he whinnied?' She laughed. 'How could I forget him? Didn't you call him "Horse By Name But Not By Nature"?'

'A veritable nub of a knob.' Katie smiled. She looked at her elegant feet propped up on the sofa. Would anyone else give her a job? Once she had been young and thrusting. Now there were so many others – much younger. And still capable of thrusting without the hips squeaking.

'You'll get another, don't worry,' said Andi.

'What? Man?'

'No. Job.'

'Who'll want me after it gets out I've been sacked? There'll be some crap statement about how it was mutual, how I want to spend more time with my microwave, how I'm happy for Keera and wish her all the best, and in ten years' time, I'll be invited on to the forty-eighth *I'm A Nonentity Get Me Out of Here.* I'll be the first to get voted off. And the only way I'll get back on air is if I develop some sort of terminal illness or something. Which, let's face it, would be terminal. And unpleasant.'

She paused. Then: 'Do you think I should disappear?'

'Well, I suppose you could go and bury yourself in Yorkshire for a bit, let your parents take the strain. Would your mum and dad mind you hanging round the house like a depressed weather front, all cloud with occasional periods of heavy rain?'

Suddenly Katie thought that might be exactly what she needed. Dad trying out recipes from his Jamie Oliver cookbook, practising the saxophone to drown out the sound of her mum 'wittering on' to her friends and relations. 'Actually, you're right. Mum's taken up art. I can paint black canvases, slash them and sell them to the Tate Modern. A new career. And I can get fat on Dad's food because it won't matter any more. And eat Jaffa cakes with Mum. And sell the flat and live with them until

I get wrinkly. Talk about how I used to be famous, as I pick hairs out of my chin and dribble egg on my saggy jumper.'

'You'll be fine,' murmured Andi.

Katie thought of her bedroom at the back of the house, looking over the orchard and Dad's vegetable patch-cum-burial ground: three dogs, two rabbits mown down with a rotavator, one inexpertly hibernating tortoise, and a pigeon that had broken its neck by flying into a window.

She put down the phone and burst into tears. She cried as she put the washing on and cried while she was watching television, in the absence of anything more constructive to do.

She ran a bath, put on Richard Strauss's *Four Last Songs* and cried some more. She cried until the bath was cold. She got out and looked in the mirror. A swollen, red-faced, rubbery-lipped thing gazed back at her. With a clump of lashes missing on the right eyelid. 'Oh, yes,' she said with a thick voice. 'No doubt about it. I'll get a job just like that. First sign of madness, talking to yourself,' she added.

'Right,' she said, and opened the medicine cabinet. 'Party time.' She took out the Benylin for throaty coughs. Went upstairs and got the whisky bottle. Put on a CD by Leonard Cohen. Sank into both bottles and further into misery.

Hours later, she woke up. Not an ounce of moisture in her entire body. She had not felt so wretched since Matt Dougal had dumped her when she was sixteen. She had cried non-stop for three days and sworn she would never let anyone dump her again. And she had held to that promise. Any man who had got close, she had split up with as soon as she'd seen signs of waning interest. One had told her he had wanted to knit his soul with hers and had mapped out a future with her in the stars. He had been the most romantic boyfriend ever. She had arrived at his flat one night to be serenaded by a violin and cello duo in the corner of the sitting room. They had tactfully left and he had led her through to his bed, strewn with rose petals. But one day he had said idly that the new girl at work reminded him of Catherine Zeta-Jones. And that had been it. The end. Many years later, he told her he had been planning to propose to her.

Anyway. No man had dumped her since Matt. But now she had been dumped as publicly as it was possible to be. Or she was *about* to be dumped as publicly as it was possible to be.

No point in thinking about that now. She'd be better off trying to get some sleep that didn't involve whisky and Benylin, so that she would look all right if the photographers took shots of her tomorrow.

Tears were leaking again.

She decided to clear out her wardrobes. She cried intermittently as she made an enormous pile of colourful suits in one corner of the room. Her breakfast-television outfits.

The Boss who had employed her to replace the veteran newscaster Beatrice Shah had told her that the viewers wouldn't care if she fucked up her interviews, but they did like to have a nice bright splash of colour in the morning while their kids were throwing the hamster around. 'It's not whether you're good or not. It's how good you *look*. Frankly, we could put a talking gorilla on the sofa as long as it wore nice clothes,' he had said. 'But they're more expensive than humans. Never make the mistake of thinking you're irreplaceable.'

Maybe she had. She'd felt too secure in her work. She knew she'd done a good job. But Keera was younger, prettier ... exotic.

Keera had come to *Hello Britain!* after losing her job as a radio disc jockey in Devon: she had done a raunchy video that had been featured in most of the tabloids. She had got herself an agent, and the management at the breakfast-television station had agreed to her doing a stint as a reporter in a small civil war they hadn't been thinking of sending anyone out to – no one from Britain holidayed there so most people hadn't heard of it. She wouldn't be paid, but she'd get a little bit of air-time. 'Nothing guaranteed, mind you,' The Boss had said.

She had worn tiny little vest tops and combat trousers, which had shown off her lean figure. And a little Tiffany heart necklace ... the station had been swamped with replacements when she lost it.

She had come home to a heroine's welcome and endless pieces in glossy magazines. 'Beauty and the Beast of War'. 'My Heart Remains In Africa'. 'Out of Africa and Into the Top 10' – that was about how she'd become one of the top ten icons of the year. No one ever revealed that her reports had been written for her and faxed over for her to rehearse.

Katie had been supportive when Keera had started at *Hello Britain!* 'You don't need to be a trained journalist to do this job,' she had told her, over coffee at the canteen one morning. 'Obviously it helps. The main thing, though, is to be interested. And as informed as possible.'

In the last few months, she had belatedly recognized the threat Keera posed to her previously unchallenged spot as queen of breakfast television.

Mike, her co-presenter, had told her not to be silly, that she had his unwavering support: 'You know I could never work as well with anyone else. We're like an old married couple, you and I. There'd be an outcry if Minnie Mouse pointed her bony arse at the sofa.' That had been his nickname for Keera ever since she'd squeaked during a live interview when she had mistakenly thought a car backfiring was a sniper.

Katie had laughed, but thought that *he* would have done more than squeak in that situation: he would have had to wash his little white Calvin Klein pants.

She checked her tear ducts. Almost dry. She took two Nurofen, and went to bed.

She woke up at dawn, and managed to wait until six o'clock before phoning her agent.

CHAPTER THREE

Katie had been one of Jim Break's most lucrative clients – he had bought his house in leafy Surrey almost entirely on the back of her groundbreaking *Hello Britain!* deal. Although they had fallen out a few times, they had a genuinely friendly relationship.

While Katie was on holiday, he had been called in for a meeting. He had had an inkling as to what it was about, so had gone in to salvage what was left of her contract. Unless they could prove she had done something immoral, illegal or downright unpleasant, she'd get some cash.

He hated dealing with the management there. Half of them were virtually related – he had felt the need to check surreptitiously that they all had thumbs. He could only assume they had information on someone at the top. How else could you explain the barrel-chested simian Barry Spicer, who was paid a huge salary and had never been seen to do anything but organize his holidays.

Whatever you thought of Katie's presenting skills, she turned up for work five days a week, wrote most of her own scripts, did as much research as she could, and never moaned.

'Hi, Katie,' he said, when she phoned. 'Hold on a second. I'll just take the phone downstairs.' She could hear his girlfriend grumbling about people phoning at this bloody hour of the night. 'Katie? How are you feeling?'

'Oh, fine. Fine. Obviously. Just been sacked. Mortgage to pay. Never felt better. Naturally. How are you?'

'I know. I did try to warn you.'

'When?'

'When I came over six months ago and showed you the audience research I'd got my hands on through an exchange of dirty info.'

'But it said the viewers didn't particularly like anyone, except the newsreader. And the only reason they liked her was that she didn't frighten the horses. About as interesting as a damp flannel. Although at least flannels can germinate something interesting.'

'Yes. But they hated your jokes, which had been getting increasingly bizarre.'

'Not bizarre. Just silly.'

'And you, of course, are so clever you've been out-manoeuvred by Keera.'

'Was it Keera who stuffed me, then?'

'That's what I've heard. She's been very quietly having conversations with the people upstairs about where she's going to go now that she's such hot property. She's got a publicity agent.'

'You told me I never needed one.'

He ignored that. 'And the publicity agent's been busy sowing all those trumped-up stories about megabucks being offered by NBC, ABC, ITN, the BBC, et cetera, et cetera. Plus, let's face it, she looks bloody gorgeous in a swimsuit and those wet photos in *Loaded* can't have done her any harm. Particularly since the soaking was in the name of rescuing refugees from that African country that's permanently on the verge of starvation.'

'They said in *Private Eye* she did those pictures in southern Spain.'

'Exactly. She's canny.'

There was a long silence.

'Well, what do I do now?'

'We say that it was your decision to leave. That you're pursuing other projects. You've had enough of getting up at a ridiculous time in the morning. You're thankful for the experience, blah-blah-blah, and that you wish Keera every success with one of the best jobs in television.'

'And then what do I do?'

'You lie low until we get you another job.'

Jim ended the phone conversation and went back to bed.

'Who was that?' asked his girlfriend.

'Katie Fisher.'

'Oh, right. She in a state?'

'She sounded all right. Pissed off. But she's level headed. I suspect she'll go to ground for a bit. Hopefully, we can sort something out pretty quickly. Although at the moment there's nothing around that's even remotely in her ballpark.'

Had he seen Katie at that moment, he wouldn't have felt quite so sanguine. She had looked over the Cliff of the Television Career and seen the River of Smiling Through Gritted Teeth running down to the Sea of Z-list Parties and the Desert of Invitations. And had set about what was left of the bottle of whisky. Who gives a toss what time it is? she thought. I'm on Barbados time and the sun is so far over the yardarm there it's almost … oh … last night. Who cares? I can have as many lie-downs, lie-ins, or whatever, as I want from now until I die alone in a shed and get eaten by cats.

Was there anyone she should be phoning? Her fuzzy brain sorted through the Rolodex of Very Important People, Important People and Other People.

People. What a weird word. Pee-pull. Pull-pee. Imp-potent pee-pull.

She closed her eyes.

'To sleep. Perchance to dream.' What a weird word. Perchance. Perch-aunts. Puh.

She woke up a few hours later, suddenly aware that the answerphone was going mad. She turned over on the sofa, feeling woozy and peculiar. She had twenty-four messages. The news was obviously out.

She would stay in.

The intercom buzzed. Katie went to pick up its phone, chewing her lip. 'Yes,' she said gruffly.

'Katie Fisher?'

'Sorry, she's still on holiday.'

'When will she be back?'

'I don't know. She may be out of the country for a while.'

'Are you a friend?'

'House-sitting. Must go. I've got a … got a – got a lithp,' she said limply. She hung up.

So, the press had wasted no time. They were outside her front door. At least one of them, anyway. Wanting to see her depressed and miserable having been booted off the sofa to make way for a younger woman the size and shape of a whippet.

She felt wretched and ugly.

She drank one and a half litres of water and ate some chocolate Brazils she'd found at the back of a cupboard, left over from Christmas. She did three sit-ups and phoned Jim.

'Jim Break.'

'It's Katie again.'

'I assume you've heard my message that they've released a statement?'

'I've got twenty-four calls on my phone that I've no intention of listening to at this stage. Where did you say my career was going from here?'

'I told them what we'd agreed. Other projects. When they asked what they were I said there were a number in the pipeline and that we couldn't discuss them until they were further along the production route.'

'So, basically they know I've got nothing to go to?'

'Katie, if you'd listened to me instead of becoming more and more convinced of your own unassailable position, we wouldn't be in this position now,' he said acerbically. 'I warned you that you were on dodgy ground. That even The Boss told me you needed to sort out the jokes. That you were going to have to do more publicity, get yourself in the papers, generate a buzz. But you decided you were going to keep your job by being good at your interviews. Like, who gives a flying fox that you managed to stitch up the home secretary with his general amnesty for thieves or whatever the hell it was? Who gives two shakes of a limp knob whether you can hold your own with some two-bit actor or comedian? You're too clever by half. And there's Mike, who's handsome, well turned out –'

'Uncultured.'

'*They don't care.* He comes across as nice. His jokes may not be particularly funny either, but at least they understand them. Yours are sometimes so far off the planet they're nearing the heliosphere and heading towards the last-known solar system in the universe. I told you you needed to get more real. Take a leaf out of Mike's book and sound shocked that anyone could pay more than twenty quid for a pair of shoes, that you couldn't imagine anything more boring than reading a book, that your idea of a good night in is watching back-to-back soaps, while eating chicken curry and a packet of Penguins. But no.

You'd talk about your opera, your books, your obscure European cinema – and you kept on with the jokes, like that one about Nietzsche.'

'Finding my own Nietzsche in the philosophy world. I still think that's good.'

'It's not. It wasn't. You're supposed to be talking to women with children. Women who have got twenty pence and a bag of sprouts to last them till the end of the week.'

'Well, the advertisers wouldn't want them, then.'

'You know what I mean.'

There was silence.

'Incidentally, Mike's been very supportive, according to my inside sources. He's apparently been saying you're a great presenter and he wants you to stay on the sofa. But The Boss – and the chairman – want you off it. Have you been out of the front door yet?'

'No – there are reporters there. And, I assume, photographers. No idea how many are out there. How big do you think this story is?'

'Sadly, no mass deaths anywhere at the moment, no politicians shagging their secretaries, no celebrity marriages on the rocks. It's a slow Monday on a damp spring day. Could be page five. Could be front page, if nothing happens between now and ten o'clock tonight. Do you want me to come over?'

'No. I'm going to have to deal with it at some stage.'

She phoned her mum and dad and left a message telling them that under no circumstances were they to talk to anyone they didn't know, about anything. She phoned her brother, Ben, and told him the same thing.

'Can I speak to my patients?' he asked, *faux*-serious.

'No. Anyway, no doctor speaks to his patients,' she said.

He laughed. 'So, you OK?' he asked.

'How would you feel if they told you you'd been replaced by a performing monkey because it looked good in a stethoscope?'

'Keera's hardly a performing monkey.'

'Yeah, right. She's got bags of presenting experience and is a bundle of laughs.'

'Viewers don't necessarily want funny women, Katie. *I* think it's great. Wakes my brain up in the morning. I like the one you did about "Time flies like an arrow. Fruit flies like a banana." I've been using it on some of my mates. But, you know, there are people out there who prefer Mike's gentle humour. Easy, self-deprecating. He doesn't talk about anything complicated or use long words.'

'That's because he doesn't know any. And thanks for being so supportive.'

'Well, I am. But I think you're better than that bollocks anyway. I only watch it to check whether you're still living.'

'You should see me today. Barely breathing.'

'Do you need me to come over and check your pulse?'

'Thank you, Doctor, but I think I can manage that.'

Ben had made her feel slightly better. Maybe she should get out of the flat. She checked in the mirror.

No, she should most certainly not go out – or, at least, not looking like that.

The intercom buzzed again.

'Yes,' she answered, in the gruff voice she'd used earlier.

'Is Katie Fisher there?'

'No.'

'Can you tell me when she'll be back.'

'No. I'm the house-sitter – sitting in the house until she gets back.'

'Which is when?'

'No idea.'

She hung up.

The intercom buzzed yet again. She ignored it, and decided she had been idiotic. How was she going to go out of the flat for photographs, now that she had said she wasn't in?

'Moron,' she berated herself.

Did it matter? Yes. Some reporter would make a big thing of how she had 'lain low, pretending to be out ... dah-dah-dah.'

She searched through the fridge. No, still nothing but beer and vodka. She took the vodka and lay on the sofa to watch television, her mobile phone on vibrate. She might as well get some enjoyment out of this hideousness.

The home phone rang. Then again. And again.

She wondered how many messages the answerphone would take before it conked out.

CHAPTER FOUR

That Monday morning, *Hello Britain!* was abuzz. Katie Fisher had been replaced by Keera Keethley. Nobody could quite believe it. There had been rumours, of course, but any news-room with more than two journalists in it was awash with them.

Most of the women were not fans of Keera. Katie might have got to the top through 'hard grind', as she was fond of saying, but she was also a good journalist. And *they* found her hilari-ous, even if the bosses didn't.

Keera wasn't funny. She was desperately ambitious. She was ingratiating. She was political with a small *p* but had a large ego. She was very good with men. She didn't care what anyone thought of her journalistic skills because it didn't matter. You asked questions. Full stop. End of story. Not difficult. No, she wanted to be thought of as pretty and sexy. And famous.

The men in charge, who had seen her lithe body, didn't mind that her interviews were often tedious and that she was more interested in making sure her long, shiny black hair was in tip-top condition than whether she asked the right questions. Or that she overran virtually every live report she had ever done, which meant that the producers had to cancel interviewees who had spent a day, sometimes, travelling to London to have their three minutes in the sun. There were few producers who had not had to do The Grovel. 'I'm *so* sorry, but unforeseen circumstances … Of course you'll be recompensed for your time … Last-minute breaking story …'

And Keera was always in the editor's office. Bringing him little gifts.

Katie had once quoted a line from *A Midsummer Night's Dream* to Dee, the weather presenter. 'Tempting him with knacks, trifles, nosegays, sweetmeats …' Now she was the ass. Keera had planned this moment since her last year at school, had laid out her ten-year plan – had decided she wanted to be on the famous breakfast-time sofa.

And here she was. Her first day when she wasn't a stand-in. Her first day when she had the status she deserved.

She surveyed the newsroom from her new position and found she liked it. It was quite small, considering the three and a half hours that had to be filled. There were the researchers and producers, the VT editors flitting through. A camera crew waiting to film a minister who would be coming into the building at seven a.m. One of the executive producers outputting the show looked up from typing to ask a younger man whether the SOT – sound on tape – was done, the VT (videotape) ready, and the graphics sorted on the story he was checking. The guy nodded and went back to his phone conversation with a reporter out in the field.

Keera went to sit at the computer and look through the links and interviews she would be doing that morning. Her first morning. The first morning of the rest of her life. She was going to make this work. It was her right.

She accepted the congratulations of Kent, a producer on her first show. 'Nice to be working with you again,' he said. Sincerely. Kent was one of the producers whose heart had *not* sunk when he heard the news. He thought Keera was one of the most stunning women he had ever met. She had been discreetly keeping him up to date with all of the offers she'd been getting.

'God knows how they keep getting into the press,' she had said to him one morning in the canteen. 'This place is like a leaky boat.'

'Well, it absolutely wasn't me,' he had said, horrified.

'No, no. I'm sure it wasn't, silly.'

'You know you can depend on my discretion,' he had said, handing over the money for two coffees.

'I know I can,' she had said, and given him the most delicious smile.

He wasn't to know that he was the man she had decided to blame if any of the stories she had planted resulted in fingers pointed at her.

She had already commented on the veritable confetti trail of stories to the news editor. 'Who on earth could it be, do you think?' she had asked, a little crease between her beautifully arched eyebrows. 'It's quite dreadful, isn't it? I mean, it's not just that so many of the stories about me are wrong, but it's not nice that they seem to involve not very kind things about others. I assume these people just think of the cash – they don't care about the damage to the station ...'

Mike also came in early on Keera's first day – The Boss's suggestion on Friday morning. Normally he barely made it to air. He never read the links because he ad-libbed most of them, some so poorly that they were virtually incomprehensible. But people liked his bumbling delivery, and he had discovered early on that as long as you laughed about your mistakes, everyone laughed with you and forgave you pretty much anything. Although God save anyone else who might mention *his* shortcomings.

Dee had once suggested laughingly that he might like to read a book without pictures in it after he had said on air that books were a waste of time. He had smiled rather oddly, and tripped her up later by asking if there were any damp patches that morning – a pointed reference to her disastrous one-night stand the week before. The man involved had immediately sold the story to a newspaper, revealing that Dee was obsessed with the cellulite on her bottom and had sent a fan letter to a member of Take That. The papers had used the opportunity to go over the old ground of her divorcing her husband after his long fling with the au pair.

Dee walked through the newsroom and noted the little knot of people circling round Keera. All the usual suspects, she thought. The editor, Simon, was in early too. He was virtually resting his tongue in her ear. Disgusting. And the director, Grant – the biggest creep of them all. The buttering-up process with some presenters could have taken a whole lorryload of Lurpak. And there was Kent with his gormless smile. Yurk.

She kept out of everyone's way as the programme went to air, going into the studio only when it was time for her to point out the fluffy bits sweeping in from the west.

It seemed that the gallery, the nerve centre of the programme, contained more than its normal quota of people. The director had to keep telling everyone to pipe down – noticeably Heather, who was nursemaiding Keera through the show. The Boss had told her to devote herself to Keera. Heather liked Keera because she liked her job as an executive producer. If The Boss said Keera was to be dressed as a hedge, Heather would ask how high. If The Boss told Heather to hang upside-down and act like a bat, Heather would be squeaking like a pipistrelle before you could say vampire. Heather was long, lanky and grateful to have been given a second chance after a libel case that had almost stymied her career.

Keera began an interview with a man from a water company who was trying to defend the company's appalling record on fixing leaking pipes.

Heather leaned forward and spoke quietly into the microphone on the desk: 'Keera, ask him how come more of the profits go to shareholders than they do to fixing leaks.'

She dutifully put the question, then another one about whether the water that flushed the loo was the same as the water that came out of the tap.

Those in the gallery glanced at each other in confusion.

Heather got back on the microphone: 'Keera, ask him when the company plans to fix the old Victorian pipes instead of just talking about it. They've had years to sort it out.'

And Keera could be heard asking exactly that – with a supplementary of her own about what the pipes were made of.

The bosses were thrilled.

Keera looked perfect: shiny black hair, tight little pink suit with a hint of cleavage and the highest stiletto heels this side of a massage parlour. Glimpsed, occasionally, in a cross-shot.

After the programme, as the backslapping began, Dee tried calling Katie again. She had already left five messages on her friend's answerphone, asking if she wanted company. On a whim, she decided to go round to the flat.

She rang the doorbell at the white stuccoed building, and suddenly noticed that, considering it was eleven o'clock in the morning, there were rather a lot people hanging about near lamp-posts, behind wheelie-bins and in cars. As she took her finger off the bell, they shouted questions at her about Katie and where she was. She said nothing, but scooted round the corner and took refuge in the porch of a block of mansion flats. Well, that'll be why she hasn't answered the phone, then, she thought. And possibly why she didn't answer the intercom. Which poses a problem.

She phoned Katie for the nth time and was surprised to get an answer. 'Thank God,' she said. 'I was beginning to wonder how I was going to get hold of you. Don't you ever answer your phone?'

'Sorry. It's been on vibrate. I've got to the stage where I don't even bother to look at who's calling. You caught me between programmes.'

'How are you? Whoops. Silly question. Can't be feeling exactly wonderful.'

'You ain't wrong,' said Katie, 'and I now look how I feel. I think I may have overdone it on the vodka front. And I'm stuck here until I come back from holiday.'

'What?'

'I rather stupidly said I was the house-sitter. I can't work out how to get out of here without looking like a right twat.'

A delivery man asked Dee to move so he could get a parcel to the basement flat.

'Hey,' she said, 'I've got an idea.'

A few hours later, a pizza delivery-boy rang the flat below Katie's, accidentally pressing her buzzer at the same time. Katie let him in.

A few moments later, Dee appeared at her door with a beaming smile, a motorbike helmet in one hand and a delivery bag in the other. 'Howzat?' she asked.

'Brilliant,' said Katie, stuffing a few items into the delivery bag. Pyjama pizza and large tube of toothpaste to go . . .

Outside, the reporters and photographers were still keeping an eagle eye out for Katie Fisher. They had had information that she had definitely returned on a Virgin flight from Barbados. She might have gone elsewhere, knowing that there would be interest in the story of her demise as sofa queen. Phone calls to her parents and brother had turned up nothing, and they were now in limbo. Most were hoping to be allocated a different story. Even if she came home, she probably wouldn't say anything, and they'd just get shots of her letting herself into the flat.

They had perked up as the delivery-boy had rung the buzzer – but the snappers with their long lenses had told them it was the flat below. They didn't spot that the delivery-boy who had just left appeared to have grown about six inches.

Katie popped on to the scooter and let it roll down the hill without turning it on. That she had no idea how to ride it had almost scuppered her and Dee, until they had come up with the idea of getting it to the end of the road where a strategic corner meant she could hop off and wheel it to the pizza joint.

Within an hour of leaving her flat, she was on her way home to Yorkshire with her brother, and Dee had phoned gleefully to tell her that she had left the building to a cacophony of camera shutters and shouted questions, all of which she had ignored.

'How long are you going to stay with your mum and dad?' she asked.

'Until I can keep a smile on my face without it falling into Dad's soup. It's chestnut and prune today, apparently. He's being creative. I think I just need to shout a bit, and use my body as a repository for pies. Thanks for all your help.'

Ben had managed to swap his shift with a fellow doctor at the hospital, in response to her emergency call for help in getting home. She couldn't face the train. And anyway, someone might alert the media.

He was looking rather handsome, she thought, like someone out of *Young Doctors*, wearing jeans and a pale blue T-shirt with a pink logo. 'Is that some smutty reference?' she had queried, looking at the logo, '"Potting the Pinks".'

'No idea. Is it? I thought it was about geraniums. I bought it at a gardening shop. Or was it a gay shop? Anyway, what could it possibly mean?'

She smirked at him.

'I'm sure it's pure filth. We'll ask Mum. She's bound to know.'

She had rarely been so happy to see him as she had when he pulled up beside her outside the pizza joint and drove her away from its cheesy wafts.

As they headed north on the A1, and London slipped away behind them, she noticed that the daffodils were out. Lambs were gambolling. Did they go to Gambollers Anonymous? Easy to get fleeced. Shorn of money.

Was that the sort of thing that got me sacked? She dozed off.

Ben looked over at his sister as she lolled beside him with her auburn hair tied scruffily back at the nape of her neck.

She looked drawn and a bit blotchy. And smelled very slightly of pizza.

CHAPTER FIVE

Ben had phoned ahead to alert the parents to their imminent arrival. His father said he would immediately get on to it, which Ben took to mean that there would be more than just the afore-mentioned soup. His mother had merely said, rather vacantly, 'Who?'

He skidded up the drive in a shower of gravel, undid both their seatbelts and went round to open the door for his sister, not from chivalry but for the joy of watching her fall out since she was still asleep.

'Thanks *very* much,' she mumbled, as she untangled herself from the seatbelt and put on her shoes.

'No, no. Thank *you*,' said Ben. 'You were such an entertaining passenger to have on a long trip. The mistress of quick-fire wit and repartee.'

'Well, sorry. I was a bit knackered.'

'And it'll take weeks to get rid of the smell of pizza.'

'You were lucky it wasn't extra anchovies.'

'Oh. It smelled like it *was*.'

'Beast.' She laughed. 'Wonder what's for dinner, talking about delicious-smelling things.'

The house was grey stone with pillars at the front porch – a legacy from the mill owner who had felt they befitted his status. Their mother had wanted some sort of creeper growing up them, but their father had vetoed it, saying he would have to deal with the extra spiders and the work involved in pruning and general tidying.

It was their father, wearing the full chef's outfit of checked trousers and a white jacket, who let them in. 'Present from myself for my birthday,' he said. 'She', he nodded in the general direction of the sitting room, 'forgot. As usual. Now that she's on her way to becoming the new Matisse, she's far too busy to notice that that I've turned pensioner. I've started calling the paints cads. As in cadmium. The colour?' he said to Katie, giving her a hug.

'It's OK, Dad. I got it. Utter cads. You know you never have to explain them to me. Maybe to your thicko son, though.'

'Anyway,' he said, brightening, 'we've got the soup, followed by sea bream baked in coconut milk, yellow chillies, lemon grass and fresh lime leaves, then Moroccan rice pudding with pistachios and rose petals. Only I couldn't find any pistachios, so I've had to use almonds instead. It was either that or peanuts. It almost wasn't anything, mind you. Hercules had his nose inches from the bowl when I popped back into the kitchen to make sure everything was ready. Bloody dog.' He looked at her questioningly. 'You all right?'

'I'll tell you later, Dad. I'll go and put the bag upstairs.'

Katie went up to her old bedroom – now a testament to her mother's ex-loves. Full of abandoned items from spent passions. It was a beautiful big room with a large window that looked out on to the slightly distracted garden. It had felt spacious when she had lived in it. She had never been much of a collector and preferred being able to lie on the carpet with lots of space round her to make cardboard boxes into everything from spacecraft to ships. She had also liked to write fairy stories – endless fairy stories that had handsome princes, beautiful princesses, lots of danger and invariably death as she'd sought ways to bring them to a conclusion. So much easier to say, 'And then the spectres ate them up and put their skeletons on display,' than be bothered with more plot when it was time for dinner.

Now, though, the room was stuffed with bits of tapestry, a defunct potter's wheel, a Workmate, half-made cushions and a badly stuffed badger.

In the kitchen, she challenged her mother about the badger. 'You must have forgotten to tell me you were getting into animals,' she said. 'Otherwise I'd have nipped to the Tower of London and brought you a flock of ravens.'

'It's an "unkindness" of ravens, I think you'll find,' replied her mother, wiping paint-stained hands on a cream smock. 'And the badger was thumped into by your father two months ago. Made a very large dent in the car's radiator. I thought it was a waste of an animal so I took it to the taxidermist. I told him not to bother too much – I just wanted to see how I felt with stuffed animals. And I've had second thoughts. I think your father would prefer to keep putting them in pies.' She nodded sourly at her husband as he checked his soup.

'And, Mum,' said Katie, with a smirk, 'that's a nice top.'

'Sod off,' said her mother, smoothing it down. 'I discovered it in an Oxfam shop the other day. Perfect for a budding Turner Prize winner, I thought. And it flatters my arse. Talking of which, what's this about being sacked?'

'Thanks, Mum. Not exactly sacked, more replaced by an upstart who just happens to be younger and prettier. And, talking of arses, has no doubt licked a number to steal my job. Scheming little witch called Keera Keethley. Should have known she was up to something. She was always in The Boss's office. She'd have fluttered her breasts and stuck out her eyelashes – he'd never have been able to resist.'

'Odd-looking woman, then,' commented Ben, as he opened a bottle of wine. 'Must get her to come to the hospital and see if I can't get her into the *British Medical Journal*.'

'You know what I mean,' Katie said. 'Anyway, here I am. Trying to escape from the press, so that the story dies away and I can sink into oblivion.' She ended on a happy smile, then burst into tears.

Her dad hugged her and patted her shoulder. Her mother muttered something about turps and left the room. And Ben drank his wine, apparently unable to think of anything constructive to do or say.

As Katie showed no sign of stopping, her father took her to the sitting room and put her in front of the television. He went back into the kitchen. 'Daytime television's a Godsend, isn't it?' he said to his son.

'Couldn't do without it,' said Ben. 'I only passed my exams by watching hospital dramas.'

'Actually, since we got the satellite dish, I can watch some really interesting stuff while I'm waiting for my peppercorns to soak,' his father added robustly. 'Soooo,' he said, after Ben had refilled his glass, 'what say you to a fish?'

'I say yes please to a fish.'

'And I say yes please to a glass of wine, which you haven't offered me yet,' shouted Katie, from the sofa. 'A schooner of alcohol to take away the pain of watching this shite on the telly.'

A few hours later, Katie had finished what was left of the bottle, had downed another, and was still crying. Her family decided to take the dog for his evening stroll and leave her to watch *How Green Is My Valley*, a makeover show involving whole villages doing up everything from their houses to their rabbit hutches.

The dinner had been delicious, only moderately ruined by the occasional sniff from Katie's corner.

'Oh, enough now,' said her mother brusquely, as Katie blew her nose over the broccoli. 'I know it's a bit bloody, but there are worse things that can happen. As your brother will testify.'

'Oh, yes,' Ben perked up, who'd only just stopped crying himself after eating a hot chilli. 'Let me tell you about the bloke who came into A and E with his dick stuck up the end of a vacuum-cleaner.'

'Do you mind if we don't?' asked his mother.

By the time Ben had finished his story, even Katie had raised a watery smile. In fact, she was finding that the red wine helped quite a lot and, with a muttered, 'Is it OK?' opened another bottle.

They decamped to the sitting room and sat in front of the television to ruminate. Katie drank her way steadily through the Merlot until the late-night news began. Ben made the by-now-habitual comment about the well-known newsreader putting the emph-ARSE-is on the wrong syll-ARB-les, and their mother pressed the off button. 'Time for bed, I think?' she said pointedly to her daughter.

Katie had about two hours of blissful drunken sleep before the quest for water sent her to the kitchen. The dog turned in his basket, farted, then went back to twitching and worrying about next door's ferret.

Katie returned to bed.

Got up again.

Went to the bathroom.

Went downstairs for more water.

Went back to bed.

Then decided that what she really, really wanted was more wine.

She opened the cupboard and perused the contents. 1986. Was that a good year? Château Lagune. Definitely something that shouldn't be drunk alone. Methylated spirits? Oh, that must have been Mum. She squinted. A Spanish Rioja squinted back.

She poured a large glass, went into the sitting room and turned the television on low. Rock Hudson hove into view in a black-and-white film involving doctors and nurses. He nudged another male doctor and said, *sotto voce,* 'She's the one I want.'

Katie giggled. 'No, she's not. He wants you,' she whispered at the screen.

She didn't remember seeing the end of the film – or the end of the bottle – when she was woken by the dog, giving her a wet patch. 'Erk,' she said experimentally. Her mouth tasted disgusting. I wonder if this is what my kidneys would taste like if they were marinated.

In the bathroom mirror, she viewed the cushion crease on her face, which resembled a fresh scar, and prodded a spot that had arrived on her cheek. Must've taken the overnight bus, the bastard, she thought, which is what I'll be doing soon, now that I haven't got a job.

Tears welled.

Ben walked in wearing his boxer shorts, his hair looking like it had been licked by the morning gorilla. 'Oh, God ... Bit early for that already,' he said, as he yawned and scratched and reached for the toothpaste.

'I wasn't crying. I yawned too big and made my eyes water,' said Katie, stalking out of the bathroom.

A little later, Ben headed off for the journey back to London and work.

Her mother flitted about with unhelpful suggestions. 'You could always go back to writing for a local newspaper,' she said at one point.

Katie rolled her eyes. 'For God's sake, Mum, I've come a bit further than that. That's like telling you you could go back to painting by numbers. Or Dad that he should try making coconut pyramids.'

'I *love* coconut pyramids,' announced her father, as he flicked through his mountain of cookery books to see what he fancied making for dinner. 'Anyway, you don't have to do anything for a while, do you? You must have got some money stashed away. Why don't you give yourself a month off and then make a decision? You could even stay here while you do it ...' He noticed his wife's expression. '... for a couple of weeks,' he finished lamely.

Katie shot her mother a look. 'Thanks, Dad. And if you don't mind, Mum, I *will* stay for a few *days*, then go back to the flat. No point in eating you out of house and home, eh?'

'Or drinking us out of house and home,' said her mother, who had not seen quite so many bottles for a family dinner since her daughter had last come to stay for a weekend.

The next day, Katie mooched round the house.

The day after, she woke up to find the house surrounded. 'Sorry,' she said to her mum and dad at a crisis meeting round the kitchen table. 'I thought they'd have given up. After all, it's not *that* much of a story. Must be a slow news day. To talk or not to talk, that is the question.'

'And answer came there none,' added her father. 'And that was hardly odd because they'd eaten every one.' *Alice in Wonderland* had been a favourite bedtime story and was often quoted inappropriately.

Katie sucked her bottom lip, then her top lip, then both of them together. Then made a decision.

'I'm going to phone my agent,' she told her parents, 'who will no doubt recommend that I go out and tell them I have nothing to say on the matter, although I wish Keera well in one of the best jobs in television. Then I'll say I have a number of projects in the pipeline, which can't be discussed at the moment because, as we know, I have bugger-all. No, Mum. Obviously I won't say that.'

'How are you?' Jim asked.

'Been better. How are things there?'

'We've been fending them off. Saying you've been having meetings with various people to discuss your new projects. Too hush-hush to talk about at the moment, obviously.'

'Same old rubbish that old has-beens always spout, eh?' said Katie.

'You're not a has-been. You're a coming-round-again. A born-again presenter.'

'A BAP – a sort of BAP that's the last on the shelf.'

'Stop it.'

'Anyway, I was hoping to have a week or two to compost here in Yorkshire, and not say anything about those toads at work.

Sadly, the press studs are on the gravel, hoping to tempt me out, and I'm thinking of getting the support of the blond and gorgeous Hercules and my Victoria's Secret bra.'

'You think the dog's a good idea?'

'You think the bra's a good idea?'

Jim laughed. 'Well, you sound like you're going to be OK.'

'Thanks. But, let's face it, we both know there are lots of women out there who can do the job and who aren't on the slippery slope to fifty. I knew I should have had a penis implant.'

'You still can. I'm sure I have a number here …'

'Very funny. I'm off to put on a face, a bra and a dog.'

'Just remember to put them where they're supposed to go.'

'Thank goodness you reminded me. I was just about to adjust my la-bra-dor straps. 'Bye.'

It took her an hour to get ready, mostly because her escape from London had involved no luggage and she had to root through the detritus of her past in the wardrobe in her bedroom. Luckily, the eighties were coming back in …

Her dad was chatting to the reporters and had given them cups of tea and coffee, telling them she was on her way back from a walk. Peering out from behind her bedroom curtains, Katie smiled. He was in his element, holding court, being witty and erudite.

She took one last look at herself in the mirror, put on a bit more lip-gloss and went downstairs. 'How do I look?' she asked, as she stood poised in the hall, with Hercules gazing up at her expectantly.

'Nice dog,' said her dad.

'Thanks.' She smiled. 'I always like to have a handy Lab coat when there's an emergency operation.'

'Good luck,' said her mum, as she opened the front door. 'I quite fancy the one from the *Daily Mail*. He smells lovely.'

The *Daily Mail* ran the worst article. 'Katie Fishes Bottom of the Barrel' was the headline on page three. The best was in the *Sun*. 'The Dogs of War – Katie Fights Back'.

'Hercules looks good,' said her mother, as she peered over her daughter's shoulder, and burnt the toast.

The papers had been pored over at *Hello Britain!* since the first editions had dropped at eleven the night before. Keera had tried hard not to look smug and ended up looking smug and arch at the same time. Mike had harrumphed and said he wasn't reading the rags until he'd finished the show. 'Nice dog,' was his only comment.

Richard, the day's producer, said under his breath, 'Unlike you.'

The show that day had sparkled as Mike and Keera seemed to have decided they needed to prove something. Off-screen, though, they had been demanding. Mike had complained about every script and was throwing papers on the floor, describing them as 'absolute shit'.

Richard was in the gallery, sitting next to the director and the director's assistant, listening to the tirade and rolling his eyes.

Eventually he had had enough. He leaned forward, opened the button to connect the microphone to Mike's earpiece and said, 'If you think they're so shit, why don't you get in a little earlier and rewrite them, instead of turning up five minutes before you need to go to Makeup and shouting about them now?' Richard could tell from Mike's face that he'd be for it later, but what the hell? He was fed up with being shouted at by an egotistical wanker – even if he was one of the best presenters around. There was no need to do all that posturing in front of everyone else: he could easily have had a word in private but, no, he liked to get out there and puff up his toady chest even more than it was puffed up already.

And as for Keera! That damn stupid question she'd put to his reporter – who, even now, was getting it in the neck from the smitten editor. 'Why is anorexia so popular?' she had asked.

Judith, the reporter, had winced and said, 'I don't think "popular" is the word I'd use.' Afterwards, she had got on to the squawk box and instructed Richard to tell her not to use that word the next time they did the Q and A.

'I'll speak to her,' Richard had said.

When they'd done the interview again an hour later, the bloody woman had gone and said the same word. Just to make a point.

'If only she had a mere shaving of the intelligence she feels she has,' muttered Richard, as he gazed at the beautiful profile of his female talent. Richard had been a big fan of Katie. The weeks that Keera had stood in while she was off had felt like months to him. He had been stunned to hear she was Katie's permanent replacement. It meant a lot more work for him: not only did he have to write the links and pussyfoot around Mike's gigantic ego, he had to *explain* the links and pussyfoot around the minefield of dealing with Keera.

She was in with so many people. She'd go straight to The Boss and tearfully tell him they'd been getting at her. Next thing you know, he'd be defending his use of the word 'twat'. Even though 'complete twat' would have been more appropriate.

He watched her on air now, flirting indecently with a member of a boy band. If she crossed her legs in that Kenny Everett manner once more, he thought, the boy closest to her was going to stop talking. Poor sod didn't know where to look, with her flashing her knickers like that.

She was having the time of her life, sitting on the sofa that should have been occupied by Katie – a woman who could hold her own in a political interview, who could coax the best out of a difficult interviewee, who would never have asked why anorexia was *popular* – as though it was football or dog racing.

Mike and Keera signed off the show, Keera doing her little wave and a giggle – one of the newspapers had commented on it and she had now decided it was her 'signature pay-off'.

Ten minutes later, he arrived at the morning meeting where a post-mortem was being held. Keera had sent her apologies: she had a photo shoot for *OK!* magazine and they wanted to get her straight after the programme to talk about her marvellous new job.

The editor was swinging on his chair and looking casually out of the window as the rest of the group responsible for putting out the show waited silently for Richard's arrival.

'Richard,' said the editor, pushing his fringe to one side, 'the scripts today were a disgrace.'

Richard shot Mike a filthy look. Mike stared back innocently. 'No worse than normal, I thought.'

'No worse than normal? Well, bloody pull your finger out. For fuck's sake, this is supposed to be the premier breakfast station in the land, and we have scripts that are no worse than normal?'

'I was taking the piss. Which particular scripts are you talking about? Take me through one and I'll attempt to defend it.'

'Show me one that was good and I'll allow you to.'

The two men faced each other.

There was a silence, then Richard finally said, 'Well, shall we get on with the rest of it?'

'I want a word with you later about dealing with the talent, too,' said Simon.

'Great. Something to look forward to.'

It was ten o'clock in the morning. Richard had done his twelve-hour shift and was wondering if they were going to feel more and more like twenty-four hour-shifts now that he had lost the one person who had made the exceptionally long nights a little less gruelling. He used to drive home, but he'd been so knackered one morning that he'd dropped off at the wheel and disappeared down a hole in the road. He was lucky he'd not taken out two of the workmen – fortunately they had decided to brew up and were sitting on a low wall a few feet from the scene. Now he took the tube. If he slept, he'd wake up at Ealing Broadway and could take a cab back to Acton.

He was on his way down the steps at the station, when his mobile rang. It was Katie. 'Hello. Can you speak?'

'I'll be on the tube in a moment. How are you?'

'Getting over it, I think. Still can't quite believe it, obviously. It feels weird not to see the sunrise every day. But I miss you – well, you and the others I got on with. I don't miss the awful bear-baiting in the morning meeting. Or the money. Joke.'

'I assume you've seen the papers?' Richard grasped the elephant in the room by the scruff of its neck.

'Yup. Anyone say anything interesting when they saw them?'

'Well, nobody said much to me, but they know better. Obviously. Mike said he'd read them later.'

'Oh,' said Katie, sounding disappointed. 'And the beautiful Keera?'

'She loved it. Particularly the bit about your new projects. She asked in a concerned way whether we thought you'd be all right. Like she cared. As for me, I thought you looked very nice with Hercules. His hair is perhaps a little shinier than yours, but your nose was definitely wetter.'

'Look, I'm staying with Mum and Dad for a bit before coming back to London. Can you keep your ears peeled for anything you think might be useful?'

'Like how to make a small bomb to put under the sofa?'

'Mm. But it would have to be a *Heat*-reader-seeking device. I still hold out vague hopes of presenting with Mike again. Actually, I'm going to phone him now. He generally has his ear to the ground. He might know if there's anything out there.'

Richard grunted, wished her luck and clicked off the phone.

Katie found Mike sympathetic.

'I sent you a couple of texts. Did you get them?'

'No,' she said. 'They'll probably come through in a lump when I least need them. Like some of my friends. Anyway, what did they say?'

'Oh, just the usual. Sorry to hear you were dumped on. How I'm having to try bloody hard to get it to work with Keera. She's not like you. You're a joy to present with, but my hands are tied. I can hardly walk off like some child who's had his ice-cream stolen. Much as I'd like to. But listen, I was at the BBC the other day and I mentioned your name to the chaps and chapesses I'm working with on a new show that's right up your street. It's a sort of *Pop Idol* meets Woody Allen. They choose ten people, out of a cast of thousands, to become directors. They get to produce a ten-minute short with all the help they can possibly need and at least one famous soap star will act in their master-piece. They're looking for two presenters … one in the studio to link everything together, and the other on location to speak to everyone involved – chat to the would-be directors, the soap stars, et cetera et cetera. I suggested you should be the one doing the location stuff.'

'God, that would be fantastic! And what a great concept! Should be perfect. A few golden nuggets among the dross at the beginning, then ten people who'll never be heard of again after they've sold their soul to the television devil. How long would it be for and when does it start?'

'They're still in the early stages. A few months before they get all the contestants and check them out. It won't happen until July at the earliest. But I've been pushing for you, so fingers crossed.'

For a nanosecond the conversation perked Katie up. Then she remembered the rather pressing problem of her enormous mortgage. Bugger. Bugger. Bugger. She looked at the clock. Eleven a.m. She had put a bottle of wine in the fridge for a sharpener while she made calls round her mates in the business to see if there was any voiceover work she could do.

But she hadn't been particularly clever in her choice of friends over the last few years. They were loyal, intelligent and fun. They knew marvellous facts. They could tell her whether it was true that earwigs were the only insects that suckled their young, the origin of the word kiss, the best way to get to Ikea, how to operate her mobile phone. But they were not very useful if you'd been sacked. 'The trouble is, Hercules,' she commented, as she circumnavigated the golden rug, 'that I'd prefer to eat my own head than spend an hour talking about a piece of jewellery on QVC. But I may, at some stage, be grateful for an offer.'

She poured a glass of wine.

'And there's the distinct possibility they wouldn't employ me anyway because I know next to nothing about lampshades and cubic zirconia. Do you think I should retrain as a carpet-maker and specialize in dog rugs?'

Hercules farted. Sniffed under his tail. Put his ears down and walked over to his basket.

CHAPTER SIX

Mike let himself quietly out of his house. His trophy wife was sleeping, her hands covered with moisturizer and encased in white cotton gloves. The Patterdale terrier they had bought at vast expense from a breeder in Devon looked up expectantly as he was collected from his bean bag on the landing. Mike tied a red spotted handkerchief round Buster's neck, and tiptoed down the stairs. He had taken the precaution of parking the car away from the house – not that Sandra would have woken up. She was always exhausted from the four hours' exercise she did every day and the lack of food that kept her in sparkling bony condition.

He opened the passenger door and Buster took up his position on the velvet cushion Mike kept under the carpet in the boot. He didn't want to have to make up any excuses to Sandra about what it was for. And, anyway, it smelled unmistakably of dog. 'All right, boy?' he whispered. 'Let's go and make mischief.'

* * *

The next morning Keera was ultra-solicitous. 'Are you all right, Mike? You look knackered.'

'The dog kept me up. I may have to take him to the vet today.'

'Oh dear. How old is he?'

'Only six. I don't think it's terminal.'

Richard, the producer, was leaning over a researcher's desk. 'That reminds me about the man who goes to the vet with his dog because it's got a cough. And the vet says, "I'm going to have to put him down." And the bloke says, "But he's only got a cough." "I know," says the vet. "But he's heavy."'

The researcher laughed.

'That's not funny,' said Keera, 'not when Mike's dog isn't very well. How would you like it if your mum was ill and we all made jokes about it?'

'Oh, lighten up, Keera. Mike just said he didn't think it was serious. And, anyway, the vet only put the dog on the floor.'

'No, he didn't. You said he put him down.'

Richard looked at her. 'Yeah. Right. Hadn't you better get to Makeup?'

Keera checked her watch, stood up and turned on her heel.

Richard watched her leave. 'And, Mike, since you're here a full fifteen minutes before the show starts, maybe you can look at the scripts and make any changes now instead of complaining later.'

Mike raised his eyebrows. 'If you were a better producer, I could come in five minutes before the show and not have to worry. What with you and that bloody director laughing at your gloriously unfunny "jokes", it's a wonder we manage to get on air. Thank God I can make a silk purse out of a sow's ear. If it was up to me, you'd be out on your arse.'

'They wouldn't be able to find anyone else to put up with your bullshit,' said Richard levelly. 'And, frankly, I don't think the show is anywhere near as good now Katie's gone. There's no edge. You're finally exposed. As I knew you would be. Until now I've been kind because I know that, for some reason, Katie thinks you're a good bloke. Don't push me too far.'

There was a pause.

Richard added, 'And don't forget, I've been a long time in this industry and know an awful lot of people.'

Mike pushed back his seat. Yawned. Stood up and scratched his scrotum right in Richard's face. 'Don't threaten me. I think you'll find I have a number of very useful friends too.' He headed for the studio.

But Richard's comments had hit home. Was the show worse since Katie had left? Surely the whole thing hung on *him*. Ratings were the only judge of what was happening, he thought. He'd go and check them at the end of the programme. Or did Richard know something he didn't?

To get rid of the doubt and uncertainty, he went off to harangue the head of Wardrobe for putting his expensive suits on inappropriate hangers. Little did he know that his weekly tirades merely resulted in much worse indignities perpetrated against them – and that the occasional crop of spots on his thighs was nothing to do with heat rash.

Katie's mum was having trouble. She was trying to do a still life with a jug, a hare and some potatoes. The potatoes had come up a treat and looked nice and earthy. But while the hare looked properly limp and lifeless, it wasn't remotely like a hare. Her attempts to give it a glossy sheen had made it look wet. 'Too much white,' she muttered, as Katie appeared at the door.

'Too much wet,' said Katie. 'I know seals come from the sea, but by the time they're that dead there's not much moisture left on the outside.'

'It's a hare.'

'Well, it doesn't appear to be very hairy.'

'Thank you so much for your kind and unnecessary remarks,' her mother said drily. 'Can I help? Has Dad forgotten to get in another vat of wine?'

Katie continued to walk towards the window, without giving any hint that she had heard the barbed comment. She had been there for five days and the bottles did seem to pile up, but she resented the implication that she was drinking too much. 'Sorry, didn't realize you were counting. Or, actually, that it mattered. I'm what they call "chilling", having had the rug pulled out from under my feet.'

'Just be careful you don't end up *under* the rug,' commented her mother cheerily. 'Remember when your brother got so drunk he stayed the night at Bob's and ripped up a corner of the carpet so that he could sleep under it? He's still got that carpet-tack scar under his arm.'

Katie's eyes managed to sparkle. 'Whatever happened to Bob?'

'Got divorced. He doesn't live too far away from here. Near Hawes. The Old Coach House – that lovely big place with the huge garden. He invited me to come round and paint there the other day. May take him up on the offer – give up with the lank hare, try harebells and hydrangeas instead.'

'He was rather good-looking, as I recall,' said Katie, as she checked her watch. Another quarter of an hour and she could legitimately ask her mother if she wanted a drink, then join her.

'Well, funnily enough, I think he's better-looking now. A bit like Richard Gere. Sort of pretty but rugged, with a hint of sadness and a *soupçon* of debauchery.'

Katie had thoroughly perked up. 'Maybe I'll come with you. I need some more gear. Sorry. That was one of the most rubbish puns ever. Anyway, let me know when or if you go.'

A week later, she and her mother were at the Old Coach House. Katie was thrilled. She might have no job, no prospect of a job, no way of paying her mortgage, no visible means of support in the near future, and parents who were getting a bit scratchy about her cluttering up their environment, but Bob was, as Kirstie Allsopp would probably put it, a des res with all mod cons and a particularly pleasant aspect. If an Englishman's home is his castle, I wouldn't mind seeing his flying buttresses, she thought.

Her mother, after the formalities were over and done with –
Yes, he was well. Yes, his parents were well. No, the cat had just
been neutered, that was why his tongue was clamped between
his teeth. And, yes, he did think he'd put the kettle on for a cup
of coffee – had gone through to the garden and was setting up
her easel by a verdant patch of hostas, flanked by snapdragons,
hollyhocks and fading peonies. 'I can already feel the muse
upon me,' she shouted back to them in the kitchen.

Katie was flirting over a gin and tonic. 'Ah. Thank goodness
for that. Always nice to have good muse.' She swallowed a pip
and choked. 'I am *so* sorry. I keep doing it today. Not the pips,'
she added, as he looked concerned, 'the puns. As my old editor
used to say: "Avoid puns like the plague." But I appear to be in a
bit of an Oasis soup.'

Bob raised an eyebrow. Very sexy, thought Katie, then sang
aloud, 'You know … you get a roll with it. As in, I'm on a roll.
Or not …' She tailed off.

'Maybe …' said Bob, as he squashed down the coffee
grounds in the cafetière '… your editor was right.' He poured
the coffee and took it to her mother, leaving her with time to
worry if she'd cocked it up already.

Well, whatever. It was hardly the end of the world. But
bloody annoying. She had obviously lost her touch. That was
what getting sacked and being away from the city did for you.
The sharp edges got blunted. It was only a matter of time before
she started wearing comfortable shoes, nylon slacks and a
housecoat.

'So ...' said Bob, as he came back to join her in the kitchen. He was smiling so she assumed she hadn't completely blotted her copybook.

'So what?' she asked brightly.

'What's new?'

'Apart from me losing my job? Not much. I've eaten so much good food because of Dad's cooking craze that I can barely fit into my pyjamas and Mum kind of hinted today that I may like to leave before I become an embarrassment. But as George Burns said when he was asked how he felt about getting to a hundred, "I feel fine, considering the alternative."'

Bob sipped his coffee and gazed contemplatively out of the window at Katie's mother, frantically daubing pink paint on the canvas. 'What's the alternative in your case?' he asked.

'What – to death? I suppose a kind of living death where I don't get another good job in television, don't even get offered a reality show, and end up running a dog-dependency unit in Penge. Where occasionally someone says, "Didn't you used to be someone on breakfast television?"'

Katie stopped. She hadn't meant to sound so bitter. But being sacked wasn't the same as moving on in the television world. Everyone knew what had happened because the papers, so keen when you were on the way up, were even more excited about chronicling the way down. And because it was all so public, it was almost impossible to gloss over it. You couldn't tell people you'd decided to leave because you wanted to widen your experience, spend more time with your family, have a change of scenery when they all knew you'd been dumped.

In many ways, it was like an actor leaving a soap. You *could* go on to bigger and better things, but often you sank without trace.

Unless, of course, it was the BBC. There, they cherished you. Nurtured you. Even if you were a patronizing, irritating woman with no sense of humour like that awful Saskia Miller. 'How *are* you?' she would ask, hand grasping forearm, eyes gazing upwards as though she'd heard you were in terminal decline.

'Pah.'

'Sorry?' she asked, missing what Bob had just said.

'I wondered what the exclamation was for.'

'Oh. Nothing. Well, nothing much. Another presenter who still has a job and who I bump into periodically,' she said. She caught Bob's eye and added, 'I'm not normally like this. It's all a bit new. Hey, Mum's painted a blancmange – or a baboon's anus. Shall we go and encourage her?'

Dee was having the most hideous day. Mike and Keera had been talking so loudly through her weather bulletins that she couldn't concentrate properly and the Met Office had phoned to complain.

As soon as she'd handed back to the sofa she knew she'd mixed up the wind speeds with the gusting speeds. The editor had torn her off a strip and she'd had to apologize – even though it was damned hard not to say that it hadn't been totally her fault. You had to take into account other people's professionalism – or lack of it.

But no. She had sat on his plastic sofa without complaining.

He had stared at her from his seat – deliberately set a lot higher than the sofa to make sure he was in the superior position. 'Pull your socks up,' he said. 'Plenty of people out there are simply itching to get into your shoes. They'd probably do the job a lot better and a lot cheaper.'

There was nothing Simon liked more than giving his female staff a 'damn good bollocking', as he called it. He got such a buzz from it he'd sometimes hunt them down in a corridor and harangue them at close quarters, standing with his hands thrust deep in his pockets and his head forward, like a primate about to fight over a choice melon.

He preferred to deal with the men by email.

Dee had sat on the low sofa, looking troubled. He had peered up her skirt. She had seen him do it and slammed her legs together.

Dee had taken her beating, stood up and apologized. Said it wouldn't happen again and headed back to her warm flat. She sat in the back of the car on the way home, thinking of what she'd eat for lunch.

On a whim, she redirected the driver to her boyfriend's home in Islington. To cheer herself up, she'd go to Franco's Ristorante with him, drink a bottle or two of Rioja, have a huge plate of cuttlefish in its own ink with polenta, and crash out in front of some trashy movie after a nice drunken romp on the sofa.

She arrived to find him in bed with her hairdresser. Her male hairdresser – the only one she had ever found who could make her thin hair look thick and healthy.

She stood at the door as they scrambled for clothes. She was tired. She couldn't think of any articulate words that would adequately convey her feelings. 'Fuck off,' she said, as her now ex-boyfriend tried to explain.

With tears coursing down her cheeks, she left. No more hairdresser. No more boyfriend. And an awful worry that maybe she should visit the STD clinic to check whether he had left her with any little presents. It would not be her first attendance. Her ex-husband had donated a number of lifetime gifts after playing the field during the last months of their marriage. 'Well,' he had said, as if right was entirely on his side, 'you were never around when I needed you. What was I supposed to do?'

'Abstain. Like me,' she had suggested, blowing her nose on a wet tissue as she had packed the few possessions she cared about.

But to discover that the moron she had been dating since her divorce was not only playing the field but playing over a couple of other acres was too much.

What a fool. Would she ever learn? Why was she the one it always happened to? How come none of her mates had noticed he was gay? How come the queen of gaydar, Katie, hadn't spotted it?

She lay on the pink sofa in her flat, unable to cry any more.

She had a headache from crying. Her nose ached from crying. Even her toes seemed waterlogged.

She couldn't think of a single thing that might have alerted her to the dreadful fact that she had been competing with the whole of the human race for the affections of a man who was probably, right now, coming out of the back of her hairdresser.

She watched the television through tear-soaked eyes and wondered if it hurt to die of painkillers – or if that was an oxymoron. Or just ironic.

CHAPTER SEVEN

Keera was beyond excited. She had been asked by *GQ* to pose naked with a panther for their section on 'The Ones to Watch'.

It wasn't a complete surprise – her publicist had been phoning all the magazines every week to get her something.

When Keera had hired him, she had said she wanted publicity at any cost. He had taken her at her word. She had said she did not want 'the usual stuff' – soft interviews of her at home – she wanted something that would make people sit up and take notice.

It hadn't been difficult to sell her the idea of a nude shoot, although he had been nervous initially. 'After all,' he had said, 'you do so much exercise that it's a shame to waste the result under clothes. And it would be very tasteful. They were desperate to get you. You'd be one of ten people they say are going places.'

'Excellent,' responded Keera, a gleam in her eye. Her only anxiety was whether they'd get it past the press office.

'Well, I was hoping you'd help out on that front,' said Daniel. And he had left it to her.

God knows how she'd managed it when one of the other presenters had been virtually put on rations for doing a photo shoot in which she had featured wearing nothing but paper-clips for a recycling campaign.

Keera's strategy had been simple. She had gone straight to the top. She had avoided the press office, on the basis that the man in charge didn't like her very much, and was gay, so her wiles would be wasted. She had knocked on The Boss's door and sprawled alluringly on his black sofa, allowing him a glimpse of her lace lingerie. She had given him a whisper of more to come. So much more. After ten minutes he had caved in.

It had taken her hours to get the outfit right. Nothing too obviously tarty ... don't want to frighten the pants off him. She giggled at the thought. She did find him strangely attractive – but with no pants on?

She didn't want anything too girly ... She wanted him to know she meant business.

In the end she had chosen a tightly fitting black suit with a low round neck and a thin pink stripe, from a new designer she had spotted at Selfridges. Sounded French, looked French, but actually American and lower cut at the front. Just where it needed it. She had hesitated over the stockings, then decided on hold-ups. If he caught sight of them – *if?* – it wouldn't look as if she was trying too hard.

Finally, the high-heeled Charles Jourdan court shoes with an ankle strap. It had taken her almost as much time to put on her makeup. Less is more, she thought, as she expertly applied base and powder. A touch of mascara and pink lip-gloss, and she was ready. Her hair, specially blow-dried for the event, framed her face with its soft, black shininess.

With one last glance in the mirror, Keera set off for the twelve o'clock appointment. Friday was always the best day to see anyone who worked in breakfast TV. No programme on Saturday – people could let their hair down. The Boss was guaranteed sober if caught before lunch. Too late in the day and he'd be under a table, if not under a woman. He'd once been found with a fifty year-old Russian countess in a broom cupboard at the Savoy Hotel after a particularly late lunch. It had been hushed up but, like most things in the media world, the news had leaked out. No journalist could resist a juicy piece of gossip like that.

Laughing coquettishly and doing a Princess Diana-type peep up through her lashes, Keera had asked The Boss if he could limit the number of people he told to the bare essentials. She thought, as he laughed too, that she had made some sort of joke about being naked. She could have hugged herself. 'I'm on my way. I do know where I'm going,' she hummed, as she left the building.

To tell Mike – or not to tell Mike? He was a bit of a prude and would probably be mildly – if not hugely – horrified. However, if she didn't keep him in the loop he was likely to be severely miffed and do that horrible thing he used to do to Katie when he was in one of his pre-menstrual moods: he had turned his back on her when he was interviewing someone on the sofa, not responded to comments and – the only thing Keera was scared of – made witty comments she didn't entirely understand.

On the other hand, she knew the viewers were on her side. They liked her natural girl-next-door approach. Never mind that someone had described her within earshot as a lobster short of a seafood platter. They'd got rid of Katie because she was too sharp. Unpleasantly so. She tried to think of a simile. As sharp as – a lemon? ... No, she was partial to lemons.

As sharp as a shark! she thought triumphantly. If she, Keera, was like a lobster, then Katie was a nasty old shark. A nasty old dead-in-the-water shark. Yes, the lobster was taking over the aquarium. Although, now she came to think of it, she wasn't sure she wanted to be a lobster. But, then, was there anything pretty in the sea?

At that particular moment Mike wouldn't have cared if Keera had told him she was having *sex* with a panther for *GQ*, wearing a strap-on dildo and a pair of reindeer ears. He was having a major worry about his nocturnal visits. He had 'taken the dog for a walk' the night before and been spotted by a drunken viewer who had yelled at him in his car. He was seriously concerned that, with papers paying thousands of pounds for news of scandalous activities, the now sober viewer might be doing a deal to feather his no doubt filthy and unkempt nest.

Would it come down to their word against his? He hoped so. He'd always been very careful. But careful wasn't abstaining. He couldn't do that. No way. Should he wear a disguise? No, that would be too silly. And even more embarrassing if it ever came out. Maybe he'd have to keep his head down for a bit, though.

He should have been going out with his wife that night to a charity function but had told her he was too tired, and would try to have an early night. He only went to those unspeakably tedious events to up his profile. He really couldn't be doing with the usual people you had to converse with at them.

He had come into the house as the sun was glinting obliquely through the trees on the drive, and told her he was going to have a literally early bath. His think tank, as he described it. He sat there, long legs splayed out, steaming. It's an odd phenomenon, he thought, that the more you sit in water, the more wrinkly you get. He rubbed his fingers together, noticing how they were furrowing as the boiling hot water did its work. Eventually he got out, noticing in passing, that he was as red as a skinned tomato.

He wrapped a towel round his waist and went downstairs to pour himself a whisky.

'Yes, it is two fingers of whisky,' he said loudly to his wife, who was doing sit-ups while watching *Richard and Judy*. 'Do you want anything?'

He knew the answer before she said it. Of course she wouldn't be having anything. She'd have her bottle of water with her and, later on, she'd guzzle an entire stick of celery. If she was *really* hungry.

He took the whisky and stood at the door, watching his wife putting herself through her endless routine. She had her feet under the side of the chintz sofa so that she could see the television, and was counting under her breath. She was up to 129 ... 130. What an awful lot of effort, he thought, when there are so many fun ways to get a workout.

If the viewers didn't get in the way, that was.

He wondered how much she had minded being told that tonight was off. He had said she could go on her own if she wanted, but she hadn't wanted: nobody would take her photograph if she wasn't with him, so what was the point? She had gone to one ball at which she hadn't spoken to anyone the entire evening. As they had sat together in the black Mercedes taking them home, she had said that some of the other guests had tried to make conversation, but they were dull. 'Why do we have to sit with non-celebrities?' she'd asked. 'Surely they know we want to talk to other interesting people.'

Secretly Mike agreed with her, but was aware that the driver was overhearing their conversation so he confined himself to a comment about the raffle.

'How's it going?' he asked now, nodding to the leg lifts she was embarking on.

'Fine.' She grunted.

He watched her for a while, wondering how she could bear to spend so much of her life lifting separate bits of her body like a daddy-long-legs trying to get through a patch of strawberry jam.

'Be careful not to overdo it ...' he threw over his shoulder, as he made his way upstairs. As he turned the corner, he finished the sentence '... or they'll turn into antennae.'

He and Sandra had separate bedrooms – a result of ten years doing breakfast television with its unpleasant early-morning regime. Not that Mike could complain. A huge salary and a four-hour day because he was arrogant enough to think he could get away with minimal preparation. He woke up at five-thirty a.m, although in every interview he said it was three.

His bedroom was enormous, the giant bed covered with carefully coiffed cushions. That was Sandra's touch. She had also forced him to have dark green sheets and duvet cover because he insisted on reading newspapers in bed. 'I'm not having white sheets with black streaks in my house,' she had said. And, actually, he wasn't bothered. She could do what she liked, within reason. As long as she never found the little hiding places ...

Katie's mother had forced her to go shopping. 'I do love you,' she said, 'but since you've come to stay, and show no sign yet of going, you may as well make yourself useful. We're down to dog biscuits and tinned rice pudding unless someone makes the effort to drive into town and get some food.'

There was a pause. And a look.

'And drink. We're out of everything apart from sherry.'

It was Katie's first trip out among the public since she'd been sacked. She was looking forward to it in the same way that she looked forward to having her verrucas frozen by Nigel at the chiropodist's in Marylebone. No, on second thoughts she didn't mind that too much because it felt like she was getting tidied up. She was looking forward to it like ... She pulled her mouth into a line, pushed it out into a cat's bottom shape, and decided it was like looking forward to A-level economics. Knowing you were going to hate it, but also that you had to do it unless you could convince everyone you were suffering from something major. Like your arms had dropped off in a freak cactus-juggling incident.

Her parents' car smelled quite strongly of dog. Dog, food and turpentine. She sniffed appreciatively. For a moment she forgot about her feelings of desperation, degradation and depression. She was safe. Wrapped in family.

It would all be fine. And what was so bad about doing QVC, anyway? As Keera had for her special meeting with The Boss, Katie had dressed carefully. She was wearing her favourite pink cashmere zip-up top, her jeans and her pink R. Soles cowboy boots. She had washed and blow-dried her hair, then applied the minimum of makeup. Unbeknown to her, she was also wearing exactly the same shade of lip-gloss as her nemesis in London.

And so arrayed, she had set forth in the battered old orange Volvo to purchase essentials. 'Although,' she said to the wind-screen, 'I do think that drink is the *most* essential of all the essentials.'

'Perhaps,' she posed to the traffic-lights, 'I should buy my own so that Mum doesn't need to have a go at me.'

'And,' she pondered to the parking spot behind the supermarket, 'I should get them from a grog shop because they might offer me a discount for a box.'

And also because Mum's friend didn't work there.

She trundled up and down the aisles, perusing the offerings. And for the first five minutes, as she fondled the plums and hesitated over the horseradish, nothing hideous happened.

Then a small, round, sweaty man, wearing a windcheater, grey slacks and an excited expression, came up to her and said, 'You're that girl off the telly, aren't you?'

'I used to be in television, but I'm pursuing other avenues. Thank you for asking,' said Katie, firmly. She turned back to decide whether her mother had meant washing-up liquid or washing liquid.

'I don't like that new girl at all,' said a woman standing near Sweaty Man.

'Can I have your autograph?' asked a girl in a stained white Barbie T-shirt and tight black trousers, egged on by her mother.

'Yes, of course you can,' said Katie, smiling tightly and using the proffered sticky pen to write her name on the 15p-off Jaffa Cakes coupon. She then fled round the corner to the soft-drinks section. But there was to be no peace. A middle-aged woman with a Hermès scarf sidled up to her and said it was nice to see her out and about after that 'perfectly awful stuff in the newspapers'.

Katie agreed it was, and moved away.

She spent more time than she had meant to in the super-market, mostly in a fruitless search for items her father required. She assumed that these particular ingredients had either been renamed or would be available from the deli down the road.

She paid for the food, put it into the boot of the car and walked briskly to the deli, where she had to stand in a queue of people who nudged each other. Just the really useful shop, then I'm home and dry, she thought, as she entered Oddbins.

A handsome young man was only too pleased to help her make her selection. Originally she had planned to buy half a dozen bottles of wine, then decided she'd get whisky, vodka and gin too. No point in being stingy about the important aspects of living.

'A party?' he asked, as she placed the bottle of ten-year-old Laphroaig on the counter.

'No, not yet,' she answered, smiling and looking directly into his blue eyes.

'Do I know you?' he asked.

'I don't think so. Common face, I expect,' said Katie, quickly.

'Yes, I do – I do. Give me a moment, and I'll remember.'

'Mm. My parents live round here. I've been in loads of times before.'

'That'll be it, then.'

Katie smiled and hoped that was the end of the matter.

But no.

As she handed over her credit card, he read the name, and suddenly said, 'You're the one who was sacked from breakfast television, aren't you? Katie Fisher. I thought I knew the face.'

'Thank you. Yes, that's right. I think I'm going to need double bags round these. If you pass me another, I'll do it my side.' She couldn't wait to leave the shop, and because she was fumbling with her handbag, and the double bags, there was suddenly an almighty smash and she was bent over the pavement with the whisky bottle in pieces on the ground – with splashes on her clothes. Just as a photographer from the local paper, alerted to Katie's appearance in town, took a snap of her. Followed by another as she rushed down the street, with her three carrier-bags of heavy bottles. 'You're not helping, you know,' she puffed, as she sped along to the car park.

He took another five pictures.

'Will you please stop that? You must have enough now,' she said, as she put the bags into the car.

The shutter whirred. 'Katie, look this way,' he shouted, as though she was miles away.

Now without the bags, she turned and smiled her best fake smile. 'Thank you. You've really made my day,' she said to him sarcastically, and stalked round to the driver's side.

He continued to take pictures as she drove away. She hoped – but without much hope involved – that the pictures would appear in the local rag and nowhere else. She felt like crying. There was nothing they liked better than kicking you when you were down. Why couldn't he have appeared when all she'd had in her bags was fruit, vegetables and things with unpronounce-able names?

At least the car had started first time, and she'd been able to accelerate slightly towards the photographer. She felt like doing a wanker sign out of the window, but managed to hold on to her common sense for long enough to realize that it would look worse than any of the other photographs.

The thing about those pictures was that she couldn't do anything about them. If she phoned Jim Break and told him to get on to the newspapers, first, it would merely alert them to the pictures' existence, and second, they wouldn't let her put a spin on the copy anyway. She was stuffed. She was as good as rolled up with pâté, baked in pastry and called Wellington.

She'd have to grin and bear it.

Or gin and bear it.

That was the solution.

She drove home, mouth watering. She could almost see the slice of lemon. Smell that petrolly smell. Hear the ice crackling in the glass.

Yes, after a few of those, nothing ever seemed quite as bad.

At home, her parents had been having 'a conversation'. Her father, always her champion, had been defending her right to spend as long as she wanted with them. Her mother, who generally had the bigger picture in mind, thought it was about time she went back to her flat and got herself sorted out. 'You have to be cruel to be kind, Jack,' she said. 'The longer she stays here, the worse it will be in the long term. If she's on her own, she'll get things done. You know how she is. But while she's here, everything's on hold. If she had no money and nowhere to go, it would be another matter.' Her eyes strayed to the large number of bottles in the recycling bin outside the back door. 'If she's not careful, she'll sink into a Slough of Despond and be unable to crawl out. There's quite a lot of alcohol being consumed here – and you know how she hates to put on too much weight. You keep cooking, she'll keep eating, and before you know it we'll be back to those slimming tablets she took last time, when she was bouncing off the walls and we virtually had to get everything reinforced in case she literally brought the house down.'

Jack huffed, and said she'd been too thin when she'd arrived and he was making her look pretty again.

Eventually, a compromise had been reached: Katie could stay until the weekend. 'And I'll have nothing to do with telling her,' said her father, 'since I'd be quite happy if she moved back in permanently.' And with a flash of his pinny he was into the kitchen to reduce the sauce he was making for the duck.

CHAPTER EIGHT

Bob was settling down to a microwave cod in parsley sauce with oven chips and an early episode of *The Simpsons* when the doorbell went.

Katie Fisher stood there leaning against the pillar, her green eyes sparkling as she regarded the hunk before her. He was wearing a faded, slightly ripped pair of jeans and a navy T-shirt with a scattering of holes. 'I've come to, er ...' she hesitated, eyeing him gravely '... get rid of your moths.'

'I haven't got moths,' he responded, then looked down at his T-shirt. 'Oh, this,' he said. 'A favourite, and very, very old. At least I don't *think* I've got moths. *Have I?*' Suddenly he looked worried.

'I doubt it. Pesky little beggars, though, if you have. I've been smelling of mothballs for years, ever since I had to go into a rented flat when I was having mine done up. I had to burn some of the more juicy specimens. And I still get the odd munch mark. But enough of that. I actually came round to see if you needed any help eating your dinner.'

He laughed. 'Well, it's specifically designed by scientists at Marks & Spencer to feed one adult. But I'm sure I have something else in the cupboard designed to feed an unexpected additional adult. If that suits, madam?'

'That will be fine. And I've brought my own bottle, if that's all right. Obviously I'll pay corkage.' She followed him into the house and took in the scene. 'Sorry if I'm interrupting a seriously good night in for one,' she said apologetically. 'This is one of the best *Simpsons*. Although generally I find Krusty the Clown a bit irritating. Are you sure you don't mind me gate-crashing?'

'No, really,' Bob said, reappearing from the kitchen with the open bottle of wine and two glasses. 'I was going to be a sad single and sit in with my fish, watching telly and possibly getting pissed on strong ale – which I would have had to go out and get at some stage. You've interrupted nothing. But I do admit I'm a bit surprised. Why didn't you phone?'

'I was taken by surprise too. My mum says I have to leave by the weekend and I was so annoyed that they hadn't even consulted me about it that I couldn't stay in case we had a row. And Dad was cooking the most delicious-smelling duck in cherries. Broke my heart. I could still smell the hot cherries at the end of the drive.'

She took her glass of wine. 'Whoops. That wasn't very politic, was it? I'm sure Messrs Marks & Spencer can do an interesting alternative. And cherries are overrated. Have I done enough? Shall I keep digging? Shall I ask another question?

What am I having for dinner?' She made a slurping sound as she buried her head in the wine glass.

Bob smiled. 'Choice of chicken curry or some sort of pork thing with potato.'

'What do you recommend?'

'Well, pork sounds vaguely rude. And curry sounds fast. So it's whichever.'

'Pork, then, since I've been very rude in inviting myself round in the first place.'

She settled back on the sofa with the glass of fruity red and made sure she looked appealing. The olive-green V-neck cashmere jersey was soft and inviting. She arranged the long green skirt so that it draped round her feet. Then she took off her brown leather boots and put her feet on the sofa. That was better. She hid her boots at the side of the sofa. Better still.

She tucked her hair behind one ear and waited for her pig.

She rearranged herself. Then lay slightly supine on the sofa.

Nope. That looked too obvious.

She sat up again.

Just when her skirt was tangled and she was in transit to a more suitable pose, Bob reappeared with an oven glove and a grin. 'Sorry, madam. Pork's off. The chicken is what we recommend this evening.'

'Oh, pluck it. Just when I had my mouth organized for a good pork,' said Katie, and gave a saucy smile.

'The microwave instructions were not followed correctly by the kitchen staff. I'll have them sacked and served for breakfast.'

'Oh, good. I like a hearty breakfast.'

Bob gave her a quizzical look and retired to the kitchen.

'Damn. Hope that hasn't frightened him off,' thought Katie. She wondered if she was doing the right thing anyway. Seducing old mates hadn't been on the cards. But, then, being sacked hadn't. Being photographed stained with alcohol and carrying bags of drink certainly hadn't. Being turfed out of your own home definitely hadn't.

This would cheer her up. She would have half a bottle of wine, possibly go to bed with Bob – or at least snog him until there was nothing left but his socks. And if she could make it all last until lunchtime the next day, so much the better. That would teach Mum to kick her out of the house.

Two months ago, she wouldn't have given Bob a second glance. She preferred the company of men who were powerful and persistent, preferably with pockets full of cash. Having said that, they didn't last more than a year, tops.

Some were so perfect on paper it was like bacon and egg. Toast and honey. Chips and curry sauce. Months later, it was all over.

There had been one who ticked all the boxes. He could hardly have been more powerful, running a multi-million-pound dotcom business. His persistence was legendary, and involved a number of excellent diamond pieces delivered by courier. How could she have known he was incapable of being nice to those he called 'minions'? Or that he would refuse point-blank to reciprocate on the oral-sex front? She had withheld services in that department to see how he coped.

Admirably, it seemed. He didn't appear to care, as long as sex was still on the table.

She giggled quietly.

'What's funny?' asked Bob, returning with her chicken curry on a tray.

'Nothing. Somebody I know who would *never* have used the table.'

'Oh, sorry. Shall we sit at the table? I'm so used to sitting in front of the telly with my food on my lap. It is a bit slovenly, isn't it? The disadvantage of living alone. You become a slovenly sloth.'

'I didn't mean that. This is lovely. Isn't your cod going to be a smidge cold now?'

'There's a limit to how many bloody times I can press that microwave button,' he said. 'And anyway, it was hot before. Do you want one of my chips?'

'I'm honoured. Few men would allow me to steal chips. And the weird thing is, one of my favourite things in the whole world is chips and curry sauce.' She leaned over and pinched three from his plate.

He gently removed two as she lifted her fork. 'I said *one*,' he reminded her sternly, then smiled.

Bob, she thought, was gorgeous. Thick, dark-blond hair sticking up in all directions. And a nice thick tuft of chest hair protruding from the top of his T-shirt. She could just see a hint of flat stomach above his slouchy jeans. All in all, it was pretty much a Diet Pepsi thing.

Suddenly Katie didn't feel hungry. She cut up the chicken and moved it round the plate. Luckily, the wine was delicious. As was the conversation, which rapidly steered a course through microwave meals and plunged straight down into the murky world of relationships.

She found out that he had split up with a girlfriend a few months ago. It had lasted a year (good, shows staying power), he was still friends (good, shows maturity) and he wouldn't reveal anything about her beyond her name and what she did (good, shows discretion).

She tried to pretend that her love-life had been more put upon than putting out. And he pretended not to know all the stuff that had been in the press. Or the stuff that hadn't, but was fairly well known round the area. She was, after all, their own personal celebrity. He even knew one of them, Peter – a millionaire with short arms and long pockets, who had gone out with her for six months. He was a friend of a friend. And he had described Katie as 'suffering from relationship bulimia' – swallowing men and vomiting them up soon after. But at the Old Coach House, all was going down well.

The night drew in. The chicken lay unloved in its nest of rice. There was a frisson. A tangible something in the air. A sparkle.

Katie forgot that the wine had run out. She was getting high on conversation. She moved infinitesimally closer to the navy blue T-shirt.

'Are you cold, or are you, erm, are you . . .' Bob left the words hanging.

'I think I may be,' she said.

Their lips touched and Katie felt as if all her follicles were standing on end. She felt fizzy. And hot. And his arms were strong. She was in love with falling in love. And she was falling in love with Bob, her brother's friend. Handsome Bob. Bob who wasn't wearing his T-shirt any more. And then they were upstairs and throwing themselves into musty sheets that had a faint aroma of toast about them.

The next morning at the *Daily Mirror*, they were poring over photographs from one of their regular paparazzi in Barbados. They weren't of the best quality – the angle was slightly too low. But you could clearly see the erstwhile queen of breakfast television practising her deep-throat technique on a banana. She was obviously the worse for wear and, even better, there was a hint of nipple, which they could enhance to make it stand out more. In every sense. The question was not whether they were going to use them. The question was *when* they were going to use them.

Just as they were debating the issue, they had a call from a stringer in Yorkshire. Would they be interested in photos of Katie Fisher coming out of Oddbins, splattered with whisky and carrying rather a lot of bottles? There was no more discussion of when they were going to use the Barbados photographs.

* * *

Katie's evening had been utterly fluttery. She had woken up the next morning, feeling warm, squidgy, a bit nervous and altogether in a state of excitement.

To be fair, she hadn't slept well. It had been a while since she'd shared her bed space with anyone else and she had periodically come out of tangled dreams to discover herself in contact with a sinewy, hairy body. She had been surprised for a nanosecond, then caressed it lightly, and smiled her way back into strange images of wild seas about to swamp her.

Luckily, she had woken first so she could get the fur off her teeth. Then she had found an old comb in the bathroom cabinet and broken a couple more of its teeth in an attempt to sort out her hair, which looked as if it had been set upon by squirrels. Finally, she had put on a soft blue shirt she had discovered in the wardrobe, before she got quietly back into bed. Now that she had hit her roaring forties, she hated the sight of body bits hanging around in the cold glare of the day. She also hated the way that creases could last at least four hours.

There had been times on-air recently when they had almost got to the 'soft furnishings' (fashion and makeovers) element of the show before they'd dropped out. That morning, she had developed a scar through one eye, courtesy, she suspected, of the scrunched-up pillow on her side of the bed.

Bob, on the other hand, was looking as gorgeous as he had the night before. He had turned over as she got back into bed, smiled at her and rumpled her newly unrumpled hair. His own was sticking up. His chest hair was sticking up. The corners of his mouth were sticking up. There appeared to be things sticking up in all directions …

Katie had had the most blissful morning with him. They had only opened the curtains as the sun was getting ready to lower itself gingerly into the afternoon. She had left, feeling cuddled, cosseted and rather roughed-up round the edges, promising to meet him for lunch the next day since he had a dinner party to go to. 'I would ask you to come,' he had murmured into her neck, as they stood at the door saying their farewells, 'but it was arranged aeons ago and I know that Diane will have a brain explosion if I mess up her placements.'

'And we wouldn't want that, would we?' nuzzled Katie. 'Brain explosions are hell to get out of the carpet. It would be offally difficult, even with Cillit-Bang. Which is the official cleaning agent for internal-organ explosions.'

'You do say the most romantic things,' said Bob, caressingly.

With a last lingering kiss, Katie had left for an evening at home with her parents. In some ways, she wasn't unhappy. She could get herself tidied up, and give her lips a break. The poor things were looking like a pair of guppies left out on Whitby beach during a hot day in August. Any more attention from Bob tonight and they would never swim again.

Keera was having a lovely day. She had been asked if she wanted to be considered for the Rear of the Year award. She had to agree to be available on the day they were going to announce it, and she had to agree to a certain amount of publicity. And, no, there wouldn't be any obvious payment to her that would compromise her position at *Hello Britain!* But they were sure they could do something that involved some form of pecuniary advantage. Everything in the garden was rosy – apart from a couple of producers whom she knew were not 'on-side', as she liked to call it. But she was working on that. She had organized a lunch with The Boss and Colin, the news editor, and had asked them if they could get Kent and Richard along too. Richard might still have been pining for Katie, but she was sure he could be brought round, particularly if he felt outnumbered. The third producer, Helen, would have to be dealt with at a later date.

Keera had booked Langan's in Stratton Street. She knew the owner and he would make sure she had the right table. All she had to do was keep everyone's glass topped up – except hers – and wear the right thing. The rest she would leave to her native charm.

She had chosen the next day – a Friday. (One infamous *Hello Britain!* lunch had gone on until midnight, with one of the executive producers driving home so tanked up that when the police stopped him he couldn't remember where he had been or with whom. According to the police interview, he had repeatedly denied drinking too much, saying only that he had eaten some liqueur chocolates on an empty stomach. The fine had been heavy. But the five-year ban had meant relocation to central London, and a family on the verge of anarchy.)

It was all coming together slowly but surely. All she had to do now was find a suitably attractive and preferably famous man to have on her arm and she would be exactly where she'd planned, all those years ago.

And that morning, on *Hello Britain!*, she had interviewed a man she thought would fill the position very nicely. William Baron. He was a lifestyle guru who was making a name for himself after getting one of the porkiest stars on *Big Brother* into the most amazing shape. He was also very handsome and had flirted outrageously with her. She had let him know that she was single, and available most weekends.

Grant, the director, had spoken to her when they were on the ad break. 'Have you got your dance card marked, then?' he had asked.

'Oh, I do hope so,' she had said, holding her lapel mike to her mouth.

'Mmm. Thought there was a whiff of pheromone in the air.'

'Ferret what?' she had asked.

The *Daily Mirror* had decided to go big on the photographs. The front-page headline accompanying the picture of Katie on holiday in Barbados was 'Fishing for Friends', with a line underneath promising more pictures. 'Can Katie Hold Her Drink?' was that headline, with a series of photographs showing her dropping one bottle and carrying many others.

The overnight producers had been the first to see them as the first papers off the presses were delivered at ten p.m.

Richard had laughed. 'Typical Katie,' he said, as he pored over the copy. 'Always did like a bit of a tipple and now she doesn't have to get up at that ungodly hour of the morning, she's partying hard. Good on her.' But he thought he might phone and warn her. And he could fill her in on the gossip from work, including the latest on Keera's clothes allowance – she had managed to double the amount everyone else got, after being closeted with The Boss for an hour.

At ten that night, Katie's happy musings had been cast upon stormy seas by the phone call. It came as she and her parents had been vaguely watching a documentary about a giant jellyfish.

'What do you think is the collective noun for jellyfish?' asked her father. 'A squish? A flibble? A wobble?'

Her mother had been absentmindedly drawing a peony on a sketchpad. 'Do they have to be pink?' she asked no one in particular.

Katie recognized Richard's number on her mobile and went out into the kitchen.

'*Monsieur Richard. Ça va?*'

'*Oui, très bien. Pourquoi on parle en français?*'

'*Pas de raison. Quieres hablar en otra lengua?*'

'Oh, stop it, you old polyglot. Or polymat or whatever it's called.'

'Polly-wolly-doodle all the day, it's called at the moment, since I have very little else to do. How are things at the funny farm?'

'The usual,' Richard said, and told her about Keera's wardrobe allowance and Mike's response when he had 'accidentally' told him. 'He was beyond pissed off, even though no one can tell whether he's wearing his navy suit from Marks & Spencer or his navy suit from Savile Row. Nobody cares. But you know what Mike's like. He can't bear to think someone's getting something he isn't. Even if he doesn't want it!'

'Yeah, bless him. I must give him a ring. He was trying to see if he could get me a co-hosting job on some programme he's been offered.'

'Now,' he said, 'don't worry too much, but I did phone you for a reason. There are some pix of you in tomorrow's *Mirror*.'

'Oh, bugger,' she said, after a slight hesitation. 'Of me and my shopping incident?'

'Yup. And I'm afraid you've also made the front page – a photo of you and a banana, which you may not remember because you look like you were a little tired and emotional.'

'Oh, no,' she wailed. 'Oh, God. That bloody banana. Shit shit shit shit shit! Do I look ruddy awful?'

'Surprisingly sexy, actually, in the banana photo.' Richard laughed. 'And, erm, perhaps less sexy in the buying-up-Oddbins photos.'

'Damn. I could have done without those. I could have fobbed off my parents with the banana incident, but they'll just look at the others and go quiet. They think I drink too much anyway. Damn. Oh, God. This might have a bearing on that co-hosting job. Why, why, why did it have to happen *now*? I was just thinking I could come back to town because the fuss had died down. Maybe I'd better go to Burkina Faso for a bit and take up whatever they do there.'

'Starve?' asked Richard.

'Maybe not, then.'

'Look, no one here seems to think they're that dreadful. Go and buy the paper tomorrow. You know how things always seem much worse when you don't know what you're dealing with. It's not as though you're embezzling grannies out of their life savings or using crack cocaine.'

'Yeah, right,' said Katie, ruefully. 'They'll print those photos next week.'

'Don't be daft. You won't be famous next week.'

'Gee, thanks. What a pal. OK. I'll wait until I see them before I book my ticket to West Africa.' She clicked her mobile phone shut and chewed her lip.

Apart from her parents, there was now Bob to consider. Or was there Bob to consider? Who decided whether or not one-night stands were one-night stands? How much would he care about photographs in a newspaper he probably didn't read?

She poured herself a large glass of whisky and went back into the sitting room as a transparent blob cast its baleful eye from the television.

Her parents exchanged an anxious glance.

'Anything important?' asked her dad.

'Mmm. Er. Well, I might as well tell you, since someone else will at some stage. There are some photos of me in one of the papers tomorrow. And they probably won't be very nice. Some are from Barbados, and the others are from the day I replenished the drinks cabinet.'

Her parents watched as a rival to the jellyfish hove into view. A giant squid. It was shown in its murky home while the narrator talked about its lonely existence.

'Are you worried?' asked her dad, as the squid danced in the current, before turning tentacle and slowly receding.

'I don't know. It's difficult to tell. I suppose it depends on what they write,' she said.

The squid started eating something green in close-up.

'Urgh. Get a room,' muttered her father.

Her mother turned to ask if another batch of reporters would be demanding tea and buns from the bottom of the garden. On hearing that it was unlikely, she stood up and wondered if her daughter would like a nice cup of hot chocolate. 'I was going to make one for myself,' she said, as she made her way to the kitchen, 'and I thought it might draw the sting from that whisky,' she said tartly.

'Only a few more days to put up with it, Mum, and I'll be out of your hair,' said Katie, as she addressed herself once more to the giant squid and its apparent lack of a Mrs Giant Squid. 'Oh, and by the way, Dad, the bloke on the phone said it's a smack of jellyfish.'

CHAPTER NINE

There was a sense of excitement at *Hello Britain!* as one of their own was featured on the front page of the *Mirror*. She might not work there any longer, but everyone shared in the vicarious thrill of seeing Katie caught unawares. And some of the men were particularly pleased to see her revealing so much of herself during the banana incident – not knowing (or caring) that the photo had been subtly enhanced.

In Makeup, Keera did her best to appear suitably sympathetic as she put the finishing touches to her hair and waited for the sound girl to sort out her microphone. 'There but for the grace of God go I, as they say,' she commented.

'I didn't know you liked a tipple,' said a makeup girl, peering again at the photo of Katie covered with alcohol and lugging half of Oddbins out to the car.

'Oh, yes. I can drink like the proverbial fish,' she responded.

'Proverbial, do you mean?' asked Richard, coming in with an amendment to the top of the show.

'Of course,' said Keera. 'I was using the word metaphorically.'

Richard made a face, left a pause and told her they were no longer doing diabetes as the lead item. It was going to be immigration. 'Sorry it's a bit of a late change,' he said, glancing at the clock. Fifteen minutes to on-air. 'We've got some bids in for various guests. We'll let you know as we go along. Mike's just got here, but once he's up to speed he'll probably do most of them. OK?'

'No, it's not,' responded Keera, her mouth turning down at the corners. 'Why should he when I'm perfectly capable of doing them myself?'

'I thought you might prefer to do the ones you've already got. That's all,' said Richard, emolliently. 'And we have given you the big showbiz interview of the day.'

'Hardly big showbiz. Julie Christie? She must be a hundred and eight. And what's she been in? Some films no one's ever heard of. *Far From the Maddening Crowd* and –'

'*Madding Crowd*, a Thomas Hardy classic, with Terence Stamp and Peter Finch.'

'Whatever. And *Dr Zhivago*. I saw the one with the lovely Keira Knightley in the lead role. On television. She was brilliant.'

'Fine. If you want to do more of the immigration chats, I'll leave Miss Christie in Mike's tender care,' said Richard. It would probably make for a better chat anyway, and he and the other producer would ensure they fed Keera the questions for the new guests.

Keera was sitting on the sofa, swotting up on the Press Association copy off the wires about immigration when Mike came in at five seconds to on-air.

'Morning.' He nodded to the floor managers and cameramen. 'These bloody early starts don't get any easier, do they?'

Nobody made much response – they all got up at least two hours earlier than he did, and for a squillionth of his vast salary.

The director, Grant, spoke in their earpieces. 'Cue Mike,' he said, as the titles showing saccharine pictures of the two hosts cosying up together faded from view.

And they were on the roller-coaster, three and a half hours of 'fun, facts and chat'.

Dee was in a foul mood, but doing her best to get over it. She missed her early-morning conversations with Katie in the dressing room. And Katie's silly, and often rude, humour in Makeup. By the time they got on air, they were usually giggling over some hideous image they'd conjured up together. Instead there was Keera, with her self-absorption and her irritating little comments designed to get you on her side. If she tells me once more that she thinks I've lost weight … thought Dee, as she ran through the graphics and waited to deliver the weather forecast. She was carrying at least an extra stone, after finding her boyfriend in bed with her hairdresser. It had pushed her into the welcoming bosom of the Cornish Pasty Company, which she passed on her way home from work. Her thighs were getting on with each other so well that if they got any closer she'd get friction burns from her tights.

'Sorry,' she heard Richard say in her earpiece. 'Sorry, Dee. We're going to have to nudge you round to after the break. We've overrun.'

She smiled into the camera at him, so that he would see her on the preview shot in the gallery.

They went into the two-minute break. She checked through her graphics again.

Mike watched her bending over, and glanced at her capacious bottom. She caught him looking.

'What?' she asked.

'Nothing. Just thinking how badly slapped together my bacon butty was this morning,' he smiled, delivering the line as they were about to go on air.

Feeling instantly unattractive and unconfident, she fluffed her way through the entire thing, talking about the frog lifting in Suffolk and winds gusseting at forty miles an hour in the north of Scotland.

Between weather bulletins she sat in the star changing room, feeling distinctly tearful. She had to get a grip, go on another bloody diet. On the other hand, only the other day, William Baron had given her his number when she had been moaning on in the green room, and told her that if she needed help to lose weight he'd be only too willing. He had said that with a very direct look deep into her eyes. And then he had said, 'Not that you need to lose any weight, of course.'

Dee didn't trust her instincts at the moment. He was handsome and funny. He smelled nice. He was immaculately shod. He was probably gay.

She went into the studio to do her next hit.

Keera was interviewing a low-ranking immigration minister. 'So,' she said, listening to Richard in her earpiece, then repeating the question he had told her to ask. 'So … why is immigration so bad?'

'No,' shouted Richard, in her ear. 'I said, why has illegal immigration been allowed to get so bad?'

Keera reached round to her back and turned down the talkback button. She could no longer hear anyone from the gallery. It gave her a little thrill. She was skiing off-piste without an instructor. 'I mean,' she said, enjoying her freedom, 'what would we do for cleaners if there were no immigrants?'

The minister looked confused.

In her earpiece Dee could hear Richard saying, 'No, I didn't bloody tell her to ask that.' She smiled. In a weird sort of way it was quite refreshing to hear someone asking a random question.

The interview continued its erratic course until Mike decided to rescue the situation with a few questions he had heard Richard trying to shout at Keera, which put the minister on the spot.

Keera threw to the break and then, smiling sweetly, turned to Mike to ask him if he would mind awfully not coming in on her serious interviews. 'Just at the moment,' she said, 'while I'm finding my feet. I think it probably undermines my authority with the audience. You're *so* brilliant at them, but I do need to appear competent. Is that OK?' And she squeezed his thigh in an intimate manner.

He looked at her speculatively. 'Sorry,' he said. 'I thought it was getting slightly off track. But I won't do it again.' Then he added, 'By the way, they're wondering in the gallery whether your talkback is working.'

Their on-screen relationship was barely out of nappies, and already the crew were sensing that Mike was contemplating infanticide. There was a veritable stampede to get to the morning meeting to watch the fireworks. But there wasn't even so much as a sparkler. Keera had phoned from her dressing room to say she was going straight out on business.

Her agent had organized a meeting with the PR from a watch company. Although the presenters were strictly banned from promoting anything, there were ways of getting round it, and Keera was determined to meet as many top-brand PRs as possible. She had heard you could earn quite a lot on the side from 'accidental' product placement.

Richard, meanwhile, had to defend himself against accusations from Simon that he had let Keera down. 'I did try to get her to ask the questions that had been mapped out by the producer,' he said, 'but her talkback suddenly went.' He left a beat. 'And then, rather oddly, it came back on again, shortly after the interview finished.' He gazed innocently at the editor, knowing he would now be aware of exactly what he thought about the alleged equipment failure.

The meeting continued with a discussion of the next day's stories.

'And by the way,' said Simon, 'can we not have any more old has-beens in the entertainment section? Julie Christie must be a hundred and eight. And our viewers are more interested in *Hollyoaks* than Hollywood.'

Down in the dressing room next to Keera's, Dee had been given a message from the presenters' secretary asking her to ring a mobile number, which belonged to William Baron. While her heart did a little extra beat, she told herself it would just be a follow-up to the offer of personal-training sessions. Did she actually fancy getting down to her skimpies, being hot and sweaty, in front of the Baron?

She stared pensively at a picture on the board she had in the dressing room of herself at an awards ceremony. She had been younger then, and a lot slimmer. Why do we never think we look good until it's too late? she thought, remembering how fat and frumpy she had felt that night.

No, she decided. She would say thanks very much to Mr William Baron, then go running. Or walking. Or swimming. Or eating less. Or only eating vegetables that began with *c*.

Oh, it was so wretchedly boring when all she wanted was a pasty and a pint of beer.

She dialled the number. He answered on the second ring. 'William Baron.'

'Oh. Hello. Good morning. It's Dee here, calling because you left a message.'

'Good morning,' he said, drawing out the words.

She wasn't quite sure if she was supposed to be saying something. Then they both spoke together. 'You go first,' she said, as they apologized over each other.

'Yes. Sorry. I called because when I saw you the other day, I mentioned I could help you out in the personal-training area, not that I'm sure you need it,' he added.

Nicely rescued, thought Dee, who was always ready to hear the implied criticism of her lack of self-control in the food-and-drink department. 'What did you have in mind?' she asked carefully.

'Well, I thought we could maybe meet up, have a drink or something and discuss if there was anything in particular you thought I could do for you, lifestyle-wise.'

There was a slight hesitation before Dee answered. She was going to say that all she needed in life was a dependable man. How to sound desperate ... 'That would be good,' she said.

And before they put down the phone, they had organized a date.

Katie woke up with a hangover and the feeling that something unpleasant was waiting for her.

Now, what was it she had been worrying about?

Then she remembered.

She steeled herself for the worst.

And then discovered she had been inadequately steeled.

She was prepared for photographs that would make her look like a drunken slut. What she hadn't bargained for was that they would make her look like an old and dumpy drunken slut.

So when Dee phoned from work to share her glad tidings of an impending date with a glorified personal trainer, she had been hard pushed to sound as thrilled as she probably should have done, considering her friend's recent history.

'What's up?' asked Dee.

'Haven't you seen the *Mirror* this morning?' asked Katie. 'I felt sure that certain elements at *Hello Britain!* would have drawn your attention to it.'

'Oh, God, I'm sorry,' said Dee, 'droning on like an idiot. I forgot about you and that *Mirror* thing. The photographs weren't too bad, were they? Did you think? I didn't look closely, but they could have been worse.'

'I suppose they could have shown me completely naked, so that people could have said that not only was I fat and ugly but I needed ironing as well,' said Katie bitterly. 'I thought they were horrible. I feel soiled. I feel like someone's come into my house and looked at my dirty pants.'

'Oh, come on, Katie. I mean, I'll go and have another look, but I think you're being over-sensitive. Hey, it was you who always said this sort of thing was a price worth paying for an upgrade or two and your favourite table at the Ivy.'

'I was never old and sacked before,' Katie retorted. 'And, also, I've got a lunch date with a very handsome man, who may yet run a mile.' She told Dee about Bob, and all about the very attractive parts of him. 'Talk about tent pole. It could hold up a marquee suitable for a family of nomads.' She smiled.

'So how long have you and Mr TP spent together so far?' Dee giggled.

'One very lovely night. And we may, perhaps, be sharing a very lovely lunch. And that might be it. Depending on his attitude to those frigging awful photos.'

'I'm sure he'll be fine. It's all new and exciting. He won't care what you look like in the photos, he likes what you look like in the flesh. Did you say he was your brother's best friend? I don't remember you mentioning him before.'

'That's because he was one of Ben's schoolfriends. I haven't seen him for years. Anyway. This may be all immaterial – it could be over by this afternoon. Listen, I'll speak to you soon. Thanks for cheering me up, but I've got to lose ten years within a few hours. If you don't hear from me again, I've stabbed myself to death over lunch.'

'Ah, the Caesar salad, then.'

'The knife in the back, eh? *Et tu, Brute*. Or in my case, *et three* – I'm so hungry.'

'You haven't changed. Still the mistress of the fine pun.'

'Ha!' said Katie, and ended the call.

* * *

Keera had been in the next dressing room to Dee, and her door had been slightly ajar; she was awaiting her agent. She had opened it wider when she heard Dee laughing on the phone and realized that she was speaking to Katie Fisher. As the call ended, she smiled and, later that day, made one herself.

CHAPTER TEN

Mike was at home, going through his bank statements and totting up his monthly cash haul when he had the call from a mate of his at the Vice Squad. They had met when Mike had hosted a police conference. 'Just to let you know, Mike, as a friend, that you might want to curtail the nightly, erm … perambulations. I've managed to sort it out with the chap concerned so he isn't going to put it on the computer. He knew you were a mate of mine, so although he checked the number-plate, he's not going to do anything about it. He also owed me a favour about a little incident involving a red light.' He cleared his throat. 'A different sort of red light, of course. Anyway, I owe him now. Or, rather, you owe me …'

Mike was silent for a minute. 'Yes, of course. Whatever. I understand. And, obviously, this will go no further?'

'No, as long as you behave yourself. Consider it a friendly shot across the bows. And maybe, in return, you can introduce me to Keera. I've always quite fancied her.'

'And your wife?'

'She doesn't have to know. Anyway, who's going to tell Keera I'm married?'

'Point taken. Thanks.'

'No worries. Email me some dates, eh?'

Bugger. He pursed his lips, picked a sideburn for a while, then went back to his accounts, wondering if there was a different area ...

Katie was making a real effort to look good for her lunch with Bob. It was a beautiful day, and the fresh smell of new-mown grass wafted up from the garden. She put on a slim-fitting – snugger than it should have been – short-sleeved dress that she had found in her old cupboard at home, with a pair of high platform sandals she had bought when they'd been in fashion the first time round. Her outfit was perhaps a little over the top for a local lunch, but she needed to feel in control when she presented the newspaper.

Bob looked pleased when he saw her making her way past the tables at the gastropub where they had arranged to meet. She attracted a number of other glances and furtive conversations, as people spotted the local celebrity moving among them, but she had got so used to it over the years it barely registered.

She had eyes only for the handsome man with the blond hair propping up the bar. It was all she could do not to throw herself on him and get to grips with his lips. They ordered a couple of pints and went to a table at the back of the pub, looking out on to the garden.

Katie perused the menu. She wasn't sure she was terribly hungry, what with the knot in her stomach. The smell of lamb coming from the next table was making her feel bilious. 'Just one course, do you think?' she asked.

'Not hungry?'

'For food? Not particularly.'

He touched her thigh under the table, and she decided she need never eat another thing. If only she could get the newspaper stuff over and done with. With his hand still on her knee, she leaned down to her handbag and pulled out the *Daily Mirror.* 'You know how sometimes, as a presenter, you attract unwelcome – possibly unpleasant – publicity?'

'Yes,' he said. 'What horrible item have you got there? Should I be worried? Have they taken a photograph of my fungal toenail?'

She slid the paper on to the table, with the photos facing him. He looked at them, then said, 'And?'

'And I thought it might be a bit offputting.'

'In what way?'

'That you might think twice about seeing me, considering that there may even be someone here at this very minute, waiting to take a photo of us on their mobile phone. And also . . .' she took a sip of beer '. . . they might dig up something about you that's a tad more gruesome than your fungal toenail. Have you tried tea-tree oil, by the way? My mother swears by it.

Or has it gone too far? Or one of your exes might do the dirty. Or something ...' she finished lamely. Because while she wanted to let him know that it *was* a possibility, she really didn't want him to say he couldn't see her again. That would be too cruel when she had only just rediscovered him.

Bob looked at her, musing. 'I'd have to be a complete idiot if I thought you didn't come with extras,' he said. He picked up his beer and drank almost half of it, then put it back on the table. 'And I think I can cope with whatever they throw at me.'

He smiled at her. 'Now, what are you having to eat? I could eat the arse out of a low-flying duck.'

That had been the end of the conversation.

The food had come, and Katie's had been taken away virtually untouched.

They had started a conversation about her imminent removal back to London. 'I need to go and check on the flat,' she said. 'Open letters and do paperwork. I'm going to call my agent and see if he's managed to get me any meetings with anybody. It's a shame I can't do an advert or two. I got asked to do the voiceover for a car ad a few months ago. They seemed surprised I couldn't do it, considering the cash they offered me, but you can't when you're dealing with the Truth every day. People would think if I said it was the best car in the world it really was. And it wasn't. In fact, it was as much the best car in the world as this is the best dress to wear if I was planning to eat any more than a blade of grass,' she said ruefully.

'It's a fantastic dress,' Bob said in a measured way. 'But it would look much better if it was on the floor ...'

And that effectively signalled the end of lunch.

When she arrived home, her parents were busy in the kitchen. Her father was chopping vegetables into narrow strips, her mother was painting a still life of the peelings and a gnome. Mozart's *Don Giovanni* was shaking the speakers. 'Are you two going deaf?' she shouted.

'What?' yelled her father. 'Can't hear you. The music's too loud.'

Katie went through to the sitting room and turned it down to bearable.

'You don't get a better ending than *Don Giovanni*, do you?' queried her mother.

'What?' asked Katie. 'You sit down to dinner with a dead bloke and get carted off to Hell? I think I'd prefer to sit down to one of Dad's dinners and get carted off to bed by George Clooney. But each to his own. What are we dining on, dear Papa?'

'We're just having Swan Cornetto,' he sang.

'Ha, give it to me,' she sang back, battling against the Commendatore from *Don Giovanni*.

'And really?'

'Fish and chipped vegetables.'

'Mmmm. Good oh. Now. I have news. I'll be leaving tomorrow. I'm sorry for all the bad things I've done while I've been here. I'd apologize individually for everything, but because I've drunk so much, I've obviously forgotten.' She nodded to her mother.

Her mother looked up from the strip of beetroot peel she was contemplating to contemplate her daughter instead. 'I assume you have a new beau?'

'Yes, there is a new beau to my string,' she quipped.

'Hey,' her father interjected, 'that really wasn't too bad. The break's obviously done you a power of good.'

'Thank you so much for that,' she said, pretending to sound annoyed. 'But, seriously, thank you very, *very* much for putting up with me. And, yes, I'd like to come back fairly shortly so that I can continue seeing the aforementioned person.'

She smiled. 'Don't I deserve a nice flirtation, Mum? And you wouldn't want me to be discomBobulated when I next come up, would you? Yes, I know he's Ben's friend,' she said, putting up a hand as her mother opened her mouth to speak, 'but I'm sure Ben won't mind. In fact, I'll have a word with him. How can he possibly object?'

'Actually,' said her mother, wiping the brush absentmindedly on her dress because she had forgotten to put on her smock, 'I wasn't going to say anything about Ben. I was going to say it would be difficult to carry on long-term with Bob if you're going back to London permanently.'

Her father, in the middle of squashing a garlic clove, turned round to give her one of his special looks. 'Lynda,' he said warningly.

'It's OK, Dad, I got the hint. I'll be going home tomorrow, and if I come back, it'll be for flying visits. Honestly. I've booked the afternoon train. Bob did offer to drive me, but it's probably more sensible if I go on my own. And, also, we're not talking wedding bells here. It's whatever it is, and if whatever it is is supposed to continue, it will. Wherever we end up.'

She went to pack. The sun was out and all of a sudden her heart felt lighter. Did it matter what the papers printed when she had Bob and his delicious chest to rest on? She had a good feeling in her waters, as her mother would have said. Everything would end up all right.

She would call Steve Nighy at London Talks radio station. They had worked together many years ago on the newspaper and he had always been keen to work with her again. And she had always liked doing radio. You didn't have to dress up, and somehow it was easier to concentrate when you were wearing flat shoes and no makeup.

By the time she came down for dinner, she was positively humming.

'Thunder flies,' muttered her mother, swatting at them ineffectually.

'Oh, I didn't think I'd put on that much weight, Mum,' said Katie, helping herself to a strip of carrot.

'What?' her mother queried, hand in mid-air.

But her father was smiling as he handed her the cheese-crusted halibut.

The dinner was delicious and devoid of any pointed remarks from her mother, who was desperate to have the house back to normal.

She didn't think she was an unnatural parent, but as soon as the children had left home, she had thoroughly enjoyed the freedom to do what she wanted, when she wanted and without any interference from anyone. She didn't count her husband. He was the cleaner/chef/mechanic. She only noticed him when a meal was late or he wasn't there when she sat down to watch a television series they'd been enjoying.

And she was glad she wouldn't have to take the empty bottles to the bottle bank. She could swear the neighbours had been looking at her in a funny way. Actually, they had. Not because of the empties, but because on her last visit to the recycling bins, she had been wearing a pair of Jack's old underpants, a T-shirt, her painting smock and a pair of wellies in case it rained.

Jack Fisher loved having his daughter around, but she always rubbed his wife up the wrong way and he'd be pleased not to feel like an emergency fire blanket, constantly on hand to put out the embers.

Kent, the producer, had been thrilled that morning to be asked by Keera if he wanted to go for breakfast with her after the show. She was so beautiful, natural and friendly, and today she was adorable in a halter-neck top, jeans and a little pair of white sandals. They went down to the canteen for a cappuccino where they chatted for ages about work, workmates and what the future might hold for them.

Kent couldn't have been happier. He told her about the tired and emotional reporter who had been given a ticking-off after wining and dining the head of spin for the Labour Party, and who had fallen asleep during an interview Katie had done with the new foreign secretary just before she left. 'Which wouldn't have been so bad,' he said conspiratorially, 'but while the foreign secretary was talking down the line from Bournemouth, you could quite clearly hear Dave snoring. Apparently he was supposed to be taking notes so he was sitting in the corner with his notebook but he keeled over and ended up stretched out on the carpet with his head virtually under the Minister's feet. It was brilliant. He was carpeted when he got back. And carpeted when he was there, actually,' he added wittily.

He sipped his cappuccino.

'And you know that the news editor's in secret talks with Channel 4 to take over their new afternoon politics show? Big heavyweight interviews and such stuff. He's haggling over the price at the moment. But it would be quite a step up. I know it's daytime, but that's where the battleground is at the moment,' he continued self-importantly, keen to impress Keera with how much he knew about the goings-on in Telly Land. 'And he'd be editor. Have his own train set to play with. Employ his own presenters.'

He gazed out of the window. 'Hey,' Kent said suddenly, 'is that something *you'd* fancy? A politics show?'

Keera peeped at him from under her eyelashes and smiled slowly. 'No, I don't think so. Although you never know. Do you think it's worth me speaking to Colin about it?'

'Hmm. I'm not sure whether it's common knowledge about the job yet. I heard it from a friend of mine who works in the next office. I can ask him.'

Keera leaned forward and accidentally-on-purpose brushed his leg with hers. 'Well, thank you for keeping me informed,' she said, checking her watch. 'Anyway, I really ought to go. I've got an interview to do today with *GQ* to go with a photo shoot I've done. You're my favourite producer, you know,' she said, as she stood up. 'Thanks for being so helpful.'

And silently she thought how *very* helpful. Money-in-the-bank helpful. Things really were going her way. She almost felt sorry for Kent. But not sorry enough *not* to make the phone call, after the interview. She thought she'd conducted it all rather marvellously. Flirty, sexy, but a hint of ambition to let anyone reading it know she was on the way up the ladder, big-time. If they wished to furnish her with her own show ...

Katie had finally got through the mountain of post, answer-phone messages and general maintenance at the flat and was lying on her sofa trying to decide how to tackle the looming cash-flow problem.

It wasn't as serious as she'd first thought. Two rather attractive cheques had bounced out of envelopes – payment for an article for one of the national newspapers she'd written months ago, and a personal appearance she'd forgotten about.

She had left a message for her agent, saying she was now available for weddings, bar mitzvahs and children's parties. She had left messages for her two singleton friends, Dee and Kathy, asking if they fancied a drink. She had left a message for Andi, asking if anything at all was going at Greybeard Television. She had left a message for Steve at London Talks. And she had left a message for Bob, which was less message than random pornography. And then, because she wondered whether anyone was in anywhere, she dialled Mike.

She could hear the television on rather loudly in the background, and he sounded a bit distracted, but he promised to phone the BBC the next day to check on how the search was going for a co-host. 'I'll tell them again that it should be you, although I'm not sure there's much more I can do,' he said, and put the phone down.

Mike's wife looked up from *OK* magazine. 'Who was that?' she asked, as the soap-opera stars shouted at each other in hideous close-up.

'Katie,' he explained.

'But I thought you'd suggested that other woman as your co-presenter on the BBC show? That Saskia Miller?'

Mike eyed her with distaste. 'I'm going out to the wine merchant,' he said. 'Do you want anything in particular?'

'No,' she said, and returned to the article about ultra-thin celebrities and their dogs, checking whether they showed small signs of the cellulite she had noticed that morning in the bathroom mirror. She was pleased to see that one appeared to have crinkly thighs, until she read that the marks were attributed to a wicker seat. She peered closer, and sighed. It really wasn't cellulite.

Instead of heading to the wine merchant's, Mike got into the car and headed to a small back-street shop in Euston. He parked round the corner, checked that the coast was clear, and walked in quickly through the black-painted door.

Ten minutes later, the same door was opened by a small, bald man in a grey shirt and trousers. He looked up and down the street, then stood back to let Mike out.

Dee was in the taxi on her way to her date with William when she picked up Katie's message. She phoned her to bring her up to date and promised to call later with all the news. 'If I'm not busy.' She smiled into the receiver.

William Baron, she thought, as he came round to pull out her chair in the restaurant, is a very handsome man. He was wearing a dark suit and a dusky pink shirt. He smelled intoxicating – a mixture of spice, black pepper and frankincense. 'I hope you don't mind,' he said, 'but I've taken the liberty of ordering a bottle of champagne. You don't have to drink it, but I thought it might be a good way of starting what I hope will be a long and, er, satisfying relationship.'

Dee felt her lower stomach tighten with excitement. 'Mmm. Yes. No. That would be lovely,' she said. And didn't say much more for quite a while because William was witty, interesting and talked for both of them.

She ordered soup and a salad, thinking it would show William she was only carrying extra weight because she had the fat gene they were talking about in the news the other day. Some people got fat on virtually nothing because of their genetic makeup. Nothing to do with a Cornish-pasty problem. Which he couldn't possibly know about. Could he?

And while she was having her internal conversation, she missed his question. 'What?' she said, trying to tuck a bit of frisée lettuce into her mouth.

'I was wondering if you wanted to come to a première with me next week? I've got two tickets. I helped one of the guys in the film to shed some weight and tone up. It should be good. It's an action movie where this guy, Dom, is a computer geek who saves the world in a kind of Batman meets Superman way. He needed to look more sleek than geek so that one of the aliens would fancy him.'

'So it's a sci-fi rom Dom romp?' she asked.

He laughed. 'He's not the lead but, yes, it is science fiction in the comic-book-hero mould. Do you fancy it? A week on Wednesday.'

Dee tried not to choke on the lettuce, which appeared to be unfurling in her oesophagus as she was trying to breathe. 'Can I let you know? It's just that I'm not sure what I'm doing next week,' she asked, eyes watering, knowing full well that her diary was as empty as her fridge after she'd spent a day home alone.

What a result! William Baron! Sexy, handsome William Baron! Asking her to a film première! God, she couldn't wait to tell Katie.

She managed, with a supreme effort of willpower, to say no to pudding, and gave him a chaste kiss on the cheek to thank him for buying dinner, as he put her into a taxi, his hand on the small of her back.

She skipped into the flat and phoned Katie. 'I am in lust. Big, big lust. He's gorgeous. And we're going to a première a week on Wednesday. Have you got anything I can wear?'

CHAPTER ELEVEN

The head of Wardrobe was holding his breath as he steamed Mike's suit. Why Mike had to take so many of them home every day so that they never had a chance to be cleaned he didn't know, but it was like ironing a sumo wrestler's pants. Although the windows were open, the stench was on the verge of making him sick. As if getting up at three o'clock in the morning wasn't bad enough, he thought, this smells like he's been on the nest all night.

Keera went past, waving breezily. 'Like the bloody Queen,' muttered Derek, as he put down the steamer and followed her to her dressing room. 'So what'll it be today, then, princess?' he asked, slightly ironically.

'I'm in a pink mood,' she said, as she rummaged aimlessly through her suits. 'Actually, I saw one of the newsreaders on Sky in a gorgeous suit that would be fantastic on me. It had one of those necklines like this ...' she indicated a sweetheart neckline '... and it came in here at the waist and then who knows?

Couldn't see because of the desk. Do you think you could get me one?'

'I'll see what I can do for you, Madame.' He bowed.

Keera was too busy perusing her outfits to notice the mock-deference.

After five minutes, she turned, gave him one of her aren't-I-pretty? smiles and said, in her girly voice, 'Can *you* find me something? Vanda's waiting for me, and she wants to do something different with my hair.'

As she headed off to Makeup, Derek surveyed the collection of outfits. Puce, he thought meanly. That's what you *should* be wearing.

Keera was in a very good mood. Today she had managed to snaffle the top interview from Mike. The minister for Education had announced he was resigning to spend more time with his family. There was a distinct possibility that this explanation was a euphemism for bad behaviour. He was an attractive man, with a frumpy wife and a flubber of a child.

Richard, the producer, had gone through her questions with her, and written them down on autocue to make sure she didn't forget them. She was excited that it might be picked up by PA or Reuters, with her name quoted as the interviewer. And Vanda would make sure she looked her best in case there were any 'takes' of her on air in the papers. That was why she wanted pink – it always stood out in a photograph.

She was getting her microphone and earpiece sorted out when Mike stomped past on his way to Wardrobe, with a face like a bag of smashed crabs. He had gone ballistic in the newsroom, shouting at all and sundry that he would be *damned* if he'd sit by and watch '*Minnie Mouse make a pig's ear of this fucking interview*'. And then he had cast aspersions upon their parentage, and told them that there would be repercussions. '*Don't you worry about that, you bunch of useless tossers.*'

He would have spent longer haranguing them, but since he had come in with only ten minutes to air, he had to get down to Makeup.

Keera was already composed on the sofa by the time he stalked in. 'Oops,' said one of the cameramen. 'We're in for a bumpy ride.' Mike was renowned for making life as unpleasant as possible if he was in a bad mood.

The director had already been warned about Mike's filthy temper today, and the reason for it. 'Morning, Mike, looking good,' he said jauntily, into the earpiece.

Mike nodded brusquely.

And the show started.

Mike refused to look at Keera during the two shots, even when she addressed a comment directly to him.

But nobody mentioned the frosty atmosphere.

You could have heard a pin drop in the studio. The guests were wheeled in in silence and none of the crew spoke unless spoken to.

Mike treated a man whose holiday had been ruined by a forty-eight-hour wait at Gatwick airport as though he was personally responsible for global warming and had possibly melted the icecap single-handedly with his foreign trips.

And then the big interview was upon them. In the gallery, they were holding a 50p-a-go sweepstake. Everyone had signed up to a selection of minutes before the eruption/interruption from Mike. Richard thought he was in with a strong chance on two minutes fifteen seconds. The autocue operator was quietly optimistic that she would be going home a few quid richer with her choice of one minute thirty seconds. As it was, nobody had gone for less than fifteen seconds, which was all it took.

Keera read the link. 'The Education minister has stunned Parliament by saying he's going to resign to spend more time with his family. The prime minister says he will be sorely missed and wishes him well with his future projects. And the Education minister joins us now.' She turned to him, pen in hand, her head on one side, and asked him, 'So, are you going to resign?' Mike couldn't help himself. His 'Phagh' could have been heard by whales foraging for krill off the south coast.

The Education minister was clearly confused. 'Yes,' he said hesitantly. 'Erm, actually, I did make that announcement yesterday.'

Keera was pleased. She'd got that sorted. Now to ask the questions Richard had written for her.

In the gallery, they weren't watching the interview. They were watching Mike on the preview camera. Not even Grant the director, a big Keera fan, could excuse that first question.

Mike's face was the colour of a bilberry with suppressed rage. And Richard sympathized with him. If he wasn't so knackered from five nights on the trot, he would have been shouting down the earpiece. But he'd got to the point where he felt like the dung beetle trying desperately to push his ball of dung up the hill. He had his head in his hands. As long as she stuck to the rest of the bloody questions, and didn't decide to throw in any more of her own, he'd be able to get through the morning meeting.

The vision mixer was wondering if he'd won the sweepstake with his thirty seconds since no one else had come up with anything shorter.

Resembling a small thundercloud, Mike read a link into the break about the weather. And as the adverts started, he stood up abruptly and strode purposefully past the cameramen. No one dared tell him that there were only two minutes on the break, and it was his item next.

They heard his entry into the gallery, but were disappointed when the microphones were cut on Mike's orders.

One minute, fifty-seven seconds later he reappeared, sat down, cold-shouldered Keera, and conducted an amusing interview with a woman who had spent her entire savings on a visit to Indonesia so that her pet lizard could see his homeland.

* * *

Katie was up early and, for the first time since her sacking, had turned on *Hello Britain!* to watch her replacement.

She could imagine the scenario after that first question, and immediately dialled Mike's number to leave a message, then thought better of it. What was the point? Nothing was going to get her the job back, and bitching about her replacement wouldn't make her feel any better. She turned over to watch an old episode of *Friends* instead.

She was pleased to notice that, on her wide-screen television, Jennifer Aniston looked positively porky.

She opened a tin of rice pudding and ate half the contents. Watched a bit of *Bewitched* and ate the other half so she could tidy away the tin into the bin. Right. She really must get on. Now, where was she?

Oh, yes. The fridge.

She took everything out and switched it off. It needed defrosting, and this was as good a time as any. And, there were items that obviously ought to be thrown away – or eaten. And while she was at it, the cupboards were still a mess. What on earth was she thinking of with a tub of mini muffins? Into the bin. Out of the bin. Delicious. A waste not to eat them. Put them back into the cupboard. Or eat them all and throw away the carton. Much better idea.

It was midday before she noticed the time.

She felt slightly sick. And very guilty. As if she wasn't spreading like the proverbial chestnut tree already, with all that home cooking and the occasional small sherry.

And she'd probably see Bob at the weekend so an effort had to be made, otherwise it was lights out and lying on her back at every opportunity so that the fat wouldn't be so noticeable. She would eat just fruit until then, and only if she was really hungry. Otherwise she'd make do with water.

She went to her vast wardrobe and chose a long soft jersey dress that wouldn't constrict her stomach, then went out for a coffee and accidentally ate a large, chewy biscuit.

London was looking perfectly glorious. May, she thought, was shaping up to be a wonderful month all round. The trees were clothed in early green leaves, and everyone was smiling – apart from that hideously dressed woman and her ugly child. Or was that a dog in the pram?

She loved Chelsea. Nice clean people with nice clean teeth. Nice clean streets. Nice clean shops.

She walked down to the river and watched it sparkling past. There was barely a cloud in the sky. The one that was there looked as if it had wandered off from the herd and was merely emphasizing how blue the sky was. 'God's in his heaven, all's right with the world,' she quoted.

In Marks & Spencer, she went randomly round the aisles, checking what was on offer and chucking two-for-ones into her basket.

'That'll be forty-two pounds thirty-seven please,' said the man at the checkout.

'Eh? How can it be that much?' Katie asked, raising her head from the basket that she felt made her look a little French.

'Cherries, eight-fifty. And there's the wine at twelve. That's already twenty pounds,' he said apologetically. 'Do you still want them?'

'No. Yes. Yes, it's OK. I didn't realize the cherries were so expensive.'

'They fly in from South Africa,' he explained.

'Goodness! All that way! Their arms must be exhausted,' said Katie, with a smile. 'Or maybe they're brought in by storks.'

He seemed confused.

'Stalks,' she added, smiled inanely and handed over her card.

Her agent was right. She was fatally addicted to rubbish puns.

But, hey, Bob was going to be feeding her soon. What did she care?

At about the same time that Katie was making the bad pun on cherry stalks, the picture editor of the *Mirror* was having a conversation with the stringer who had given them the photos of Katie and her bottles. The stringer said he had been trailing her on and off since he had spotted her leaving the supermarket and going to Oddbins, and had a number of interesting new pictures. He had shots of her going to a place called the Old Coach House in one outfit, and leaving the next day in the same one, with kisses being exchanged on the doorstep. He had photographs of the man who lived in the house getting into a car, and he had nice close-ups of her and the same man at a pub where they appeared at one stage to be glued together at the lips, in the manner of a fly on a lump of sugar. 'I asked around, and his name's Bob Hewlett. Divorced. No children.'

The phone call couldn't have been more fortuitous.

The *Mirror*'s gossip girls were thrilled. Now they had photos to go with the snippet of information provided by their *Hello Britain!* mole. They would run it on Wednesday as their main picture story with the headline: 'How Can You Fisher in a Tepee?'

The *Express*, meanwhile, was going to run a gossip item about *Hello Britain!*'s news editor being in talks with Channel 4 for a politics show. That, of course, was hardly interesting for their readership. What *was* was that Colin was possibly going to take Keera with him. Hardly surprising, after that searing interview she did with the Education minister recently. There can't be many people not left thinking that she should be the new host of *Newsnight*. They then used the article as an excuse to print a big picture of Keera in a bikini, kindly provided by her agent.

'Please don't tell anyone you got it from me,' he had told them. 'Keera would kill me.' He texted Keera afterwards to tell her that the mission had been accomplished and that the evidence had been deleted.

Wednesday dawned fair and fresh. Those going into *Hello Britain!* could feel the nights getting shorter. Sleeping during the day was becoming more difficult, but it was so much easier to get up when it was light. It was almost a joy to watch the sunrises. Almost. Few people would go for the sunrise option if sleeping was the other possibility.

Helen was the producer of the day, and had most of the programme in hand by the time Keera came in, pulled up a seat and logged on to the computer. 'Anything interesting in the papers today?' she asked casually.

'Yes, there is. Something about you going to a politics programme.' Helen smirked.

'Really?' said Keera, feigning astonishment.

'Mmm. That you and Colin are off together. I didn't even know he was in talks with Channel 4.'

'Neither did I. Nice to be considered as the possible presenter of a politics show, though,' said Keera, tucking a long strand of black hair behind her ear.

There was a snicker from behind one of the computers. She glanced over. 'Something funny?' she asked James, the intake editor.

'Oh, yes,' he said quickly. 'Skateboarding-duck item.'

Helen threw him a warning look. 'I don't think we have time for that today. We're a bit tight on the programme,' she said.

Even though Keera was suspicious, she was sensible enough to leave it there.

It was only when she was sitting on the sofa and riffling through the newspapers that she spotted the story about Katie and Bob. The editor of the *Mirror* had decided the item was worth taking out of the gossip pages and putting on page three.

There was even a little box at the bottom asking for information about Bob. And offering fifty pounds.

Suddenly Keera discovered herself hoist by her own petard. She had sold the story so a decent cheque was coming her way. But it was a much bigger piece than the one about her, and Katie looked very pretty in one of the pictures. She flicked surreptitiously to the one in the *Express* again. No, it was all right. She herself looked much better. And, casting a glance at Mike, she realized she had no need to be surreptitious. He was still grumpy after that interview with the Education minister on Friday and had barely spoken to her. He was doing last-minute swotting for his next item – an interview with an actress from a soap.

'Calling her an actress is like calling me a shot-putter,' he had ranted at Helen, on his way through the newsroom – running late as usual.

'I dunno,' she had said quietly to his retreating back. 'You've always been a bit of a tosser.'

James had snorted with laughter.

Mike had got his agent to phone The Boss after the Education minister incident. There had been a row about the Big Interview of the Day, and who should be doing it.

'My client, Mike, is far more experienced than his co-presenter, and should be doing anything that may be reported on PA,' the agent had said pompously.

The Boss had listened on speakerphone, with his secretary taking notes and members of the newsroom passing within earshot. When the call had finished, he had rung Mike at home and told him not to be an idiot. 'I know Keera didn't do the best of jobs,' he said, 'but if she never does these things, she's never going to learn. And she's doing the best she can. So back off. Anyway, part of the blame lies at Richard's door. He didn't coach her sufficiently. She thought she had to make absolutely sure he'd resigned before she went on to the other questions. And as for saying she didn't ask the one about the rumours that he had been caught out doing something he shouldn't have, I would draw your attention to the fact that when he was asked that later on the *Today* programme, he dead-batted it.'

'At least they *asked* the bloody question. It made us look like complete tits,' spluttered Mike.

That night, Mike thought he might try out his brand new items. He threw Buster into the car and set off in high spirits. But he had to find a new patch and was unable to discover anything he liked the look of. One possibility had been snaffled by a man in a battered old Ford Fiesta. Then he heard a police siren behind him, which gave him such a start that he speeded up and almost rear-ended a Volvo. It had ruined his equilibrium to the extent that he went home and downed three large whiskies in half an hour.

He would have felt better had he not spent that afternoon with his wife's family at the annual barbecue. It had been held mid-week because Mike refused to have his weekends ruined. ('They're the only days I don't have to get up before the dawn chorus.')

There had been a row about his refusal to put fish or vegetables on the grill for her mother. 'They ruin the taste of the sausages. If it's a barbecue, it's a barbecue. And that means meat. Not vegetables. And particularly not fish. It makes the sausages taste fishy. And I am damned,' his mother-in-law winced, so he repeated it, 'yes, I am *damned* if I'm going to serve up fishy sausages.'

Sandra had left him to it. She had put a lettuce leaf and a small quantity of tomato salad on her plate.

Her mother had gone at him like a wasp at a rotting plum.

'Next year,' he said, slamming the barbecue shut, 'you go to your mother's and I'll stay in and rearrange my face with a pair of secateurs. An infinitely more enjoyable experience.'

'It's one day out of your life, Mike,' she said, helping herself to another glass of water and staring longingly at the lone sausage he was about to feed to the dog.

She went to bed early, pleading a headache. But he heard her doing her sit-ups.

'Stupid trout,' he muttered under his breath, then threw all the dishes into the sink. The cleaner would do it – Aurelia, or whatever her name was. Not slim enough, pretty enough or with a small enough grasp of English to be useful to him. He didn't even want to see her bend over in a short skirt. By the time he got back from his aborted night out, he was in such a filthy mood that the only thing he wanted to do with any other human was kill them.

* * *

129

It was how Katie felt about the people at the *Mirror*. Her Wednesday afternoon had been ruined. How could she have been so thick? Of course that sneaky bastard had been taking photos of her after he'd made money out of her the first time.

A bottle bank in every way.

And she could think of only one person who could have revealed the information about the TP.

She was so full of rage she could barely eat the muffin she was having for lunch. She stuffed the last bit in, choking as she inhaled a raspberry. She stood outside Costa Coffee, slightly red and sweaty, with a coughed crumb on her Top Shop top, mobile phone in hand.

Dee's phone was off, so she left a message 'after the small annoying beep supplied by my provider'. It started with 'How fucking could you?' And ended 'Thank you for being my so-called friend. I hope you got well paid for it.'

Luckily, Bob had taken it good-humouredly. 'The only thing I'm confused about is TP. Are you going to let me in on the secret?' he asked.

Katie kept her fingers crossed behind her back, as she had since childhood when she told lies. 'It's just a reference to the fact that we barely made it out of the tent. I told Dee about it. Actually, I've just had a horrible thought. She probably wouldn't have sold it ... Of course she wouldn't. She would probably have said it accidentally to somebody she didn't know was a gossip journalist. Toads. Sorry. I'll call you back.'

She phoned Dee again. She left another message which started, 'Sorry about the other message,' and ended, 'But could you just be more careful in future?' Then she popped back into Costa Coffee, bought another muffin, because the last one had been ruined, and phoned Bob again.

He tried to cheer her up by saying she had warned him about photographs and that he wasn't too worried. 'My mum seems to think it's rather sweet,' he said. 'She's very pleased we've got it together. She always liked you, you know. Actually, the thing I'm most annoyed about is that I'm only worth fifty quid!'

By the time she got home, Katie was still fuming about the piece. It really wasn't terribly helpful to her career. But she felt a bit better because Bob hadn't taken umbrage. She opened a bottle of red wine – after all, somewhere in the world the sun was over the yardarm – then opened a bottle of something unpleasant she had found at the back of a cupboard when she was clearing up. It was blue and tasted funny but, hell, the person who invented coffee probably thought that it tasted weird first time round.

By the time *The Archers* came on just after seven o'clock, she could barely remember her name, let alone what Eddie Grundy was doing with the cows in her sitting room.

CHAPTER TWELVE

Dee had left her mobile at work so she didn't get Katie's messages until she turned it on at five o'clock in the morning. She was in the dressing room, blearily trying to decide what to wear. She put it on speakerphone, and smiled to herself when she heard William giving her possible dates for another meeting. She paused with her hand hovering around the blue section of her wardrobe as she listened hard to the second message – someone inviting her to a drinks party on Saturday. Then she almost stopped breathing as Katie blurted out her message with more than a hint of venom. She took it off speakerphone, pressed '1' and listened again. She only half heard the first message before Katie's voice was booming out again with her apology.

She let out the breath she had been holding, and stood with her hands on the table and her head down, trying to work out how she could have revealed the TP to anyone.

Derek came in to help her make her choice and found her in her tracksuit, staring into space. 'What's occurring?' he asked, intrigued.

'Oh, nothing,' said Dee, hurriedly, turning back to the wardrobe. She allowed Derek to pick out an outfit he had bought on a sale and no-return basis, which no one had liked. He had put it into Dee's wardrobe – and on Dee's budget – one quiet afternoon.

'Is that mine?' she queried. When assured that it was, she went meekly to Makeup to wash her hair. She blow-dried it, and put on moisturizer by rote, searching every neuron to discover when she had let the TP thing slip out. She travelled down the cranial equivalent of the back of the sofa, then concluded that getting up early was turning her from alert to a blurt.

She went to sit on the makeup chair. I'm wearing a sort of snot-green outfit,' she answered, in response to a question about eye-shadow colour.

She was very quiet as the brushes whisked over her face. With her eyes shut, she tried to remember whom she had spoken to since the conversation with Katie. Had she told William? She didn't think so. It wouldn't be the sort of thing she'd tell a prospective shag. No reason to mention another girl while flirting. And she had been to only one party where there had been reporters, a photographic exhibition of landscapes. It wouldn't have lent itself to a comment about Katie's latest conquest and the size of his tent pole.

She opened her eyes as Keera glided past with a flash of black hair, and a little wave at those in Makeup.

Her weather bulletins that morning were a disaster. At one stage, she had cupped her hand over south-west Britain and said the shaft of Cornwall was going to get slippy. Then she had lurched over Dorset and staggered around Scotland 'where there will be a bit of flog and mist'.

Mike smirked as she handed back to him. 'Did you say it was drizzling in Devon, or was it just you *drivelling* in Devon? And possibly the rest of the poor country?' he asked, with a smile.

Dee forced her face into an answering – if unconvincing – smile, as Grant barked a laugh into her earpiece.

She went back to the dressing room and slumped in front of the mirror, the green suit reflecting on her face, making it look as if she'd been steeped in limeade. God, what had she been thinking, buying this outfit? It was hideous. The colour of algae bloom on a pond. Really only suitable for an eighteen-year-old with a neck like a swan. Or just a swan.

After her nine o'clock weather bulletin, she girded her loins and phoned Katie.

Katie had been up for hours, staggering from the tap to her bedroom, to the bathroom, with her pyjama bottoms on back to front, and her pyjama top done up wrongly. She had drunk about a litre of water in twenty minutes. Her stomach was distended. But it was as nothing compared to the distention she could feel in her brain. She could feel it trying to get out. It was knocking at the skull wall. There was almost no room for her eyeballs. When she had been able to open them against the pressure of her brain, she had checked in the mirror to see if anything had been damaged.

She was horrified.

Were those your actual bags under her eyes? Or had two flesh-coloured caterpillars crept in under cover of darkness and slept in the hollows?

The phone startled her, and she held it gingerly to her ear.

'Yes?' she asked in a thin voice.

'It's Dee. Look, I'm so sorry if it was me, but I honestly don't remember mentioning it to anyone.'

'What?'

'I didn't tell anyone about the TP tent pole thing. There wasn't anyone I wanted to tell, and I haven't been anywhere where I would have found anyone who wanted me to tell them and would've put it in the paper or phoned someone who was on a paper.'

Katie sat down. Her head was pulsating like a cartoon heart. 'Right. Good. Right,' she said. 'Can I talk to you later? I think I may be poisoned. And there must be an antidote in the cupboard. If not, I may have to cut somewhere and extract the poison.'

'You poor thing,' said Dee, sympathetically; ''Shorrible when you get poisoned. I recommend a banana.'

'I'll be sick if you talk about food. I'm going now. I need –'

'Of course you do. I'll phone you later.'

* * *

At least Katie was still talking to her.

And, now she came to think of it, the photos were all right. And certainly better than the previous ones. And the TP thing hadn't been rumbled. And Bob looked rather handsome.

Thinking about which, the handsome Mr Baron wanted another date ... when next Wednesday was already in the diary! Most excellent. There was a spring in her step as she went up to the newsroom.

The morning meeting went on around her, as she pretended to pay attention, her eyes unfocused. Simon had made some sort of snide comment about her performance, but she was in the middle of taking William's clothes off and laying her face on his chest, so she nodded, said sorry, and returned to her daydream.

Jim Break had seen the photographs and was not unhappy about their appearance. He had been talking to a couple of mates in the business and had lined up a meeting for Katie with the head of a new production company, which was planning to make a series about the dating game, provisionally called *All Mine At Nine*, for ITV2 at nine p.m.

Katie was feeling ill. But less ill. And she decided to make a decision. She stood in the sitting room indecisively. Then did it.

Yes.

She was going to grasp the nettle of life and squeeze it tightly. She would put a dock leaf on her hand later.

She was going to get her house in order.

Take the bull by the horns.

Grab the future under its armpits and shake it until its gonads dropped.

And she was going to start right now.

She ate what was left in the store cupboard and fridge since the last clearout.

She put the empty bottles in the recycling. There appeared to be a fair number. She turfed out a whole lot of shoes. Too small. Too weird. Too old-fashioned. Too left feet.

And as she reached and fumbled, the wretchedness and retchedness receded. She would get slim. Watch how slim I'm going to get. A stone in a week, at least. She cleaned a window. It was exhausting. The others would have to wait until tomorrow. After all, you only looked out of one window at a time.

As the rush-hour started, she sat down with a cup of strong tea and watched the news on Sky. Followed by the news on Channel 4. Followed by a documentary about bridges on the Discovery Channel. And something about revolting diseases on Channel 5.

She lay down with a bottle of water to watch the news at ten, and was in bed by eleven p.m., reading a book about how to reduce wrinkles.

Salmon. That seemed to be it.

She flicked to the last chapter. Yup. Salmon. Every day. I will have a fishy on a little dishy every dashed day. And maybe sleep on it on Tuesdays.

I could be pre-pubescent by – she looked at her watch – Sunday.

Keera was having an early night. She was wearing her brand new turquoise silk nightie and her cleaner had put fresh sheets on the bed. She gazed at herself in the mirror. God, she thought, I really am quite beautiful.

But to stave off any ravages created by the chocolate she had allowed herself at lunch, she cleansed for the second time and applied a very expensive face pack.

While the pale cream gradually sank into her translucent skin, she tucked her feet up on the sofa and watched *Friends* on E4. Followed by *Friends* on More 4. Followed by a bit of *Lost*, which she had recorded, then caught five minutes of a show about disgusting diseases on Channel 5.

Then she phoned work to find out what interviews she was doing the next morning, carefully wiped off the face pack and slipped between the sheets. Not long now until her magazine article came out. She smiled secretively as she sniffed the sheets. When she was rich, she'd have clean sheets and a massage every day. And a facial every week.

She wanted a million in the bank by next year.

The salary from *Hello Britain!* was good – but not that good. That was why she *had* to supplement her income by selling stories to a couple of newspapers. She knew that with a newspaper column you could rake in a fortune. If she showed her commitment to one paper, she'd have a foot on the ladder.

Then there were the photo shoots, which she'd already started to charge for. She wasn't picky. Any magazine that wanted her could stump up the readies for the privilege.

And her agent had found her a number of jobs hosting corporate events, which were very lucrative. There had been a hiccup recently when she'd slagged off a caravanning conference she had hosted, only to discover that the person who had organized it was there. Whoops. But what did she care? She was the beautiful Keera Keethley, licensed to thrill. They couldn't get enough of her well-toned body. She'd get as much as she could for free, and she wasn't afraid of hard work. Or of working hard to get her way. And if there were people in the way of her getting her way … well, it was the law of the jungle. Mmmmm. The jungle. That would be a good photograph. Me in a bikini. A thin film of sweat. Who could she flog that to?

Actually, she thought, hanging her feet off the edge of the bed to let them breathe, there's one outstanding part of the plan which is, as yet, unfilled.

The post of consort. Or was it cohort? What was the difference? Did she care enough to find out?

She examined her nails. Must get a French manicure.

No, I definitely, definitely don't care.

She slid her hands under the cool pillows to find her Jackie Collins book.

* * *

Mike was having a fairly late night. He had found a promising new furrow to plough – an area that appeared to be awash with possibilities.

If he had been a superstitious man – and he wasn't – he would have put it down to Buster's neckerchief ... the very one he'd been wearing on the first ever escapade some years ago. He had driven north for about half an hour. It didn't even feel like London. He had taken another half an hour to make his choice, and the whole episode had been swift and very satisfactory. All his new toys had performed well.

He hummed and sang along with the songs on Melody FM on his way home. He could have shouted, he felt so alive.

He locked the car, checked that everything was where it should be in case Sandra was up, and let himself in through the front door. He could hear the television blaring from her room. Then the noise dropped dramatically.

Sandra had watched *Richard and Judy*. *The Six Show*. Three episodes of *CSI*. And a show about foul illnesses on Channel 5. Then she had started to paint her toenails, and was midway through watching *Must Like Dogs* when she heard the door click.

She turned down the television, switched off the light, and snuggled down in the bed, leaving her feet hanging out of the end of the duvet to stop the polish smudging. She breathed quietly. Not that she was too worried about him coming in and bothering her but it was as well to take precautions. There had been nights recently when he had looked at her in what she thought was a calculating way, and she didn't want him getting the wrong idea by drawing attention to the fact that she was still up.

Sandra liked the lifestyle she had with Mike, but she saw no reason to indulge in the sort of activities that involved sticky seepage. She found the idea of sex only slightly less repulsive than some of the diseases she had seen on television tonight. If she had been approached by a man with a clipboard demanding that she put her X next to a choice between horizontal jogging with Mike or having her leg hairs plucked out by a man with snaggle teeth, she would have gone for the full, painful deforestation. At least he wouldn't sweat on her and make that horrid grunting noise at the end.

If she thought of Mike at all – and it was difficult to find any time to think about him, with her strenuous exercise and beauty routine – it was an affliction that had to be borne.

Like her bunions.

Bob had spent the night at the pub. He had had a fruitful day. Having been left the house and a fair sum of money by his father, he had dumped his job in the City and taken up his first love, gardening. That day he had been to see a charity that wanted him to landscape a plot of land behind a children's hospice. He would be paid a nominal fee – barely enough to cover his expenses – but he had virtually a free hand and was already planning his own vision ... his own version of the Secret Garden.

He had had a long conversation with Katie's brother, Ben, who had phoned him at home when he was considering having a nice glass of wine to celebrate his commission.

'I'm ringing you because now that you and my sister are, er … erm …'

'Yes?' said Bob, helpfully.

'Well, I thought it would be better coming from me than anyone else …'

'You're scaring me. Get on with it.'

'Well, there's been a piece in the paper. About you and her. And some details that are correct, and some that I'm sure aren't …'

'You can stop right there. We talked about it yesterday. I was only worried that information on me seems so cheap. If it was worth it, I'd have phoned them myself. But not for fifty quid.'

Ben laughed. 'I would have told them that, as a doctor, I'm concerned that at your age and your stage of training you should be riding what we in the profession call "a donorbike". How's it going?'

The rest of the phone call had been about the new Triumph Speed Triple, which Bob was going to take racing. It was black, shiny, fast, and sounded like an Airbus taking off. 'It's mental,' he said. He decided to celebrate his new gardening job with a few pints down at the pub with Harry from the next village north.

Harry was a watch designer, who lived with his illustrator wife and four-year-old daughter in a beautiful Georgian house that Bob was fond of dropping in on around dinner time. He was Elizabeth's godfather. He was frequently spotted pedalling her round the lanes, on a bright pink cycle-and-bin contraption. He would be forced – less unwillingly than he made out – to wear an orange fluorescent vest for added safety as Elizabeth sat regally in the 'bin' with her bubblegum-coloured helmet on.

Bob was on his second pint, thinking aimlessly of salted nuts, when Harry arrived, later than scheduled. 'Sorry. There was this riveting programme about truly unpleasant illnesses that Sophie was watching. All in revolting close-up. You wouldn't catch me showing my naked hairy arse to the world.'

'I think you'll find,' said Bob, ordering two pints of Old Speckled Hen, 'that your naked hairy arse has been on show many times, not least in the common room at university after your team won the cup. And again, if I'm not much mistaken, after your stag night.'

'Stag weekend,' corrected Harry. 'That was such a bloody good weekend. Although I could have done without being tied to that lamp-post without a stitch on in February. If it wasn't for you, I'd probably have caught pneumonia. Nothing around but sheep. Actually, I'm thinking of going back to Kerry for a weekend of golf and fishing. Fancy it?'

'Not at the moment,' said Bob. 'Keeping weekends free just in case …'

'Just in case what?' asked Harry, looking him squarely in the face with his eyebrows raised.

'In case I need to go to London, or in case this bird I'm seeing decides to come here for a weekend.' And he filled Harry in with the details. 'Funnily enough,' he said, munching a salt-and-vinegar crisp, 'I've *always* fancied Katie. I do like an older woman. Anyway, probably nothing will come of it, but of course I'm up for a bit of fishing if it doesn't work out.'

'How much older *is* she, then?' asked Harry.

'Only a few years actually. What *are* these crisps?' He turned the packet round. 'My God. I didn't think they made anything normal any more. I was fully expecting something like chicken winnet and goat beard. How very refreshing.' And, as he had intended, that got them off the subject of Katie.

He thought Katie was gorgeous. If he was being honest with himself, she was the first woman since his divorce who had made him think about marriage. He had seen her the morning after the night before and his heart had lurched in a way that it hadn't for a very long time.

He liked her sense of humour, the way she threw herself into everything, the sparkle in her eye when she was having a rant – and the vulnerability that occasionally leaked through.

He was in grave danger of falling in love.

He had known about some of her relationships – those that had appeared in the papers – and she had brought some of her lovers home to Yorkshire with her over the years. But she had told him there had been few – if any – who had meant anything to her.

And he was very much hoping that he did.

As he ambled home from the pub, hands in his pockets, smelling more than faintly of fine ale, he was a happy man. The moon was shining, the night sky glittering with stars. He could see the Great Bear, the Plough and Orion's belt. If he looked really hard, he thought he could see Orion's underpants too. He let himself into the Old Coach House, poured himself a couple of very fat fingers of whisky and headed for bed. He threw his clothes on to the floor, climbed under the rumpled duvet and fell asleep to the shipping forecast on Radio 4.

CHAPTER THIRTEEN

Katie's week had slipped by so sneakily it was as if the days had been dressed in combat fatigues. One morning, she had braved a bit of *Hello Britain!* Mike, she noticed, was massively snubbing Keera. Good. She'd known she could count on him.

She watched Keera doing an interview with The Proclaimers. 'How did you two meet?' she asked, leaning forward for a maximum-cleavage shot. She heard Mike laugh in the background. Excellent. She could only imagine the hilarity in the control room.

By Friday, she had had enough of her own company. Her agent, Jim, had organized a meeting for Monday with the TV company doing the dating show, and she had spoken to everyone she could think of who wouldn't snitch to the newspapers about the fact that she was available.

She reckoned she had another two weeks before she would have to think seriously about remortgaging. Or even selling up and moving to a smaller flat, or a different area. But articulating that thought aloud made her feel so depressed she could feel her mojo leaking out of her feet.

The problem was, London was so darned expensive if you didn't have the readies. Money seeped from the pores of her wallet if she so much as stepped out of the flat, what with one coffee and another.

So, when Bob phoned to ask her to come and stay for the weekend, she hesitated for less time than it had taken her eyelashes to blow off during a faulty-oven incident ten years previously.

She managed to find a fairly cheap train ticket on the Internet, stopping at all points north, and pulled out a bag. What to put in it? Pyjamas, obviously. But the white cotton? Pink silk? Playful lemon with pink strawberries?

This is ridiculous, she thought. I'm a grown woman, worried about pyjamas. And pyjamas aren't sexy, anyway, are they?

Or are they?

Well, I can't sleep without them, so if he has an issue with that, then … Then what? Then nothing. I can hardly develop the physical ability to generate heat. Become the embodiment of a radiator. Radiate heat. When I'm a heat-sapper. She continued to reason as she tried on ten or eleven pairs of pyjamas. The thing is, pyjamas are comfortable. And they're useful for going to make tea in cold kitchens. And I'd rather be seen in pyjamas than naked. Cellulite. Bottom. Thighs. She shuddered.

She put in plain pink cotton pyjamas.

Was it better to have a baggier pyjama than a close-fitting pyjama when seen from the back?

This was a nightmare.

She consulted her watch. She really ought to get a move on.

She threw in four pairs of pyjamas. Just in case. By the time she had done the pyjamas, there wasn't much time to choose anything else. For heaven's sake, it's only a weekend. She grabbed her favourite comfortable clothes and one nice dress.

She could barely close the case. She appeared to be carrying more than she would have taken for a fortnight's potholing in Peru.

And only made the train by the skin of her teeth.

When the announcement came through of the stops it would be making, Katie realized that this was going to be one of the longest train journeys ever. And that she'd forgotten her iPod.

She started off sitting near a man with one that had such inadequate headphones she could hear virtually every word. She was on the verge of asking him whether the racket he was listening to was Daft Punk or Daft Rubbish when he got off.

A fat woman with two fat children got on. They started eating their way through a mountain of salty snacks. Katie glanced at her watch. A whole day that I'll never have again before I reach Yorkshire. I knew I should have booked a fast ticket.

It's like that bloody day I tried to get home from the Tory Party conference in Blackpool and the *Hello Britain!* travel department booked me a super-saver ticket, only valid on Sunday.

Mind you, she had immediately bought herself a first-class ticket and enjoyed drinking herself into a stupor with a load of political hacks – one of whom, she thought, she might have bounced on later. He always greeted her as if she had. On the other hand, there had been occasions when she *knew* she hadn't slept with them, but they acted as if she had. Having a reputation for putting out after a few glasses was not one she wanted. But it was accurate.

Thinking of which, now that she had lost at least a pound with her non-drinking regime, she could afford to cheer herself up on this dreadful journey with a nice vodka-tonic.

Her mouth was watering with anticipation as she left her seat to go to the buffet, past the fat family, who were now surrounded by pastry crumbs and empty packets. How come families like that always smell? she wondered. It's like going into primary schools where children always smell of biscuity bottoms.

She negotiated her way round a smooching couple, who were oblivious to the looks they were receiving as they noisily exchanged saliva, and joined the queue of malcontents waiting for service from the thin, spotty youth behind the bar. Either he was on a go-slow, or he really did move at the pace of a slug without a destination lettuce.

Finally she was at the front of the queue. 'Vodka-tonic, please,' she requested.

He handed her a see-through plastic cup, with a dash of vodka in the bottom, and a tin of tonic water.

'Could I have another, please?' she asked. 'You can put it in the same cup,' she added helpfully. 'Actually make it a double.'

'That'll be a triple then,' he said, picking lightly at a crusty spot.

'Yes, I'm aware of that,' said Katie, with asperity.

'Do you want another tonic?'

'No, thank you. But thank you for asking. I would never have thought of that on my own.'

She could feel the man behind her getting twitchy. But she had reached the age when she would not be put off by huffing. She handed over the money, waited until Wednesday for the change, because Mr Spotty Youth seemed unable to add or subtract properly, then went back to her seat.

The vodka-tonic lasted her until Peterborough. She managed to get in another triple during the interminable stop. Must be watered down, she thought, as the train crawled into Doncaster and she hadn't got 'the Buzz'. She'd had nothing to eat all day. Apart from the muffin she'd eaten for breakfast. And the egg-and-cress sandwich she'd grabbed on the way to the tube. She'd eaten them standing up so they didn't count.

She made her way past the fat family, who were now almost completely obscured by food wrappers. They were surrounded by so much detritus that she wondered vaguely if someone had burst. She decided that the smell they exuded was like a Dulux paint chart. Bacon butty with a hint of cloying sweetness. Do pigs think other pigs smell? she mused. Do they have a discriminating olfactory sense? If they could smell a human roasting, would they turn to their piggy friends and say they could murder a human butty? If they call them human, and not something else. After all, bacon doesn't sound in any way like pig. Pork doesn't really sound like pig. Maybe they call us rosbifs, as the French do. Only they would have to be French pigs. Do all pigs speak the same language?

She walked through the carriages, past the snogging couple – she had read somewhere that other people's saliva washing over your teeth is good for the enamel – and got to the buffet bar. The queue was so long she ended up jogging in the intersection with an occasional waft of brake fluid, which overrode the smell of stale sweat from the man in front.

What was it about men and their suits? They wear them and wear them, and never think they need to clean them. They get hot. Sweat. Eat and drop things. Possibly have sex with their secretaries in cupboards, then zip themselves up and pop themselves on tubes and trains along with other baked animals … and don't think they might smell horrible.

'Dry-cleaning's the answer,' she said aloud. And immediately realized she had. Four people in front of her turned to check she wasn't a nutter. One was a woman who did a double-take. After a few minutes, she peered round Mr Stinky, to ask, 'Is it you?'

'Of course it's me,' said Katie, frowning at the nylon-slacks-and-floral-blouse combination. 'Did you think I was you?'

The woman laughed, revealing a front tooth that was longer than every other tooth and lined with brown. 'No. I mean, are you famous?'

'Obviously not,' quoted Katie, from a reply she remembered Barry Cryer had made to the same question.

'Yes, you are,' said Mrs Slacks-and-floral. 'You're that woman off the telly. Breakfast telly. Got sacked. Read it in the paper. Can I have your autograph?'

Katie was trapped. She didn't want to give her autograph. But this was the sort of woman who wouldn't give up. Grudgingly she nodded.

'Have you got a pen?' asked Mrs Slacks-and-floral.

'No, I haven't. Sorry. Shame. I'll give you the autograph later,' said Katie thankfully. And ended the conversation.

Only it didn't end because, after a pause, the woman in front of Mrs Slacks-and-floral said she *did* have a pen. So there was a scrabble for a piece of paper. Eventually a napkin, soiled with a tea stain, was handed back to her. 'Best wishes, Katie Fisher', she scribbled. And, as an afterthought, put a squiggle at the end, which might have been a kiss. May as well appear friendly to the ugly beast, she thought, keep its ravening maw quiet. She handed it back.

The other woman leaned round. 'Can you sign me something as well?' she asked, wafting another napkin with a similarly shaped stain.

Ohforfuckssake, thought Katie, but, nevertheless, applied herself to the task and handed back the napkin. She now felt thoroughly disgruntled.

The sodding train was taking for ever to get anywhere, the drinks were watered down, she was surrounded by trolls, the heating was making her sweaty, and all she wanted was to fall into Bob's arms and be made to feel fizzy.

She was almost at her stop by the time she finally extruded another triple vodka from the pustule at the bar and had to neck it at speed before she gathered her belongings – being careful in case they had shifted during the journey.

She staggered slightly as she got down from the train. Now, where had Bob said he'd pick her up? She lumbered through the ticket barrier and out into the car park, feeling hot, bothered and – now she came to think of it – a bit peculiar.

Must have been the egg sandwich. You can never trust a non-organic egg sandwich. Bound to have been laid by a three-legged creature in a Thai chicken shed with no windows or board games, then mixed with mayonnaise by a man who hadn't washed his hands despite his recent attack of death.

Bob swam mistily into focus. 'Hello, you look very handsome,' she slurred, and sort of tripped into his arms, offering her face to be kissed.

Bob gave her a big, warm, comforting hug and took her bag as he walked her to the car. 'Good time on the train, I see,' he commented, with a smile.

'No, it was bloody awful. I think I've been on it since Tuesday. Nothing nice to look at, and everyone smelling of cheese,' she drawled, only narrowly making it up the ledge into his Land Rover.

As he drove, she strove to concentrate on what he was saying about the weekend and the plans he had made.

Suddenly, it was one bend too many. 'Stop the car, I'm going to be sick,' she declared, through tightly clenched teeth. And she was, so violently that the cow parsley was taken by surprise and launched some of it back on to her shoe.

Katie stood there, shaky and clammy. How very unpleasant. But she definitely felt better.

'Are you all right?' asked Bob, solicitously, coming round to her.

'Mmm. Fine. Dodgy egg sandwich at the station,' she explained. 'Feel better now. No, don't come too close. Sorry. I'll clean up a bit. Give me a moment.'

She heard him move away and bent forward to pick a dock leaf to clean off the mess on her shoe. And got stung on the face by a nettle. How long had she lived in the country? She *knew* that if there were dock leaves there would be nettles too. Or that where there were nettles there would be dock leaves. She grasped another dock leaf and rubbed her head.

Bob watched the theatre from the driving seat. Bless her, he thought. What a mess. He assumed she was miserable and drunk because of the state of her career, and decided that this weekend would be about her, about making it better, about wrapping her in a big blanket of love.

Whoops. Careful, Bob, he thought. Let's not do the L-word. Big blanket of loveliness. That's what's needed.

When she struggled back into her seat, the scent of vomit clinging to her, he excused her behaviour and drove carefully back to the house. Which, even if he said so himself, was looking bloody gorgeous.

The rambling roses were poking their snouts out from the foliage, the yew hedge was preening, the tradescantia was fair bursting into the sunshine ... everything in the garden was glowing.

Katie fought to keep it all together. She barely noticed the tendrils of wisteria curling softly round the door, as Bob carried her bag in and dumped it on the floor. 'Would you mind awfully if I went for a little lie-down?' she asked.

'Of course not,' said Bob, looking disappointed. 'You know where you're going. I've just got to go and turn the oven down.'

Katie trod heavily up the stairs, lugging her bag. She crouched to get out her spongebag, washed the green dock-leaf residue from the middle of her forehead ('Nice look,' she muttered), cleaned her teeth and lay on the bed. The birds outside were discussing how you could afford to be up later to get a worm if you knew where to go. Katie snuggled into the clean sheets and swam drunkenly into sleep.

Downstairs, Bob regarded the vegetable stew to which he had added dumplings on his way out to the station. Would they go soggy if he left them in and turned the oven off? He was unusually desperate for the meal to be just right. There was a bottle of red wine ready in the decanter, which he imagined was going to be an unwelcome sight to a pair of hung-over eyeballs.

He sighed.

Over the next few hours, he kept watch over his alleged girl-friend, and his alleged dumplings. Night fell, and she slumbered on, the stew got cold and the dumplings collapsed into the coagulating vegetables.

At ten o'clock, he stood up determinedly.

Katie was curled up with her feet under the duvet, her long hair waving over the pillows in a cloud of auburn softness. He gazed at her thoughtfully, then reached out a hand to touch a curl. She woke and smiled at him. He smiled back, his heart contracting. How beautiful she was, with the light of the moon shining through the window, he thought. 'Hungry?' he asked.

'I don't think so,' she said, propping herself on her elbows and deliberating. 'What time is it?'

'Gone ten,' he said. 'I thought I'd better wake you or you'd never get to sleep. As it were. How are you feeling? Better?'

'Much better, thank you. Not tip-top, one hundred per cent, but much better than I did. I'm so sorry. I have a sneaking suspicion that I may have over-imbibed on the train. I may have a headache coming on.'

Bob disappeared. He returned a few minutes later bearing two tablets zipping round a glass of water.

'I feel so guilty,' she said, slurping down the welcome opaqueness. 'I seem to remember you saying something about dinner tonight.' She couldn't help an involuntary grimace. 'Why don't we go down, and you eat it?'

He studied her contemplatively. 'I have a much better idea,' he said. 'I'll go and turn everything off, then join you in the bed, now that you've warmed it up.'

Katie felt her stomach lurch in an altogether more agreeable fashion than it had been doing since its last vodka injection, and while Bob was clattering about in the kitchen, she brushed her teeth again, gave the essential bits a flannel bath and put on her blue pyjamas.

She arranged herself in what she felt was an alluring pose to await his return. She heard him bouncing up the stairs, and positioned herself so that the moonlight shone obliquely behind her left shoulder. Those hideously long, dull photo shoots had not been in vain: if she had learned nothing else, she had discovered the value of good lighting.

And it was worth it for the look on Bob's face as he opened the door again ...

CHAPTER FOURTEEN

At about the time that Katie was broaching her first triple vodka, Dee was a-flutter because she had a date with William. On a *Friday* night. 'Oh, yes, oh, yes,' she sang, as she began to get ready. 'I can have a drink. Or four. Let my hair down. And my knickers – oops, how very, very naughty, Miss Krammer,' she berated herself, while smirking.

Legs waxed. Check.

Underarms waxed. Check.

Bikini line waxed. Fuck, yes.

Eyebrows plucked. Check.

Best underwear. Check.

Outfit to go on top of best underwear. Hell, no. There was absolutely *nothing* to wear in the wardrobe.

But that can be put right immediately, with a trip to Oxford Street before an afternoon nap, followed by a sloughing-off in the shower, a thorough moisturizing, a toe- and fingernail inspection and makeup application. How was she going to fit it all in?

At seven thirty, Dee decided she hated her new outfit. It was uncomfortable, wrong for the time of year, wrong with her shoes, wrong with her body. Wrong. Wrong. Wrong. It was as wrong as her ex-boyfriend taking Seamus up the Marmite motorway, as he probably was right now. As wrong as Christmas in California. As wrong as eating parrot.

She dragged out a pair of jeans and a long, orange, floaty item which she had bought from Karen Millen in the sale, what?, at least eight years ago. Her lipstick and eyeliner were now out of kilter, but sod it. How much did she really fancy William Baron anyway?

She pursed her lips. Actually, quite a lot. Damn.

At eight thirty, having changed into a burgundy dress from a secondhand stall at Camden Market, scraped off her makeup and applied blusher, lip-gloss and a lick of mascara, she was as ready as she was going to be. And late.

'Hi, William,' she panted into her mobile, as she ran to the tube, leaping over a tramp who tried to ask for money. 'I'm running a tad late. Problems at home. I'll explain later. I'll be there in half an hour. Sorry. Sorry. Got to go.'

The clock had never seemed to move so fast. The tube took for ever to arrive, with the sign merely flashing up that she was on the Northern Line.

Come on, come on, she willed it, tapping her foot up and down, trying not to get stressed.

She walked into the Oxo Tower on London's South Bank forty-five minutes late.

* * *

William stood up as she approached the table, flustered, with a slight sheen on her top lip.

'I'm so sorry to have kept you waiting,' she said apologetically, aware that she wasn't arriving as she had imagined. And probably not as he had either.

He looked at his watch. 'It's fine,' he said, as if he didn't mean it. 'Sit down, have a drink and relax. It's Friday night, the end of the week. What was the problem?'

'The tube,' she said. 'It took for ever to come.'

'I meant the other problem.'

'What other problem?' she asked, confused.

'The problem at home,' he stated, nodding internally to himself. Yup, she'd made it up, whatever it wasn't.

She explained about a neighbour, a cat and a hanging basket, then noticed his expression. 'You're right.' She smiled guiltily. 'All made up. I had a crisis of confidence. To be honest, I changed outfit three times, lost my keys under the mountain of clothes, and then, honestly, the tube *did* take for ever to come. I really am truly sorry to have kept you waiting.'

'Normally,' he said, 'I would take this opportunity to say that being late is the ultimate rudeness because it implies your time is more valuable than the other person's. But you're excused because you look very pretty, and I'm conceited enough to think that it was extra effort for my benefit.' He tipped his head on one side.

'Cocky,' she said, emboldened, 'but true. And you wouldn't have liked the first outfit, which I bought … which I bought … which I bought …' She ground to a halt.

'Which you bought?' he prompted.

'Specially,' she finished. And laughed. 'Enough of this nonsense. You don't want to hear me waffle on about that. Let me tell you what happened at *Hello Britain!* this morning. One of our reporters, David, was doing a piece about an inaugural flight for top nobs to LA. It was supposed to be all Secret Squirrel, because we didn't have permission to film on board ... all those celebrities and everything. Anyway, he got mashed on the plane, with all the free champagne, told the guy next to him that he was filming for television. *He* told someone else, the captain got to hear of it, came down and said that under no circumstances would there be unauthorized film of that first flight, and confiscated David's camera and everything. David got off at LA airport, or rather fell off, arse over tit by all accounts, got into a cab and headed for the studio. He was incapable of writing a script. The overnight producer had to send one over to his BlackBerry, which he then voiced, even though he could barely speak. He was so roundly abused on the phone that he says now he's going to take them to an industrial tribunal for making him cry ... Oh, yes, please. I'll have a dry martini, a dirty dry martini with olives, please,' she said, as the waitress came to ask her what she would have to drink.

'Do I take it, then, that we're in for a good time?' asked William, approvingly.

'We may be,' she confirmed flirtily. 'Oh, and Keera mentioned today about you doing some strand at work, so we may see a bit more of you.'

He seemed puzzled.

'Didn't you know?'

'No. But I don't mind at all,' he said. 'I'm gratified to be mentioned in a conversation by top television totty.'

'Do you think she's top totty?' she asked searchingly.

He spotted the heffalump trap and sidestepped it neatly. 'Not as top and tottyish as you. But you must confess she's easy on the eye.'

'It's not the eye that's the problem. It's the ear,' she said. And almost blushed because it came out sounding so eleven-year-old petulant. 'Look, she's not my favourite person because she ousted one of my best friends from the sofa, is all. And she's not the best interviewer in the world. But yes. Easy on the eye.'

'Why was she talking about strands, anyway?' he asked, reaching for his glass of lime and soda.

'Well, she said maybe you should do a strand. Which I agreed with. Helping different people to get their life on track. Harassed mums. Harassed students. Harassed pets. Harassed television presenters who are late.'

He smiled. 'You're not harassed, are you?'

'Not so much now,' she responded. 'But I did have a horrible time getting here, and it was like that scene in the film *Airplane* where everyone was wanting to accost me. In fact, there was one beggar near the tube who said, "Spange", to me. I know I was late, but I had to go back round and do another fly-past. He was definitely saying, "Spange". I was sitting on the Northern Line wondering about it, and I suddenly thought, I bet it's because he's so bored with saying the whole shebang – he's shortened the traditional "Can you spare any change?", if that's what it was, and I'm pretty sure it was. How brilliant is that? It's like speech as text. You know when you write L and then the number eight for "late"? As in how L-eight was I? No, you don't have to answer that. I do know I was unforgivably late. I can't believe you're going on and on about it . . .'

'Eh? It was you.'

'So it was. Anyway, we could do short language – like wha-dinner?'

'As in?'

'What are you going to have for dinner?' she explained.

Her face lit up as she smiled at him.

She was doing the *Annie Hall* thing. Normal words at ground level, but on the mezzanine she was about ready to strip him down to his fundamentals. It overshadowed her menu slightly because she wanted to order food that would make her mouth taste nice, yet not be too difficult to eat. She chose asparagus (smelly wee, but it would be over within a few hours) and Dover sole with green beans.

He chose soup and a salad, with no thought whatsoever as to how he would taste. 'Wine?' he asked.

'Aren't you ever going to stop drinking that water? And why do you keep going on about me being late? And don't you think the congestion charge is a tax on mobility?'

'Sorry?'

'Whine. As in whine – with an *h*. Almost as old a joke – and as terrible – as the white horse going into the pub.'

'And the barman saying, "Hey, they've named a whisky after you,"' he continued.

'And the horse saying, "What? Eric?"' she finished. 'Yes, it's almost as old as that one. And to answer your question, dry white, please. No, sorry,' she said, suddenly remembering how disgusting it made your breath smell, like three-day-old sick. 'How about another cocktail after dinner, and water with the food?'

'Hmm. I like the cut of your jib,' he said, and ordered a jug of tap.

The food was delicious. The water flowed. And the conversation ebbed and flowed with a nice undercurrent of sexual tension.

Dee entertained him with tales from *Hello Britain!* She was careful not to mention that Keera's interviews provided the bulk of the anecdotes.

One of the stories concerned a new weight-loss strand. 'There were all these people desperate to lose weight, and they were telling their stories, and they were actually very moving. One woman put on weight during pregnancy, then her husband died and she turned to food for comfort until she was about thirty stone. Another was bullied at school because he was shy, and became a tub of lard because the fridge was his best friend. And there was, erm, there was, erm, Mike ... Yes, there was Mike, watching them running down to the sea, and she – er – he says as they switch back to the studio, "Look at that tidal wave of obesity." How sensitive is that?'

It didn't get quite the response she was expecting.

'I can see where you're coming from with the sad stories,' he said, cutting a cherry tomato in half and spearing a small piece of cucumber to go with it. 'But people do have to exert more self-control. It's far too easy to blame it on someone else. Fat is a hedonist issue. I doubt that Neanderthal man – and woman, of course – got fat through grief. Or, at least, there are no known incidences of partners being gored by woolly mammoths with consequential explosion on the weight front. You had to hunt for food. You got your exercise and you ate to keep your energy up. And there were no fat people in concentration camps, were there? You starve people. They get thin. Obviously I'm not advocating concentration camps, but you shouldn't eat more calories than you expend. Run ten miles, you can eat more. Sit on the sofa watching television, eat a stick of celery.'

The conversation had lost its edge.

William was not a habitual *Hello Britain!* user, and knew nothing of Dee's battle with weight. Not so much the Battle of the Bulge as an assault on Cheddar Gorge. Dee wondered if there had been any point in putting on her scrumptious underwear. Would he simply check out her fat suit? Typical, she thought. I finally get a date with someone I fancy, and he's a body Fascist.

'I'm not a body Fascist,' said William, warming to his theme. 'I like curvy women like Halle Berry, Jennifer Aniston.'

'They're bloody *tiny*,' Dee said. 'They might have breasts, but there's more meat on a chihuahua. What on earth are you doing with me, pray tell?'

William looked at her, debating. 'I'm here because you're warm, beautiful, funny, and I fancy you.'

Dee put down her forkful of fish. She opened her mouth to say something, then closed it again. Opened it again. Looked nonplussed, then smiled her gorgeous smile. 'Top marks, matey,' she said. 'Very nicely done.'

And the evening was back on course. Although she had to have a few stiff martinis to get her into the mood in which she felt she could rip off her clothes with gay abandon.

His flat in Fulham was not quite as she had expected. Smaller, more sterile than she had imagined. But the sex was everything she'd dreamed and more. What need of a vibrator when you had a man who could breathe through his ears and had a twelve-inch tongue? as Katie was wont to say.

There was no sleep to be had that night in Fulham.

Saturday morning dawned fair in Hawes, but there was no gazing through the windows at Wensleydale unfurling in all its glory as the day threw off her morning clouds to reveal an underskirt of duck-egg blue.

Katie spent the entire day drinking water and watching Bob pottering about in the garden. Occasionally lust overwhelmed them and a tangling of limbs resulted in a crumpling of sheets.

He had told her what he'd planned for the day – rambling round the hills and a pub lunch – but she had vetoed it on the basis that even the smell of a pub would turn her into Linda Blair from *The Exorcist*, and she had brought only a limited number of shoes to decorate with slime.

'Nice,' he said lovingly, leaning forward to tuck a strand of hair behind her ear.

His revealing gesture went unnoticed by Katie. She had been too busy thinking of what a waste it would be to go hiking when there was a perfectly good way of getting in the exercise without thundering round the hills like a pair of goats. When, in fact, there was a perfectly good place to be acting like a pair of goats a mere hoe's throw from where she was sitting in a deckchair, admiring the view. Of Bob, with his T-shirt clinging damply to his firm body. His dark-blond hair sticking damply to his handsome head. His trousers clinging damply … There they went again. Not that Bob seemed to be complaining.

When he mildly passed comment on the number of T-shirts he was getting through, she told him to do the gardening without one on. He had wanted to throw out the vegetable mess from last night's aborted meal, but Katie persuaded him to make it into a shepherd's pie.

'We can go on a quick ramble, if we must, so that we can pick up a real shepherd to put on top.'

'Aha. A fellow fan of the Stephen Sondheim, I see. Should we have parson pie tomorrow?'

'It'll be Sunday,' she replied. 'I'd prefer gardener. Even if it's a bit green.'

And that had been another half an hour of lust quenched.

'I am Charlotte Duvet Rumpling,' she murmured into his chest, where she was blowing the hair gently up her nose. 'And you are Chuck Sheetz.'

'There's no such person as Chuck Sheetz,' he said disbelievingly.

'Oh, yes, there is,' she replied, threading her fingers through his chest hair. 'He's an animation director ... or might even be *the* animation director on *The Simpsons*. I saw his name at the end of the credits on the movie.'

'Well I never,' he said, impressed. 'Maybe Chuck Sheetz and Charlotte Rumpling could get together to do a film called *Lust in Space*. Or a play – *Tis Pity She's in Hawes*. Only it's not, of course,' he added, grabbing her hand and pulling her towards him again.

It had been the perfect weekend for both of them.

Bob had come to the conclusion that Katie was the woman he might very well want to spend the rest of his life with. Katie had forgotten the shabby state of her career in the all-consuming edibility of the gardener she had known for years. The weather stayed fair, the wisteria silently grew another centimetre, the birds had conversations about their favourite telephone lines, the worms squelched together in wormy harmony.

On Sunday, they lunched on crunchy bubble-and-squeak with an egg on top.

'It all began with an egg,' Katie said sagely, squishing her yolk into the potato.

'And a sperm,' said Bob, misunderstanding her.

'I meant the weekend, you idiot.'

'And I,' said Bob, 'meant your creation. And mine, of course. Unless there's something my mum hasn't told me. And, actually, it started with a vodka in your case. The weekend, that is.'

'How is your mum?' asked Katie, adding a dollop of ketchup to the mixture on her plate.

'Fine. Still missing Dad. But, then, it's only been six years and they were together for decades. Not surprising she still misses him. I do, too. But gardening helps. And I'm looking forward to landscaping this hospice. It's a pretty big job for me. I'm not getting paid vast sums for it, but it means I can do virtually what I want. Which is to create secret places … benches round trees, hidden behind bushes. That sort of thing. Places where you can go and contemplate if you need to. It's what Dad always told me. Some people can be alone when all around is confusion, but most of us can't. Nature offers us a rather more pleasant alternative to the locked room. I think he'd have approved of what I'm about to do. He was on the committee of a children's charity, trying to organize some sort of youth centre, when he died.'

'Bloody sad,' said Katie, deciding it was better to keep slightly upbeat when talking of tragedy.

There was just the sound of scraping forks for a while, and then she started up again. 'Now, this week I'm going to get to grips with the tatters of my career. I've got this meeting tomorrow about the dating show, but I'm about as likely to get the job as my pagan aunt has of making pope. They'll be wanting a twenty-four-year-old with breasts and hair. I've got feelers out all over the place, newspapers, magazines, radio, and I need to knuckle down. So if you don't hear from me it's not that I don't want to speak to you. Just that I'm busy. And then I can't quite remember what I'm doing next weekend, but I have a faint memory of something on Saturday, so I probably won't see you.'

'Excellent. I might get my mulching done,' said Bob, putting down his knife and fork and pushing his chair away from the table.

'You romantic young thing, you,' responded Katie, and helped him to clear away the dishes. The sink was like a map of the New York skyline since they had done the bare minimum – bare being the operative word.

Bob gave her a lift to the station, then a lingering, moist, meaningful kiss before he waved her off.

Not that Katie realized it was meaningful.

She settled into her seat, replete in every way.

CHAPTER FIFTEEN

There is no more pleasing sight on a computer than an email from somebody offering money. But a handsome man offering a date comes a close second. And on Monday morning Keera was gratified to discover one of each.

Her agent had forwarded her an *At Home With ...* from *OK!* magazine for a nice number of noughts, and WBaron1@ hotmail.com had written to say thank you very much for suggesting him for the lifestyle strand, and would she like to meet up?

Yes, she would. Very much. Although she would also like to know where he'd got his information from since she'd only mentioned it in passing to the senior producer on her way up to the morning meeting.

Curious.

She clicked on reply to her agent with a few available days, and replied to William Baron with a few available nights.

She watched her fingers on the keyboard, bashing away. Oh, yes, look at them go. I'm a journalist. Oh, yes. I'm a success. Oh, yes. I'm so going to clean up in this gig, she hummed in her brain.

Logging off smugly at 5.03 a.m., she picked her way down the stairs to Makeup and Wardrobe, watching her Gina-clad feet moving gracefully on the stained carpeting. What gorgeous feet. What gorgeous hands. I'm so gorgeous they should write a song about me, she thought, swaying along the corridor to her dressing room. 'Good morning, Derek,' she sang to the head of Wardrobe as she passed. 'I feel fitted and sleek today. Sort me out a selection, will you, please?'

Derek mimed her words back to her, his head bobbing graciously from side to side, then came out of his cluttered room and followed her. 'You're in a good mood,' he remarked, as he opened the wardrobe doors and surveyed the collection. Fitted and sleek. He let his hands roll over the fabrics.

'Navy?'

'No, that one's flared,' she threw over her shoulder, as she went through some of the mail in her tray. A satisfying collection of fan letters – and a parcel. 'Something a bit more fitted.'

'The dark green?'

She opened the parcel. 'More sleeker.'

'Rubber suit?'

'Ha-ha. No. How about the chocolate with that thin pink stripe? Tight jacket, snug trousers.'

'And what underneath?'

'I think I'll go topless,' she said, having got to the contents of the box and discovered some freebie cosmetics. What a wonderful Monday. 'Yes, topless,' she continued. 'It's a low-cut jacket, but not so low that I'll fall out. Anyway, it'll give the weirdos on the Internet sites a thrill. You know how they like to post pictures of me in various poses. Did you spot the one where you could see my pants?' she asked, as though horrified.

'No,' said Derek, finally locating the chocolate and pink. 'I must have missed it during my extensive late-night searchings for pictures of you.'

He exited to steam up her suit.

In Makeup, Keera had her hair blow-dried and revealed her two pieces of good news to Vanda. 'They're offering me a big-figure sum for the *At Home With ...*'

'Lovely,' said Vanda, concentrating on the back section of shiny black hair.

'And,' she said, in a slightly more confidential manner, 'that William Baron's asked me out on a date. The lifestyle man? Handsome? Tall, dark and handsome, to be accurate?'

'Vaguely. Came in a few weeks ago?' asked Vanda, teasing down a frond of fringe.

'Mmm. Very tasty. He's asked me for dinner.'

They nattered on, as Dee seethed quietly in the other makeup chair.

What the fuck was he playing at? The bastard. Here we go again. Another shit. I'm the worst picker in the world. Fuck. Fuck. Fuck. Fucker. Wanker. Now she knew why he hadn't phoned her yesterday. Or on Saturday. The arsehole was double-dating. And with another presenter at *Hello Britain!* Calls himself a lifestyle guru? As if he wouldn't be caught out.

Matthew, the makeup artist, was quietly applying himself to the grim face in front of him. 'All right?' he queried, as he perused his eye pencils.

'Fine,' said Dee, anything but. Boy, was she going to tear a strip off that toerag. She could barely contain herself until off-air.

Only one thing lightened her morning: Keera asking a husband-beater, 'So essentially, what you're saying is that he was asking for it?' with a solicitous face.

She phoned Katie because Katie was always up for a go at Keera.

'What am I going to do?' she wailed, after she'd explained the gory details.

'You definitely know he's asked her out?'

'Yes. She was as smug as a smug thing on National Smug Day about it. As smug as a bug with a smug rug. More smug. As smug as –'

'Yup, I get the picture. But maybe he's doing it to further his career. It may be a dinner he thinks will help his strand along, as it were. Not a dinner that will help him get his end away. Talking of which, was he good?'

'Brilliant. The bastard. Body like a Greek god's. And he has an appendage like an elephant's trunk. *And*, as you would put it, a twelve-inch tongue and he can breathe through his ears.'

Katie laughed. 'I bet he's not after *her*, just her contract. She's a stupid trout with the brain of a sea cucumber. He'll see through her immediately.'

'Well, no other man here has,' pointed out Dee.

'Richard and Mike?'

'Two men out of a barrel-load isn't many.'

'True,' said Katie. 'But I wouldn't totally condemn him. He deserves a chance. If only so you can get your paws on his love rocket again, and have your hands-free orgasms. Why not text him? We're too old to be playing games. Just say you had such a great time, does he feel like a rematch? And bring up the Keera stuff when you go out. I bet you a pound to a pickled herring he's not after her for her perfect body and perfectly pointless mind. He's just after the work. Listen, I've got to go. Talking of perfectly pointless, I have a meeting to get to and I haven't even had a shower yet. By the way, I had a fantastic weekend with Bob the gardener. I'll tell you about it when we meet up. Which is when?'

'Thursday night, Chinawhite, so we can dance and fall over with alacrity. Nine o'clock, glad rags. There are six of us.'

'Roger and out. And don't worry.'

'Oh, and I didn't tell you that originally he asked me to go with him to something this Wednesday. A première. Only he hasn't phoned me back. Do I mention that in the text, or does that make me look desperate?'

'Put it all in the text and say it's cool with you either way, but you need to know because you've been asked out to something or other on Wednesday night. I really, really have to go. See you Thursday.'

Katie's meeting for *All Mine At Nine* had gone surprisingly well. They hadn't fallen asleep on the desk, they'd laughed at one of her jokes, she'd flirted with a boy so young his bones had hardly formed (he was – of course – the top bod), and she was feeling quite positive.

She phoned Jim Break as she was walking to the tube to give him the possibly good news.

'And now a bit more,' he said. And explained about a new magazine, called *First Glance*, which was interested in her writing articles suitable for intelligent women in their forties, who were either facing empty-nest syndrome or had chosen not to have a full nest and were happily contemplating the menopause 'or whatever'.

'*Happily* contemplating the menopause? I'm assuming you've had a rush of blood to the head. And apparently men have one as well. They buy a motorbike and swap their wives for younger models. Then one vainly hopes that they develop a variety of interesting sexual diseases and die a pauper's death after they've handed over their goods and chattels to the ex-wife.'

'I *knew* I was looking forward to something,' he said. 'I'll warn Amanda now. If she leaves within a few weeks, I can have the bedroom aired and start getting in the showgirls.'

'You do that. So, do I need to meet anybody, or write an imaginary column or whatever?'

'Yes. As I know you're doing precisely diddly-squat, I've organized afternoon tea on Wednesday at the Lanesborough for you and the editor, a thoroughly nice bloke called Tom French. He's gay, so dress smart.'

'Excellent. I always seem to go down well with gays. Fingers crossed. I could do without losing my flat as well as my job. Although my mum reckons I should buy a vineyard and cut out the middleman.'

'Mm. About that … I don't want to preach but …' said Jim.

'But you're going to.'

'Only a small sermon. For verily I say unto you that perhaps you should curb your very natural addiction to the grape, grain, potato and cactus and go steady until you have another job lined up. I think you've got away with what's appeared in the papers so far, but it wouldn't do for you to look like a dipso. And also, if you don't mind my saying so, it makes you look like a sad loser. Which you aren't. Here endeth the lesson. Go forth and multiply.'

'Of course. I'll do the nine times table. My favourite.'

'I'll work on that after I've put the phone down. 'Bye.'

'Oh, just before you go … did you hear Keera's corker this morning? You know that beached dolphin in Scotland, coming hot on the heels of that beached whale in the Thames?'

'Yup.'

'So it comes back to a two-shot and she turns to Mike and says, "What is it with all these big fish?" and he looks at her in that way he does and says, "Think you'll find they're mammals." She says, "Whatever." Big fish. I ask you.'

'Not one of your best Keera stories. I saw her the other day asking a poor woman whose husband had been missing for a year why on earth people go missing.'

She laughed. 'You're right.'

'However, I also think you should stop watching *Hello Britain!* until you have a sense of perspective. You're never going to work there again. Get over it.'

'Thank you for your support.' Katie smiled. ''Bye.'

Thinking about it on the tube on her way home, sitting opposite a surprisingly attractive man (nice crotch, she nodded internally), she was finally coming to terms with the loss of the job she had loved so much. She still missed the camaraderie, the excitement when there was breaking news, the immediacy of live television – the fact that you could never be asked to do it again but with more feeling.

What she didn't miss was getting up at chaffinch fart. She didn't miss the politics, small p, the having to have makeup put on when your eyeballs felt like they were rocking in sockets lined with sandpaper, the rewriting of creepy Kent's dreadful prose.

The man opposite looked up from his paper. Katie smiled at him. He smiled back. Whoops. First rule of travelling by tube. Never meet anyone's eye. They're probably mad. Phew: he's gone back to his paper. Excellent bulge in the trouser department. Good jeans. Nice shoes. You could tell a lot from a man's shoes. Jeffery West, she reckoned. Slightly battered. And funky T-shirt. Faded blue with a picture of ... What was that? A rabbit of the stoned variety. Dylan out of *The Magic Roundabout*. And firm jawline.

He looked up again. She looked at her hands. Fiddled with her bag. Got out some hand cream. That's it. Look busy. She glanced up again. He was checking her out. This was ridiculous. Hell. Still three more stops. She studied her shoes minutely until she got out at Sloane Square. She couldn't decide whether she was happy or unhappy that Nice Crotch hadn't followed her.

She phoned Bob. 'Thanks again for a really lovely weekend,' she said.

He was in the middle of potting and sounded as though he smelled of sunny soil. He burbled on for the ten minutes she needed to get over her tube experience, and ended the call by saying he missed her.

'Hey, it was only yesterday,' she said in a rallying tone.

'Can't I miss you if it's only one day?'

'If you really want to, of course you can,' she said briskly.

Mike was having another meeting with the bosses at the BBC about his co-host. They said they were considering approaching Katie Fisher – 'A rerun of a successful partnership,' said Kuldeep, the producer.

'Excellent thought. She's a laugh. Always first to the pub over the road and always the first to dance on the bar. A hoot.' He noticed their expressions and added, 'But she always made it on-air every morning. Admittedly, she'd sit on the sofa at about

179

three seconds to go. I think that was to freak out the director, though.'

He sat back.

'And how do you feel about Saskia Miller?'

'Well, she's obviously one of the best female presenters around at the moment. Beautiful. Intelligent. Quick on her feet. Funny ...' he pressed on, as the director, Sam, raised his eyebrows. 'And I think we'd do very well together.'

'All right,' said Sam. 'You can't say fairer than that. We'll be in touch. And we'll probably be making the announcement some time this week.'

'Excellent,' said Mike, standing up, pushing his chair back and running his hands through his thick hair, in what he hoped was a Hugh Grant kind of manner. He was looking forward to the new show. It had huge ratings written all over it. And where there were huge ratings, there would be huge increases in his bank balance.

Sandra was in the kitchen when he got home.

'What have you been up to?' she asked, making a coffee enema. 'You look like the cat that got the cream.'

'Good day, that's all,' he said, reaching into the fridge for the bottle of white wine.

'Wine at four o'clock?' asked his wife, pointedly, as she walked towards the bathroom.

He pulled a face at her departing back. 'Coffee up the arse at four o'clock?' he mouthed. He slipped off his shoes, lay back on the sofa and contemplated his life. It was looking pretty darned fine. His occasional radio show had posted solid ratings – well, the same ratings as the woman before – he was about to get a prime-time show in the bag, with his choice of co-host, and he could feel his loins stirring at the promise of a trip out with Buster that evening. He stroked the terrier, who had leaped on to the sofa with him since Sandra was out of the room. When she was there, she would squirt all round him with the disgusting room spray she used to combat foul odours. 'Hey, boy. Fancy a ride in my car later?'

Upstairs, the loo flushed a few times, and shortly afterwards Sandra came downstairs.

'Successful colon cleanout?' he asked, as she put a collection of pots and tubes into the dishwasher.

'Thank you for asking. Yes,' she said, snapping on a pair of rubber gloves and wiping down the surfaces. 'I'm out tonight. You don't need the car, do you?'

'I do, actually,' he said, annoyed. 'I promised the boys I'd meet up with them in, erm, Twickenham.'

'Twickenham?' She turned to stare at him. 'Since when have you ever met up in Twickenham?'

'There's a new pub they're checking out ready for, er, the rugby season.'

'That's not for months, is it?' she asked suspiciously.

'Pre-season matches. Anyway, why do *you* need the car?'

'I'm trying out a new exercise class and I need all my stuff with me. Maybe you can drop me off. How long are you going to be?'

'It depends. Not late, though. Need my beauty sleep. I'll drop you off, but I can't promise to pick you up.'

'Fine. Seven all right?'

'Yes,' he said, and slurped the last of his wine. 'And no,' he added, 'I won't be drinking. I've just had the one to unwind. If that's OK with you?' And he went off to change out of his suit.

But if Monday had been a peachy day, and a doubly peachy evening – fifteen minutes of heaven – Tuesday was a stewed prune of a morning.

He was called into the managing director's office by a grim secretary. He had a suspicion it would be about his holidays – he had stealthily snuck in another couple of days on top of his already extraordinarily generous allocation.

But the MD had been sitting there with a pile of his expense forms. 'Close the door, Mike,' he had said sternly. 'Best this doesn't go any further.' He pushed the sheets of paper across the desk. 'Would you accept that these are your expenses?'

Mike took a cursory look. 'Yes,' he said. 'They look like mine. Any problem?' He pushed them back.

'There is,' said the MD. He shuffled the papers. 'The phone bills. Most notably,' he said, 'these mobile calls to 0906 numbers.'

Mike flushed. When had they *ever* checked the actual numbers on the bills before? 'I think that may have been when I lent my phone to a friend recently. He'd lost his,' he explained.

'I don't think so,' said the managing director, putting his fingers together and raising them to his mouth in the shape of a pyramid. 'The thing is, we were doing spot checks on expenses and yours were among them. When we saw these numbers, we went back over the last few months. There are at least three or four on each bill.' He paused, then added, 'We phoned a few to check they were what we thought they were. One of them was a foreign-sounding woman with apparently astounding breasts. Another said she was African and was wearing next to nothing. She had quite a lot to say on the subject of –'

'Yes, yes,' interrupted Mike.

There was silence in the room. Through the door, he could hear the secretary ordering lobelia. He wondered what for. Eventually he spoke.

'And what is your suggestion?' he asked finally.

'Well, I've talked to the finance department. We considered you paying us back for the calls, but that's rather time-intensive for us. So we think perhaps we should ban you from claiming expenses for anything.'

Mike bit his lip. He'd been snookered. He couldn't do anything about it, unless he wanted the whole building to know what he'd been up to.

The MD was quite enjoying himself. He didn't like Mike. He thought he was a bully. And now he had evidence to convict him of sleaze. He might be one of the best presenters in television, he thought, but he's a see-you-next-Tuesday. Who's about to get his comeuppance. He watched Mike thinking things through and realizing there was no way out. He sat back as Mike looked up from his examination of his Gucci loafers.

'Fine,' Mike said, his eyes hardening. 'And I'm assuming that if I agree to that, no more will be said about this?'

'You have my word,' said the MD. He didn't want it getting out, any more than Mike did. It wouldn't reflect well on the station.

'Well, if that's all,' said Mike, 'I'll be going. I have a radio show to record.'

'Thanks for dropping by,' said the MD, allowing him through the door, a slight smile hovering on his lips. He poured himself a small port from the bottle he kept hidden in a filing cabinet for special occasions. 'Cheers,' he said to the huge picture of Mike that hung in his office. It had been one of his favourite Tuesdays so far, and he hadn't even got to elevenses yet.

CHAPTER SIXTEEN

The meeting with Tom French, the editor of *First Glance*, went so well that Katie was virtually hired on the spot. He was a tall, dapper man, and had stood up as she approached. His handshake was warm and firm. None of that barely-touching-the-fingers nonsense. Or the clammy squeeze of a blown-up Marigold glove. He was wearing a pale linen suit, a pale blue shirt and a lightly battered pair of beige suede shoes.

'What a thoroughly handsome rig,' exclaimed Katie, looking him up and down as she sat on the banquette and was handed a menu by the waiter.

'Why, thank you, kind lady,' he said, smiling. 'Not often enough we hear that word, these days.'

'I think it should be reinstated, don't you?' asked Katie. She turned to the waiter to order afternoon tea. 'I'm assuming you've ordered,' she checked, looking at the pot of tea in front of him.

'Yes. A cheeky little Darjeeling, second flush, and I'm assured that a quantity of sandwhiches, cakes and scones are on their way too. And I've always been fond of the quirky word. It does sound so much more romantic to be hit on the head by a ruffian with a cosh than a hoodie with a brick – even if the outcome's similar.'

'And vagabonds don't sound half as smelly as tramps,' mused Katie. 'While having a husband who's a bedswerver is much nicer than putting up with an unfaithful git.'

'Words. They're all we've got to distinguish us from the animals,' said Tom, flourishing his strainer at the waiter for another cup of tea.

'And clothes,' added Katie. 'Imagine a bear in a D and G trouser suit. More or less scary?'

'Would depend on the colour. Black, with a white pleated shirt ... scarier. Lilac, possibly less so. But there are the teeth to consider. And the claws.'

For a moment they considered the question silently.

'And,' he said contemplatively, 'that's assuming it's a male bear. Would you find a bear in a ball dress more terrifying?'

'Earrings or no earrings?' asked Katie, as the waiter promptly arrived with her tea. 'Anyway,' she said, putting down her cup, and picking up a wafer-thin sandwich, 'this isn't getting the baby bathed. Should we get down to the nitty-gritty? An expression, incidentally, that I hate – but occasionally feel the need to flourish, like a G-string poking above the top of a pair of jeans.'

For the next half an hour, give or take a few labyrinthine asides, Tom and Katie discussed articles. 'Tell you what,' she said, 'why don't I knock something off today – in writing as opposed to shoplifting – and we can take it from there?'

'Excellent. On what?'

'How about starting again when you're in your forties and feel you might be over the hill?' She smiled.

'You're not over the hill,' he said, 'unless to be over the hill is to be running up and down it with abandon. Possibly with a meadow somewhere.'

'How very Timotei,' she remarked, picking out a chocolate éclair from the cake stand in front of them. 'However, I'll bash it out today, and send it straight over. Now, business over. Let's gossip.'

An hour and a half later, Katie left the Lanesborough in fine fettle. She wouldn't have to sell the flat. She would get the *All Mine At Nine* gig. And she hadn't given up on the co-host's role with Mike, who had sounded very positive when they'd had a brief chat yesterday. On a whim, she went for a manicure, then home to write her article.

Tomorrow was going to be a long old night, she imagined, so she turned in early after drinking two litres of water and eating four carrots that were marooned in the bottom of a very empty fridge. She reckoned she had lost – oh, at least three ounces since yesterday. Oh yes, she thought ironically, thank goodness she'd eaten all the sandwiches and cakes at the Lanesborough. So efficacious for the thighs. And it was the time of year when they'd be getting an airing as spring was turning into the most beautiful summer. No doubt there would be a hosepipe ban soon, but the pansies were out and the trees were wearing their greenest livery. Even the occasional cloud had looked happy to be there.

Thursday blossomed fair.

Katie tripped merrily to her favourite coffee house and ordered herself an enormous soya cappuccino.

She did a little window shopping, and was home by four o'clock to check in the fridge and see if anything had come in while she was out.

Nothing but a couple of beers and a very old bottle of champagne.

She necked one of the beers and tidied a cupboard, which had escaped the earlier frenzy, then spent a very long time getting ready to go out.

The K Club, as they liked to call themselves, met up about twice a year and always had a riotous time. Katie, Kirsty, Kathy, Carina (sounds like K), Kinsey (her last name, to fit in with the K theme – first name Jane), and Dee (who used to eat Special K, so that was all right) were journalist mates, producers, reporters and presenters. When they had first got together, they had met each month, but husbands, partners, boyfriends, children and jobs had conspired to make it an impossible schedule recently.

Dee was the lynchpin, the organizer, who emailed everyone to set up the dates.

Essentially, each adhered to a similar timetable.

Dinner.

Followed by a bar.

Followed by a club.

Followed by carriages at dawn.

Followed by hangovers.

Followed by assertions that they were never, ever going to drink again. Or, at least, not that much.

At eight o'clock on the nose (tardiness was next to untidiness), she got on to the tube, feeling marvellously racy in her high red shoes. 'Red shoes, no knickers,' as her mother used to say.

By nine, the girls were in full flow. Dee was recounting the tale of her second date with William Baron. 'It was going really well until he said fat people brought it on themselves, or some such crap. I accused him of being fattist. And he said that on balance he thought I was probably fattest. Although he did immediately say that was a joke. A pun. And we know, Katie, how flat those can fall. So, anyway I drank enough to drown a schooner, or is it drown a sailor? Which meant we had a much easier evening – from my point of view. Except ... I was still thinking about the fat thing, and my arse being on show. So we went back to his place, and I suddenly remembered what my dear old aunt Gracie was wont to say: "Beauty is only a light switch away." From then on, everything was lights off. Apart from a strategically placed candle.'

'Good God,' said Carina. 'Where the hell do you put a strategic candle?'

'You don't change, do you, you smutty-minded individual? It was – obviously – strategically on the bedside table, thank you very much. To make sure we knew where we were. Or, to be strictly accurate, where the body parts were.'

'*No*,' said Carina, mock-mystified. 'He's a murderer too?'

'Oh, shut up and let me finish,' said Dee.

'Your aunt Gracie was right,' interrupted Kathy. 'Good lighting is v. v. important as a woman reaches her prime.'

Dee continued her tale: 'And I left early on Saturday morning before he got up so he wouldn't see my haggard face without any makeup. And my hair was a mess,' she ended.

'What's the worst thing about getting old, do we think?' asked Katie.

'Wrinkles,' said Carina.

'Weird knees,' added Kathy.

'Bat wings, so you constantly have to find something to cover the tops of your arms,' said Jane.

'Getting rid of your short skirts because of the cellulite,' claimed Kirsty.

'I don't know because I'm only thirty-two,' said Dee.

'Liar,' laughed Katie. 'I've been thirty-seven for years. Why don't you join me there? And I hate my eyesight going wonky. Although it has its compensations. In the mirror, I think I look all right. So despite being *terribly* young, Dee, what pisses you off about getting less young?'

'That everything seems to be so much more urgent. In the past it didn't matter that I didn't have a bloke because there were so many other things I needed to sort out. But now ... Well. Now I want babies. And the time available, unless I resort to a turkey-baster and a willing male donor, is getting shorter. So to cut a long answer slightly short, I would say that I yearn for a meaningful man, a baby, a pension – which I really should have started by now – a house in France, and more self-control so that I can stop this constant battle against the muffin top, which wasn't quite as repulsive when I was younger.'

'But don't you think,' suggested Carina, 'that life as *une vieille dame* has its advantages? We wouldn't want to go back to being nineteen, would we, with all those insecurities? Backing out of rooms naked because you were worried about what the man would think of your wobbly bits? Paranoid that they didn't fancy you because they didn't phone the next day? So obsessed with them that you could barely brush your teeth for thinking about them?'

'It's all right for you,' said Kathy. 'You're married to a lovely man, with children, a beautiful house, no need to worry. I, on the other hand, being terminally single, have to make such an effort every time I go out that by the time I've left the flat I'm exhausted and ready to go back to bed. And,' she raised her hand to stop Katie butting in, 'it's been so long since I've had a shag, I think I may have healed up. And I'm getting to the stage where I feel like I can't be bothered either. I only have a bikini wax now if I'm going on holiday. I'm currently sporting, under my attractive and very expensive Hennes skirt, a pair of hairy shorts. And a pair of support pants over the top. I feel sure that any prospective partner would be champing at the bit at the thought of it. Not. And I'm not sure I care.'

She sat back and tossed down the last of her wine.

'It's all right for you too, though, Kathy,' said Jane. 'I've got a twat of an ex-husband, who refuses to see the children more than once a month so they're all upset, and little Hero's started wetting the bed. And although David does his best, they're not his kids and Bertie and Willow keep on shoving it down his throat whenever he tells them off. We haven't had sex for God knows how long – we're always too tired with ferrying children around to get it together. My idea of romance is a nice cup of hot chocolate and a whole night's sleep on my own in a double bed.'

'And it's all right for you, Jane,' said Carina. 'At least you have a job you can do from home. Whereas the home *is* my job, and sometimes I get such stultifying brain atrophy that I can see John nodding off while I'm speaking. I feel about as sexy as a bag of chicken giblets. Even if I force myself to climb out of my tracksuit by the time he gets home, ten to one I'll have a bit of fish-finger on my top. I have nothing interesting to tell him, and if I do, I can't think of the right words because I've spent all day talking to the children or their horrid little friends. If he's not already shagging his secretary, it's only a matter of time.'

'My turn now.' Katie laughed. 'It's all right for *you*. At least you have a man who supports you, and will continue to support you, even if he does run off with his secretary. Who, incidentally, as we both know, is such a munter that he'd need his head examining were he to take down her particulars. And you've got adorable children, who won't be little for ever.

Whereas if I don't get some money in soon, I'll be forced to sell my raddled old body in King's Cross.'

Kirsty continued with the theme. 'It's all right for *you*, Katie. You haven't had any children so you don't have empty, sagging breasts, like two small pouches, or a latticework stomach that swings from side to side when you run. And haemorrhoids. And bags under your eyes. And a partner who bloody ogles every girl he sees.'

'But it's all right for *you*, Kirsty,' said Dee – who got shouted down.

'You've already done yours!' they cried. And ordered another couple of bottles of wine for the road.

'By the way, Katie,' said Dee, quietly, 'you were right about William. I spoke to him eventually, and he said that that was exactly why he invited her out. And he says he didn't say dinner, just that he'd like to meet up to discuss a possible strand. And he said he didn't get back to me about Wednesday because he had a late session booked in so he wasn't going. We're out on Saturday night.'

'And what will you be wearing to meet your paragon of guru?'

'Paragon of guru?'

'Play on words. Paragon of virtue? Paragon of guru?'

'Seriously bad. Give it up. Now. So ... I was thinking I'd wear fishnets,' said Dee.

'Good thought. Anything else?'

'Nope. Just fishnets. And maybe a fish in the nets? Haddock, perhaps.'

'Or crabs?'

'Ha. Disgusting. But you'd never get crabs in a fishnet. You need a pot for that.'

And the night descended into bawdiness.

At about the time that those with day jobs were thinking about getting home, the K Club went clubbing. The cackling coven wound its way through the streets of London's West End and up to Air Street, where Katie had reserved a table. 'Cocktails, I think,' she said, 'and I will be having a Cosmopolitan.'

The heat in the club lay on them like a duvet.

'Maybe we should get up and dance. At least it'll be good for us,' shouted Carina, over the music. 'Like doing morris dancing in a hammam.'

The best thing, thought Katie, fuggily, about your very best friends was that it didn't matter how rubbish you looked, they all said how beautiful you were. And they didn't criticize your dancing. And they said they loved your shoes, even if they hated them. And that your hair was fine. Really fine. No, not at all like Margaret Beckett on a bad day. And these Cosmopolitans are bloody glorious. 'Another round, I think,' she said, sliding back sweatily on to her seat.

'Three more Metropolitans, two Caipirinhas and the same thingy as last time,' she puffed to the waiter.

As they sat at the table recuperating, clammy and with a lot less makeup on than when they'd arrived, Katie spotted a proposition. She cupped her hand round Kathy's ear. 'Look at that gorgeous bloke on the dance-floor,' she slurred. 'Indian. Or half Indian. Snaky hips or what?'

Kathy peered round her into the gloom. 'Mmm. Magnifishent. Hairy chesht. Jusht what you like in a man. And, amazhingly, hish friend ish attractive too.'

'I'm going to dance near them,' announced Katie, standing up. 'Coming?'

They staggered on to the dance-floor where their antics were noticed by Mr Snaky Hips and his mate, who began to undulate in their general direction.

The girls squashed up as the new arrivals joined them.

Introductions were made.

Mr Snaky Hips's name was Krishnan Casey. He was half Irish, half Indian, had the greenest eyes and a mouth made for kissing, Katie thought.

His friend was half Irish half Chinese, Seamus Chung.

'Brilliant name,' said Kathy, admiringly, her eyes lingering on the six-pack revealed by his tight-fitting shirt.

The pounding music made it difficult to have any meaningful dialogue, so the girls concentrated on meaningless dialogue. They discovered the two men worked in the City, played squash together, lived in Holland Park, and would have to be up at six in the morning.

'How do you do that?' shouted Katie.

'Drugs,' shouted back Krishnan. 'Do you want some?'

'No, thanks. Would ruin the taste of my Surbiton,' bellowed Katie. 'But don't let me stop you.'

'I was joking, actually. I drink lots and lots of water. Can't get enough of the stuff,' he said. 'Which is why I'll be leaving you for a few minutes.' He disappeared in the direction of the loo, oddly with Seamus.

'Well, *I'm* sorted for pudding,' said Katie, putting her mouth close to Kathy's ear again. 'How about you?'

'Dreamy,' murmured Kathy.

Dee came round from the other side of the table and leaned forward to Katie. 'What about Bob?' she asked.

'He's lovely,' slurred Katie, 'totally yummy. But he's not here. Sadly. And I think I need to be kissed. It's not being unfaithful. And he's very sexy, isn't he?'

Dee merely shook her head, and returned to the icy remains of her drink.

Katie was feeling decidedly woozy when Krishnan came back, and thought she might be better off on the dance-floor with him. She tried to do dirty dancing, but found it difficult to keep in time, so settled for trying to balance on the balls of her feet with a sweep at either end of the sway. 'Whoops,' she said, as she bounced off another shuffling drunkard.

Krishnan held on to her arm as she stumbled, then put his other arm round her and held her tight. Katie looked up, drowned in the sea green eyes and closed her own ready for the kiss. Then opened them again because her head was spinning. But Krishnan had already taken her lips in his – and what a kisser. She was lost within five minutes of the exquisite perfection. Katie was an expert on kissing. It was possibly her favourite hobby. She had started early. At twelve, she had kissed Geoff with the shiny dark hair. It was better than shortbread covered with chocolate. Better than jumping out of trees. Better than beating Tracy at maths. There was absolutely nothing better than closing your eyes and getting goosebumps while a boy held you close.

She gave up learning the piano. She gave up concentrating at school. She gave up on all her girlfriends who were not as passionate as she was about her new hobby. She went to the cinema with any boy who was willing. She discovered what she liked and what she definitely didn't.

She did not like the washing-machine. That was George – saliva all over her face, and a rotating movement with the mouth.

She did not like the chewer. That was Edward – no tongues, just a chewing motion.

And she hated the woodpecker. That was Chris, with his frantic pecking and jabbing.

Katie got a reputation for 'going with anyone'. But she didn't care. It was important to check whether there was anything new to learn. And, amazingly, there always was. But she never wanted to go any further than kissing. Her reputation changed to 'prickteaser'. She cared even less. She just wanted to carry on kissing. And while there were mouths to feast on, she would continue her studies.

Whether Krishnan had studied quite as much, she might never find out. But right then, right there in the hot, clammy club, he was the most delicious kisser she had ever kissed.

It was perfect. A bit of pressure, and the tongue doing a vague exploration. It was lucky he was holding on to her when he finished because otherwise she would have fallen over, swooned in a truly old-fashioned way.

'Wow,' she said, coming up for air. 'Where did you learn to do that?'

He whispered in her ear, making the follicles stand up all down her back. 'I was taught by nuns.'

She laughed, and they returned to the table for a drink. She managed another Cosmopolitan, and felt as sparkling as a seventies glitterball. She decided she was going to take Krishnan home. As a treat to herself. 'You want to come to my pad? In Chelsea?' she asked. 'I have a beer in the fridge ...' she added, knowing herself to be a little drunk, so speaking very slowly to make sure she was being understood.

'My, oh, my. A whole beer. I think I would probably like to,' he said, looking at her in a measuring way.

Katie stood up. 'Girls,' she announced portentously, 'I am going to go now. Krishnan here will be taking me home. Thank you for a wonderful night. I love you all.'

She and Krishnan made their way to the exit. There was a slight wave in her walk. A glassiness in the eyes. A heaviness to the head.

The cold air in the street pulled her up. 'This way,' she said peremptorily to Krishnan, having spotted a taxi at the end of the road.

At which point, a photographer leaped in front of her and started snapping. She could see spots in front of her eyes, and staggered off the pavement, narrowly held from flying full length by Krishnan, who seemed surprised to have a photo taken of him and a woman he had just met. 'What the fuck are you doing, mate?' he shouted angrily. 'Back off. And put that bloody camera down.'

'It's OK,' puffed Katie, standing up and pulling down her dress, which had ridden up alarmingly high during the tumble. She tried to see past the flashing light of the camera to the photographer behind it. 'Please stop that,' she said, putting out her hand. 'You've done enough now. Stop it.'

He carried on as she walked towards him.

'Stop it,' she said again.

But he didn't.

And, suddenly, she had had more than enough of him. She ran at him, grabbed his camera and pulled his head towards her with the neck strap. 'Stop it with the fucking photographs,' she shouted in his face, and pulled the strap over it.

'Give me back my camera!' He made a grab for it.

'No,' said Katie, pulling it from his fingers.

As he fought to get it from her, a young woman tried to walk past them. No one knew quite how it happened, but one moment they were grappling over the camera and the next there was a girl on the ground with an enormous gash on the side of her face where it had hit her. 'Now look what you've done, you arsehole!' shouted Katie, as she knelt down to the girl.

The photographer was taking pictures again.

'You *bastard*,' she yelled at him. '*Fuck off*. Oh, God, she's out cold. *Call an ambulance*.'

Suddenly she noticed that Krishnan was no longer with her.

He had watched the scene unfolding, and realized she was famous in some way. He really didn't want to be around. He thought he'd be in trouble.

So he didn't witness the arrival of the ambulance. The arrival of the police. And the exit of Katie and the photographer in the back of the squad car.

CHAPTER SEVENTEEN

Friday was not a good day. At least, it wasn't for former breakfast-television presenters who had spent the night in a police cell. Katie had not gone quietly. She had vociferously protested her innocence, and pointed furiously at the photographer as the culprit.

Although the policemen were sympathetic, they couldn't fail to notice that she reeked of alcohol, and that her explanation of events kept getting lost in translation, muddied by a few too many Cosmopolitans.

It also didn't help that the photographer appeared to be a decent type, who claimed he'd only taken a couple of pictures before she'd attacked him. They spotted the lie as soon as they got to the police station and looked at the digital playback.

Nevertheless an injured woman had been taken to hospital for stitches and observation. And, of course, a celebrity was involved, which meant there would be newspaper interest. And that things had to be seen to be done so the media wouldn't have a go at them.

Katie hardly slept, veering between desperate dehydration and dehydrated desperation. Just when things were looking up, she'd had to make *a small error*, and now she was on the slippery slope to ruin again.

If only she hadn't had that last drink. If only they'd gone to a club that didn't attract photographers. If only she hadn't taken the camera from the photographer. If only she ... And what the hell had happened to Krishnan? Why hadn't *he* helped her? She didn't remember him leaving. Mind you, she didn't remember much of the evening after they'd got to the club.

She remembered the heavenly kiss. She remembered flashes of dancing. And she definitely remembered the photographer getting right up her nose. She *didn't* remember the woman getting hit, except that there had been a struggle and it wasn't her fault.

At seven a.m., she was let out of the cell, and given the opportunity to make a statement. 'I need to make a phone call before I do that,' she said, and rang Jim Break.

He wasn't thrilled to be woken up, even less so to discover why. 'All right. I'm on my way,' he said, snapping into action. 'I'll get a lawyer *en route*. Don't say anything – and I mean anything – until we get there.'

The process was interminable. Endless policemen and -women seemed to be involved (most, she found out later, would have come in for a gawp), but eventually it was over and she was charged with assault occasioning actual bodily harm and released on bail.

A clutch of photographers and reporters had arrived to witness her leaving. Jim had organized an emergency delivery of makeup, but Katie was hardly looking her best. In fact the night on the tiles, followed by sleep deprivation, meant that she looked like death eating a sandwich.

'I feel like a bag of spanners,' she said, as they walked to the doors. 'I should have asked you to bring me some other clothes to change into. A crumpled dress and high heels is not the look I generally aim for when I need a new job. Now, do I do the "Here comes the skateboarding duck" face? Or the serious "Thousands of dogs to be put down" face?'

Jim suggested a smile. 'No point in looking like you think you did it. And, after all, no one's died.'

'My career?' she queried, as they stepped outside to a barrage of clicks and flashes.

'I'm not allowed to tell you anything,' she replied, to the shouts directed at her by the reporters.

Jim led her to the car as the photographers tripped over themselves to get their shots, thrusting their cameras right up against the car's windows as it drove away.

'Well, I think that was a very successful evening's work,' said Katie, cynically.

'Yes,' said Jim, turning to look at her in the back seat. 'Not much more you could have done, really. Incidentally, you mentioned you were on a girls' night out and that you left with a man called Krishnan Casey. What happened to him? Do you have his number? He might be quite useful in terms of backing up your story.'

'Rather foolishly I forgot to get it. I didn't think I'd need it. I wasn't planning on a long relationship and marriage.'

'So that's something else they can write about, as if they haven't got enough. I'm assuming he'll be in the pictures?'

'Well, they can't show those, can they?' asked Katie, horrified. 'Aren't they *sub judice*?'

'I'm sure they'll get round it. What were you doing with this bloke when the photographs were being taken?'

'Kissing?' she ventured, and paused.

'And?' he said.

'And I think I fell over and he helped me up.'

'Excellent. This couldn't be better, really. Not. Let's hope he rings up and offers his support in your court case – if there is a court case, the best scenario being that the woman decides not to press charges.'

'Or press charges against the *real* culprit,' said Katie, waspishly. 'You may be forgetting that I'm the injured party here. I was minding my own business when I was assaulted. It was *his* camera that bashed her. Wielded by *him*.'

'Only he wasn't plastered. Plus he hasn't just been released from his post on Britain's foremost breakfast-television show,' Jim stated heavily, looking out at the lunch-time traffic.

'Oh, so I'm guilty because I'm famous?'

'Something like that,' he replied. 'Don't be an idiot. You know as well as I do what the police are like in cases involving celebrities. You'll get the book thrown at you even if you only had one fingernail on the "blunt instrument".'

Suddenly Katie had the most ghastly thought. If the pictures appeared of her and Krishnan, a landscape gardener in Yorkshire was going to be about as happy as Rik Waller at a salad bar. And her brother would tear her off a strip. Several strips. Possibly using his surgical tools. Flayed so close, she'd be able to sunbathe in her bones. Oh, well. Can't do anything about it. It's in the lap of the gods, she thought. I am *never* drinking again.

'Do we cover it?' asked Colin, *Hello Britain!*'s news editor, at the morning meeting.

The editor, Simon, smirked. 'I think we do. After all, she doesn't work for us any more. There's no obvious Monday angle, but if you, John,' he said, nodding at one of the reporters, 'can work on it. Maybe we do something about binge drinking. Check through PA and Reuters, see if there's anything we can peg it to. And we can get a commentator on it, and show the shots of her leaving the police station.'

Keera was the last out, and turned with her hand on the doorknob. 'Simon,' she smiled at him, 'I wondered if I might have a word about a strand I think would be really good for our viewers.'

He assented, and she sat down, letting her thighs part gently so that he had a nice view.

Twenty minutes later, she had been given the green light to have William Baron 'stripped' across five mornings.

She emailed him the good news immediately, and suggested a dinner meeting.

William was in a bit of a quandary. Keera's email couldn't have been more obvious. This was dinner with a hint. A hint as obvious as Hagrid at a party for dwarfs. She was after him. And she was definitely a prize worth having. Did he need to put the brakes on Dee before he had dinner with Keera? He liked her well enough, but she wasn't as high profile. And, come to think of it, she ate like a horse. And she'd got stroppy with him when he'd been explaining his theory on porkers. Anyone would think *she* was fat. In all truthfulness, she was a muddle round the middle. But more of an issue was the tardiness ... the muddle in the brain.

Where Keera was as trim and toned as a racing snake.

For half an hour, he mulled over the pros and cons. Then he sent an email to Keera. '*Carpe diem*,' he wrote. 'Whenever and wherever. Look forward to it.'

The response was swift.

She had looked up *carpe diem* in the Internet dictionary. 'Tomorrow night?' she wrote. 'The Ivy?' She knew there would be a snapper outside to witness the moment. Particularly if she made sure of it. And the deed was done.

* * *

He pursed his lips. Now to get rid of the weather girl. He checked his watch. Mid-morning. She'd be asleep. He phoned her mobile and left a long message: something had come up and he had to cancel their dinner tomorrow but would be in touch to reconvene. If he was lucky, he thought, she'd get to hear from Keera where he'd been and not bother him. He hoped she was the type with too much pride to grovel. He stood in front of the mirror, flexed his biceps, turned sideways and jutted out his jaw. 'Which way's the beach?' he asked his reflection. And stretched out one long, sinewy arm. 'That way, ma'am.' He gave himself a satisfied smile. 'You,' he pointed at himself in the mirror, 'are on your way to fame, fortune and a happy future with a beautiful assistant. I am Dr Who. Conquering stars. With a star. If that isn't too complicated?' he asked himself, and gave himself a wry, devastatingly handsome nod.

The BBC press office had put out the information about their new show to be presented by Mike Dyson and Saskia Miller.

The producer, Kuldeep, bumped into Sam on the way to the canteen. 'Have you heard the news about Katie Fisher?' she asked him.

'Yes. That was a lucky escape,' he commented, moving aside as an audience stampeded past for an early recording in studio six. 'Although on the basis that all publicity is good publicity … there will, no doubt, be a lot of it about. And there's always the distinct possibility that she's not guilty,' he said.

'Whether she is or isn't, she may be a bit busy for the next few weeks. Not what you want with a new show. Sorry, the presenter can't be here. She's up before the beak.' Kuldeep laughed.

'Suppose so. Are you after coffee?' he asked, as they reached the counter.

'Caffè latte, please,' she answered. 'Double espresso caffè latte. Soya milk.'

He reached forward to take a croissant off the shelf and put it on his tray. 'God, life was so much easier before. Coffee or no coffee,' he said.

'Blah-blah-blah,' said Kuldeep. 'When men were men. And women knew their place. And children were seen and not heard. And when, as an Indian, the most you could aspire to was a corner shop. It must be awful to have to remember so many words when ordering a coffee ...' She smiled at him to take the sting out of her words.

There was a pause.

He said, 'I hate to admit it, but I've forgotten what you wanted. Double espresso with soya milk ... erm, latte?'

'Exactly. Thank you. And I do think we've made the right choice with the presenters. So does everyone else on the programme.'

Katie got home, showered, washed her hair, spent a long time cleaning her teeth, flossed, ironed some clothes to put on, blow-dried her hair, and when she had run out of things she could tell herself were imperative, she phoned her parents. 'Hi, Mum,' she said. 'Can I speak to Dad, please?'

Her mother harrumphed slightly, but carried the hands-free phone to her husband, who was in the middle of boning an organic chicken.

'Hold on a minute, Katie. He's just washing his hands. How are you?'

'Fine, Mum. I need a quick word with Dad first.' She heard her mother chivvying him, and then he was on the line. 'Dad,' she said, 'I'm in a spot of bother, you're not to worry, and I didn't do it. And now I've said that, I'll start at the beginning. Do you need to sit down while I tell you?'

'No, no,' he said, sounding concerned. 'I'll stay in the kitchen. Got to keep an eye on the chicken – you know how Hercules likes to have his lunch cold, uncooked – and first. So, what have you been up to?'

And Katie told him, including the Krishnan bit, but leaving out the kissing. No point in making things worse, if it wasn't necessary. But she needed him to be on her side if Ben had a go at her. So she stressed how many Cosmopolitans she'd had – and that all the other girls had been in a similar position. It wasn't *only* her.

'It's already been on some of the early news bulletins apparently,' she told him, 'but obviously the usual rules apply. Don't talk to anyone about it. Even if they don't say they're a journalist. That way it's safer. You can say you've spoken to me about it and that you know what happened, but you can't speak about it. I think that should be all right.' She stopped. 'And if you see Bob ... If you see Bob ...' she trailed off. 'Do you think you *will* see him? Do you see him often?'

'No,' her dad smiled at the other end of the phone. 'No, we don't. Your mother's finished the painting of the wilting wisteria, or whatever it was supposed to be. It's up in her "office", looking remarkably like a combination of an autopsy and Fungus the Bogeyman.'

'Nice,' remarked Katie. 'Well, if you do see him, say ... say ... say ... could you say that I left a message for you and you haven't spoken to me yet?'

'If I must,' said her father, 'but you know I'm not very good at lying. Shouldn't you talk to him now, if it's so important?'

'I will. Not just yet, though. I need to be a little more *compos mentis*. And at the moment I feel like compost. Full stop. With a T.'

'That's probably what you need – a nice big cup of strong tea. Anyway, we probably won't see him. Don't worry. And you honestly think you won't end up being charged?'

'Highly unlikely,' she said, crossing her fingers.

'Well, I'd better get back to my chicken.'

'I bet it's trying to get to the other side, as we speak,' responded Katie.

'What?'

'Chickens. They're always trying to get to the other side of the road, aren't they? It's a joke, Dad.'

'If you say so. *Hercules*, stop that! Katie, I've got to go. *Hercules*.'

Katie heard the noise of dog claws scraping along the floor and imagined Hercules being dragged away from the chicken by the scruff of his neck.

The phone went dead.

Katie wandered round the flat, trying to work out how she was going to broach the subject with Bob. It had to be done. But she would tidy another section of her wardrobe first – things were so jam-packed in that the day before she had discovered an unworn, new dress squished behind some of the hangers.

The day before.

The day before the wretched incident.

If only ...

She pulled the phone plug out of the socket, and put her mobile on silent. For an hour, she was able to lose her brain in the mindless pursuit of cupboard tidiness. How therapeutic was chucking things away? With each toss of a dress, she felt better. Every jacket that hit the pile made her situation less hideous. Finally she got to the other end of the wardrobe.

Excellent, she thought. I can see what I have. I only have that which fits me or makes me look nice. I no longer have size-eight items that I cannot – and never could – get into comfortably. I have ejected that which is of a colour unfashionable or of a cut unflattering. I have rejected those things that are wretched and embraced those that are harmonious. Blessed are the weak, for they will inherit the wardrobe.

Although it would have been better if they'd been weak in an area of life other than the demon drink.

Damn. I must phone Bob.

She looked at her watch.

She'd do another twenty minutes.

She set about putting all the jackets in one section, dresses in another, skirts by the trousers, then colour-sectioned them.

If it hadn't been for the doorbell, she would have spent the entire afternoon in the cupboards.

She stood stock still. Looked at her watch. She wasn't expecting anyone. Was she? The buzzer went again.

She went to the intercom and stood there uncertainly.

It sounded again, making her jump.

'Hallooo, who eees dat?' she said, in a bad impersonation.

'Katie, it's Bob,' he said. She could hear him smiling, even through the crappy intercom phone.

She hesitated. Could she pretend it wasn't her? No. He knew. And what else did he know?

Did he know about the arrest?

About Krishnan?

She buzzed him in. Rushed to the mirror to check herself, then went to open the door.

He looked utterly gorgeous, blond hair rumpled, blue shirt undone a few buttons to show the deliciously hairy chest. And he was carrying flowers. He smiled at her, and crushed her in an embrace that made her head spin. 'I heard the news and thought you might need cheering up,' he breathed on to the top of her head.

'Who told you?'

'I happened to be listening to the local radio station when it was mentioned. You as a famous local person and all that. I got straight on the train. If I'd stayed I'd only be worrying about you. Are you all right?' He moved her slightly away from him and gazed at her with concerned blue eyes.

'Fine. Ish,' she said, and moved to take the flowers from him. 'I'll put these in water. Do you want anything to drink?'

'Cup of tea? I'm desperate. The buffet queue was so long. Although,' he said, as he followed her into the kitchen, 'now I come to think of it, I could leave the cup of tea for a short while.' He put his arms round her and kissed her so hard that she wondered if one of your actual faints was coming on.

He pulled back, a sun god in her kitchen, with his tanned arms and a spectacular bulge in his jeans. She raced him through to the bedroom, staggering a little over the clothes on the floor, and tumbled on to the duvet.

She wouldn't tell him about Krishnan. Or should she? When should she? She stopped thinking, as what was happening consumed every inch of her brain.

The next morning brought a call from her brother, among the umpteen others she had had about 'the incident'.

'You are in big shit, Katie,' he said. 'What the hell were you thinking?'

'Thank you for asking,' she said. 'I'm fine. And I'll think you'll find it was an accident after a few too many drinks. It'll blow over within a week. Tomorrow's fish and chips.'

'I'm talking about the photographs in the papers today. Obviously drunk. And with your tongue down some bloke's throat.'

She should have told Bob. This wasn't going to look good. 'I was drunk,' she interjected feebly.

'Like that's a sensible excuse,' said Ben. 'But you've put me in a bloody awkward position. I never minded what you got up to in the privacy of your own home ... but it just screams that you're a – well. Whatever. I mean. At least dump Bob before taking up with someone else. He's a friend. What can I say? It's out of order.' He stopped. 'Hello?'

'I'm still here,' said Katie. 'But I've got someone with me right now,' she said, in a pointed fashion. 'Can I call you back later?'

'Is it that bloke who's in the picture?'

'No. I'll call you back.' She put the phone down.

This, thought Katie, is like a bad farce.

'Who was that?' asked Bob, as he came out of the bathroom after a shower, a towel wrapped loosely round his muscular torso.

'Jehovah's Witness. Told them I was polishing the satyr's hoofs and could I call them back,' she said. She bit her lip pensively, then made a decision.

CHAPTER EIGHTEEN

It was Saturday, the big night out for breakfast-television presenters, and it was going to be a big night out for Keera. She was going on a date. And it was going to be in the papers. Oh, yes. She swayed down the road, her long black hair swishing gently about her shoulders, thinking of how she looked.

I will move my hips a little more – like this. And now I flick my head – so. And look how my shirt gapes, with that excellent cleavage. She glanced into a shop window to see her reflection – and in the next, she got a horrible shock.

No.

Katie Fisher was on the front pages *again*.

She bought the *Sun* and the *Daily Star*.

But as she read the articles while she drank her skinny decaff cappuccino, she realized, with relief, that it was bad news for Katie. The world is smiling on me, she thought. I'm going to have a handsome boyfriend by this evening. And we will be photographed looking beautiful together.

She flirted a bit with the waiter as she handed over her cash.

'I know I shouldn't say it, but I do think you're marvellous on *Hello Britain!*,' he said admiringly.

'Thanks. Of course you can say that,' she said, peeping up at him through her silky, silky fringe with her limpid blue eyes. 'Very nice coffee. See you again.' She stood up, threw her leather handbag over her shoulder and sashayed out. Only another month before she was on the cover of *GQ* with her panther. She shivered with anticipation, and almost caused a collision between two men who had been gazing at her like pigeons faced with a fresh sprinkling of bread-crumbs.

Dee was having a miserable Saturday. She had been buoyed up for a marathon rematch with William and been cancelled at the last minute because 'something's come up'. She hadn't been able to get hold of him to find out more details – or to arrange another dinner. Her only hope was that one of the K Club would come back to her with a plan.

She had been blissfully unaware of Katie's predicament until Carina texted her back: 'Can't do tonite. R U kidding? Still got hangover! Anyway, we have dinner party. Have you seen the *Sun*? Do we think Katie is in trouble???'

Dee went out immediately to her newsagent, bought three papers, a Twix, a Bounty for later, and a scratch card. She ate the Twix on the way home and did the scratch card. How come other people always won money? Her luck was shit. People like

Mike landed in shit and came out smelling of roses. She landed in shit and smelled of shit. Or worse, landed in shit, and got Weil's disease.

She sat on her sofa, and ate the Bounty while addressing herself to the newspapers. Oh dear, she thought. Oh dear oh dear oh dear. And she couldn't help but smile. Katie was having an even worse day than she was.

She peered closer at the photograph. The guy Katie had got off with was really very attractive. And Katie didn't look too bad in the Friday-morning photos, considering she'd slept the night in a police cell.

At which point, Dee's luck turned.

Kathy phoned to say she was feeling up to another night out – as long as it didn't involve any alcoholic beverage since she was never drinking again.

'Dinner and a film? Or film, post-film snack and glass of water?' asked Dee.

'Or could we get tickets to that play at the Royal Court? It's only fifty minutes long, apparently, and has had really good reviews?'

They arranged to meet up in the early evening.

Dee's mood had completely changed. She hummed as she hunted through the chaos of her flat to find her favourite mug. Whoops. It was so furry, it resembled an installation at the Tate Modern. She lobbed a bit of bleach into it and left it on the side to soak, precariously balanced on a pile of dishes.

She'd treat herself to a taxi.

She spent an hour composing a text to Katie, which offered a shoulder if she needed it. No point rubbing salt into the wound with references to TP, she thought. And then, because the day was all clean and new-minted, she walked up to Camden Market for a dose of grime and people.

Her hair shone in the sun and more than a few men checked her out as she swung past. She noticed, and did a surreptitious check to make sure she didn't have buttons undone, or her skirt tucked into her pants. Or a spot coming.

She could do with a table lamp, she thought, as she meandered through the old-stables area, hunting through the bric-a-brac. Dee considered herself one of the world's foremost collectors. It was only a matter of time before one of her finds turned out to be worth an absolute fortune. There were those who scoffed – Katie, for example, called it tat. But she loved her disparate treasures. Her cornucopia of clutter. Her puppets, ornaments, dolls, boxes, vases, pots, papier-mâché masks. And, as everyone knew, Katie was head of the Church of Minimalism. A ridiculous tidy freak, who would never suddenly discover that she was a millionaire, that something she had bought for peanuts was now worth a king's ransom.

Katie had listened to this diatribe once, then tried to pick up one of the alleged treasures to find it stuck to the table with what looked like cheese fondue. Dee's excuse had been the lack of a cleaner. 'I've tried to get one but they don't know what's precious. They throw away the wrong things and they clean some of the others, and break bits off them and don't tell me.

So what am I supposed to do? And I don't have time,' she had wailed, as Katie had given her one of her special looks.

Well, she thought, how many minimalists would be lucky enough to find a half-eaten packet of Quavers in the bed when they were feeling peckish after watching *ER* last night? Eh? Eh? Put that in your pipe, which you would have tidied away, and smoke it.

She picked up a *faux* Tiffany lamp with the perfect combination of lilac and orange, and began to haggle. She was sure they hadn't realized it was genuine.

Mike couldn't help but laugh when he saw the pictures of Katie. He had bought the papers to see if there was any mention of his new project for the BBC with Saskia.

Katie really did have an admirable kamikaze streak. Which reminded him – he really must sort out the meeting between Keera and his 'friend' from the Met. He'd had another email from him, reminding him of his 'obligations'. He sighed. It pissed him off right royally having to do it. He was enjoying being peevish with Keera. He'd have to get it over and done with on Monday so that he could return to peevishness for the rest of the week. Meanwhile, he took the opportunity of his wife's absence at a three-hour Pilates session to sort out his box of tricks. He wanted to throw away a few things that had perished, and check what else he needed. Saturday was always a good night for nocturnal activity. And he wanted it ready for the off immediately they came back from the charity ball.

Charity begins at home, he thought, opening one of the deep drawers in his bedroom and removing the sizeable box from where it was buried under a thin layer of little-used jumpers. He should get a bloody gong for the amount he did for charity – he was constantly giving his time to help the ruddy aged, buy buses for ruddy children, drill water for ruddy parched people, in places he'd never heard of, who should just bloody move. At least it looked good in the photographs, and sometimes you made useful contacts. The last one had resulted in the radio show, in which he was able to indulge in an occasional rant against some of the people he interviewed on *Hello Britain!* It was, perhaps, a little like biting the hand that fed him but, in the knowledge that he was the best thing that had ever happened to breakfast television, he felt no compulsion to temper his comments.

Having said that, perhaps it wasn't his wisest move, saying that the gay lobby had hit a bum note with their campaign to out celebrities.

Right. He delved into the box. Where was his favourite item?

Katie ordered a cab to take Bob to the station.

'I'm going to miss you,' she said honestly.

'I'm missing you, and I haven't gone yet,' he said, with a wistful smile.

'Actually,' she said, biting her lip, 'I ought to tell you something.'

He looked at her expectantly. 'Well? Is it a nice something?'

'Not really. No. Not really, at all. The thing is …'

'The thing is …?'

'The thing is … You know that piece on the news?'

'Yes, of course. That's why I came down, if you remember?'

'Yes. Anyway. Can we sit down?' She led him to the sofa.

'Oh dear,' he said. 'What have you done? Is there a body somewhere?'

'Bob,' she said.

'Yes, Katie?'

'The thing is …'

'You've said that already. What on earth's happened?' He started to look worried.

'That night I was very drunk.'

'I know.'

'And when I'm very drunk, I get a bit amorous.'

He moved slightly away from her on the sofa, and she felt his arms tense.

'No. It's all right. I didn't, erm, well, you know. Do anything major. But I did kiss him. And they did take photographs. And they're on the front of the papers. But it didn't mean anything. Honestly,' she finished, watching him for his reaction.

He didn't say anything.

'Really,' she reiterated. 'It didn't mean anything.'

'But you couldn't wait until you next saw me to feel amorous?' he asked, sounding wounded.

'It wasn't like that,' she said, as tears welled. 'He was there. And I was drunk. I'd had so many Cosmopolitans I barely knew which way was up.'

'I see,' he said, withdrawing his arm from her shoulders and sitting forward on the sofa.

The intercom sounded.

'Why did you leave it until now to tell me?' he asked, as she went to answer it.

'Yes. He'll be down in a few minutes. Thank you,' she said into its phone. She turned. 'I didn't want to ruin everything.'

'You mean you didn't think you'd have to tell me and now that the pictures are on the front pages you had to. Coward,' he said.

'Yes, all right. A bit of that,' she said, through the tears that were making her voice thick. 'Yes, I admit it was cowardly. But it didn't mean anything. It didn't ...' She went to get a tissue to blow her nose.

He stood up. 'I need to think about this,' he said. 'I hear what you're saying about the drink. But I need to think.' He went to pick up his bag. 'I don't know what to say. Thanks for a wonderful night, ruined somewhat by this revelation. I'll let you know.' And he went out of the door without saying goodbye.

Katie burst into proper tears. But a small part of her was annoyed that he considered kissing other people such a big deal.

However.

Whatever Bob wanted to do, she would stand by it.

Definitely, most assuredly, she'd miss him if he chose not to continue their relationship.

Most definitely, and assuredly, she'd be very happy if he made the opposite choice.

She looked outside at the cloudless sky. I need food, she thought. A bagel will make me feel better.

Bob jumped on to the train with minutes to spare, grateful that he didn't have to wait for the next one. As it was he was only just going to make his goddaughter's party. He closed his eyes and listened to the conversation going on opposite.

'So I says to him, I says: "If you want me to have the meat delivered round the back door, you've got anuvver fink coming." And you know what he says?'

He says, thought Bob: 'I'm the Bishop of Southwark, and this is what I do.' And he smirked. Not that he had smirked as he read the papers he had bought on the station platform.

He had studied the photographs. He had read the story, his stomach lurching unpleasantly. He had revisited the pictures. He was sufficiently a man of the world to know that photographs could be subtly altered. But he could see no way round the fact that his girlfriend, the woman he had come to consider a possible partner for life, appeared to be passionately kissing another man. It made him feel sick. It made him feel like an idiot. He'd rushed down to comfort her, and had this thrown in his face.

He opened his eyes and sat looking out of the window at the English countryside slipping past him in a slide of Whistler green. He thought of his friends. Of his mother. Of what they would advise him to do. After many hours of deliberation, he made his decision.

He drove home from the station with such a tight jaw his teeth ached. Yesterday he had gone to London full of promise. Today he was returning with shattered dreams. He gave himself a mental shake.

He drove straight to Harry and Sophie's.

'Hello, Squidgy Bottom.' He smiled as Elizabeth opened the door, with Sophie behind her.

'I don't take kindly to being called Squidgy Bottom,' said Sophie sternly.

Elizabeth giggled. 'But it *ith*, Mummy,' she lisped, poking Sophie's bottom with a dirty finger.

'Whereas *you*,' said Sophie, 'have a peachy, edible bottom.'

'Why thank you, kind lady,' said Bob, bowing at the waist.

'She meanth *me*!' shouted Elizabeth, running off to a gaggle of small girls smelling of angel cakes and Smarties.

'Thanks for coming,' said Sophie. 'She's been excited about seeing you. And I know you had to cut short a weekend in London. How was it?' she asked, giving him a searching look.

'Fine,' he said, not smiling. 'How's the birthday girl?'

'Full of sugar and bouncing off the walls. So we're very grateful for the space-hopper you gave her. She can bounce off safely. Are you all right?'

'Yes,' he said, with a smile that didn't reach his eyes. 'A bit tired, that's all. Long train journey.' And he went through to join the party.

Later, helping to clear away the pink, fluffy, trodden-under-foot mess, he asked Harry when his weekend to Kerry was happening.

'Not a satisfactory trip to London?' asked Harry.

Bob made a face. 'That obvious?'

Harry paused, his hand on the snout of a lilac pony with its mane missing. 'Pretty obvious,' he said. 'Considering that I saw you yesterday on the way to the station in radiant good health, with "Off For A Shag" tattooed on your forehead.'

'Have you seen today's papers?' asked Bob, and when Harry shook his head, he described what was in them. 'Consequently,' he said, 'I'm not feeling tip-top, as they say. Actually, you know what? I don't want to talk about it. When's that weekend?'

Keera rang her contact to tell him that she could be found that evening at the Ivy, dining with a man whose name was William Baron, a lifestyle guru. 'We'll be arriving at eight, and leaving at about … Oh, who knows what time we'll be leaving?' she simpered.

The contact put her name on the list of that evening's possibles.

The planets were aligned in her favour. No major stars were elsewhere in the constellation that night so Keera's wish came true.

William was delighted. 'How awful,' he said, through the flashguns, as he guided her into the restaurant. 'We should have chosen somewhere more discreet.'

'Yes,' she agreed. 'I should have thought ... But then again, we're single, aren't we? So it's not as though we're doing anything illegal.' She smiled up at him, the smile she had perfected through hours in front of the mirror from the age of eight.

He smiled back, the smile he had practised every day in the bathroom mirror since he could stand on tiptoe and see more than his fringe.

He ordered consommé and grilled fish, with a side order of steamed spinach. Keera admired his choices and opted for a green salad and half a dozen oysters, with a side order of peas and carrots. 'Should we go mad and have a glass of wine?' she asked, looking up through her impeccably mascaraed lashes.

'It *is* Saturday night,' he murmured. 'We could go utterly insane and have a whole bottle.'

'But that would be insanity on a grand scale,' she averred.

'I see a perky little pouilly fumé,' he said, his eyes gesturing to the wine list.

'As long as it's white wine,' she said.

'Yes, it is. There's also a sneaky sancerre. Or a sincere sauvignon.'

'They all sound very enticing,' she said, and selected an enticing posture from her vast repertoire of poses.

The waiter waited, then told them he would come back for their wine order.

The evening flew by.

They discovered they were kindred spirits.

'Books are generally not worth the paper they're printed on,' proclaimed William.

'Although I did *love The Road Less Travelled*,' said Keera.

'But that's a self-help book. Those are the *only* books worth having.'

'And what's your favourite film?' she asked.

'I liked *Lord of the Rings*, couldn't get enough of those Orcs,' he said.

'Ooo. And Sean Bean as Aragorn,' she said.

'Actually, I don't think it was him. It was a Danish guy. Scandinavian anyway. But, yes, he was brilliant. Well, they all were. What film would you choose for your desert island?'

She thought for a minute, putting her head on one side and choosing 'winsome' from her Rolodex of expressions. 'I think,' she said, taking the minutest sip from her glass of sauvignon blanc, 'that my favourite would have to be …' She tailed off. Think, think, think, she thought. Which one should I pick? 'My very favourite would be … You know, actually I love films like *Finding Nemo*. Films with a heart. And it's funny. Obviously it's not my *favourite* film,' she added, seeing his slightly disbelieving expression. 'That would have to be – erm – *Life Is Beautiful*,' she said, with a flash of inspiration. She had been early for dinner, and had stopped to read the offerings at an art-house cinema round the corner.

'A fan of the foreign film, eh?' asked William, with renewed interest.

Whoops! She hadn't realized it was foreign. 'Mm-hmm.' She nodded vigorously. 'What about your favourite actor and actress?'

And on it went.

Apart from the minor blip with the foreign film, Keera felt she had acquitted herself well. She had drunk an adequate amount to prove she was no prude. She had eaten sparingly so that her stomach had not distended. She had been witty and entertaining.

William was also feeling quietly confident. The sofa queen was much higher status than the weather bimbo. She was also a careful eater, unlike Dee. *And* – it was a big *and* – she knew you had to be on time and not have stains on your clothing before you had even started eating. He wondered if it was too early to suggest a nightcap.

He had a rare moment of doubt. Was Keera so high status that she would judge him by his flat? He hadn't been successful long enough to be able to afford the sort of place he felt would suit him.

Should tonight be the readying of the troops before the storming of the ramparts? She definitely seemed up for it, he mused, as she faked interest in the pudding menu.

'I don't know. It all sounds so good,' she said, eventually putting it down. 'But I have eaten quite a lot. Maybe some mint tea?'

'I might order a coffee,' he said. 'I think I'll probably need to go for a run when I get home. Get rid of all this nervous energy you've created.'

'Ooo,' she said, with a sidelong glance. He was going to make a play for her. How very encouraging. A kiss outside the Ivy would be good for the photographers. And, unlike Katie, she would be sober and attractive.

It was while they were flirting over the coffee and mint tea, moving their agendas ever closer together, that Keera discovered William should have been having dinner with Dee.

'I hope it's not going to be an issue,' said William, trying to sound sincere.

'Oh, no, I don't think so. I mean, I'm assuming you weren't actually going out with her. As in dating?'

'Good God, no!' he exclaimed. 'She's very nice, in a homely way, but not really my type.' He let the implication hang. 'You know, we went to dinner essentially. That was it. Nothing more.'

As they left the restaurant, she moved very close, turned her mouth up to him as though to ask him something, and the photographer got a nice snap of something that looked like a kiss.

She got home and fell asleep thinking about her five-year plan.

William got home and found a sweet message from Dee saying she hoped his business meeting hadn't been 'too unutterably stuffy. Do you fancy having Sunday lunch tomorrow at one of the fab curry houses round the corner from me?'

No, he did not. What a revolting thought. He pressed delete, and went to bed to read the instruction manual for his new juicer.

CHAPTER NINETEEN

Bob's mother would have told him off for mooching about with a face as long as a wet weekend. He would have felt better if he could have shouted at someone. But he lived in the wrong part of the countryside for an accidental double-glazing salesman.

It was the wrong day to shout at his bank manager. It was the wrong time of year to do anything in the garden that involved chopping. And it was the wrong type of weather to be stomping about the countryside. There should be a howling gale for that, and it was too hot for anything but fuming.

What he wanted more than anything else was for Katie to be taught a lesson that would involve them ending up in bed together and her saying she would marry him and forsake all others.

At which point, he caught himself up short. Was that what he wanted? In which case, why didn't he just phone her?

No. Because she was obviously the sort of person who couldn't forsake others. She would break his heart big-time. She would be unfaithful. And he couldn't cope with unfaithfulness. It had happened before to him and it wouldn't be happening again. He needed a one-man woman. Not some ... He searched for the word ... Some slut.

He stopped wearing a path in the sitting-room carpet, and stalked out of the room. He threw on his leather jacket, grabbed his helmet and headed off to the garage.

He was five miles down the M1, risking his licence, when Katie phoned his landline.

She didn't leave a message.

The *Hello Britain!* press officer answered a call from the *Mail*. 'I'll get back to you on that,' he said, and phoned the managing director, who confirmed the story, but said it was obviously imperative that it did not get out. 'Give them something else,' he said.

'Such as?' queried the press officer.

'Has Keera done nothing recently? She's always in the papers. Come to think of it, *we* are in the papers all the time, these days. This place is as leaky as an old bathtub. We could do without all these tales of incontinence.'

'Incontinence?'

'Sorry, I meant incompetence. The old story that suddenly appeared, for example, about the reporter who fell asleep when Katie was interviewing that minister. We need to find out who the mole is. I'll put an email out tomorrow about it being a sackable offence to give stuff to the papers. As for this other matter, have a word with The Boss and Simon. You don't need to tell them about the story we're trying to bury. But we need one juicy enough to get the *Mail* off our backs.'

The press officer had been planning a rather wild Sunday of repotting his begonias and gently lobbing snails from his borage plot into next door's garden before a trip to Tate Britain to look at the Constables. He sighed, and rang The Boss, then put the phone down quickly. He had had a brain-wave.

He phoned the *Mail* back. 'There's no truth in that particular story,' he said, 'but I do know – and this is strictly between ourselves – that Keera and Dee are dating the same man.'

William Baron woke up on Monday morning as a love-rat. He couldn't have been more thrilled if he had discovered an extra inch at the end of his Love Muscle, as he called it. He knew the value of publicity, and he had no intention of telling any of the reporters that he had only had one dinner date with Keera – and that, allegedly, to discuss work.

His phone had rung so much his ear was hot. 'I'm sorry, but a gentleman never tells. All I will say is that I'm a single man, and I've done nothing I'm ashamed of.' He might have scuppered his chances of a strand on *Hello Britain!* (although there was always hope), but his newborn company had been given a gigantic kick up the radar. And, looking on the bright side, Dee had discovered it was over without the need for a tedious conversation. Friends of hers were quoted as saying she was 'devastated'. He was, apparently, 'the first man she's loved since her ex-boyfriend revealed he was gay'.

Cracker.

If he played this right, he could be on *Celebrity Love Island* next time round.

At *Hello Britain!*, the tension was so tight that even a gnat couldn't have stepped on it without pogoing out of the window.

Dee had considered taking the day off. Katie had told her to get over herself. 'Consider it a small chapter in your autobiography. I know you liked him, but the man is patently stupid. To prefer Keera to you is folly. She's a swamp donkey. And he's a bum creeper, going after the person he thinks will do his career most good. You're better off out of it.'

'Why do I keep getting knockbacks, though? Just when I climb out of a hole, another opens,' said Dee, in a small voice.

Katie couldn't help but laugh. 'Yes. And they're always "arse"-holes. But you're talking to someone who's also lurched from one hole to another. It reminds me of when I was twelve and got caught in rough seas in France. Every time I stood up I got knocked down by another wave. But I survived. Albeit by hoisting myself up by pulling down the trunks of a man standing next to me. Anyway, the point is what doesn't kill you makes you stronger.'

'You know I *hate* homilies,' said Dee.

'So do I,' said Katie. 'I was checking you were listening. Now, I may not be the example to which aspiring journalists – nay, aspiring humans – flock. In fact, as a recent email put it, I'm not going to be an example, I'm going to be a terrible warning. But this is what I'd do.'

And Dee listened to the instructions.

On Monday morning, Dee smiled as Keera flew past the door to Makeup with a furtive glance. And then with each throw to the weather, she made a comment.

'Here's Dee with the weather,' grimaced Keera, in her favourite blue suit.

The vision mixer cut to Dee, young and pretty in a short, floaty dress. 'Thanks, Keera. Well it's looking a bit barren in the weather department today …' she said, with a bad pun on William's surname.

The vision mixer cut to a two-shot of Keera looking confused and Mike smiling. Both girls were having a difficult time, and he was above it all. What a pleasant aspect it was from where he was sitting. He didn't like Dee, and Keera had been painted as a scarlet woman in the *Mail* article.

On the next throw, Keera kept her mouth closed and looked pointedly at Mike.

'Any damp around today, Dee?' he asked, with a shark's smile.

'Only in some of the area here,' she said, wafting her hand generally towards the south. Thirty-love, she reckoned. Nevertheless, she rushed to take off her makeup immediately she finished her last bulletin so she could escape the building

before Keera came through. She hurtled through the newsroom, accompanied by a smattering of applause from those she
considered her friends, and threw herself into the back of the
Mercedes waiting to take her home. She was on the mobile
immediately. 'How did I do?' she panted.

'Bullseye, double top,' said Katie, approvingly. 'You were brilliant, as I knew you would be because she's only one step
removed from a whelk. Listen, I'm at a loose end for the rest of
the day. Shall I come over and we can go out on to the tennis
court and liberate your inner Annabel Croft?'

'Has Bob phoned?' asked Dee, solicitously.

'Nope. Obviously that's all over,' said Katie, trying to keep
her voice upbeat.

'God, what a pair,' sighed Dee, sliding down in her seat. 'Do
you think we need to buy a flat together, get the Zimmer
frames, the sticky bathmat and the handle by the loo?'

'It may yet come to that,' said Katie, darkly.

The press officer who had done the evil deed popped down to
Mike's dressing room to tell him the whole story – how he had
sacrificed the girls on the altar of publicity to save Mike's skin.
He liked Mike. He thought he recognized a fellow sufferer.
'About this story we've squashed ... categorically denying it,' he
started portentously, 'on the assumption that you did not leak
the aforementioned information to anyone, and knowing that
it was not the managing director, and presuming that the
person in Finance has not revealed it ...' He stopped.

'Yes?' asked Mike, brusquely. He found the press officer creepy.

The press officer rested his tightly clad bottom against the table, revealing a thick visible panty line. 'It would be wise to play your cards close to your chest. We think there's a mole here. There has been a distinct increase in activity, which has been noted. The MD is determined to weed out the nasty little animal in our midst.' He looked significantly at Mike.

'What?' asked Mike, irritated.

'There may be stories put about from now on, that are not true. They will, basically, be planted. So that we can find out who the mole is.'

'Well, you're doomed to failure, then,' snapped Mike. 'If more than two people hear a story, you'll never find out which one phoned the papers. They'll both deny it, and then where will you be? Unless you're going to get court orders to seize their phone bills. Or their bank accounts. Bloody stupid idea. The MD needs to get a grip.' He turned to sign an autograph on a mug for Save the Whale.

The press officer withdrew, miffed, since it had been his idea for the rogue stories.

Mike stripped down to his snug-fitting white Y-fronts, and put on some casual trousers. 'As if any of the presenters would be selling stories for peanuts,' he muttered, under his breath.

He stepped over the suit he had left on the floor, walked down the corridor and poked his head round the door of Wardrobe to ask Derek to have it dry-cleaned. 'I've dropped tea on it,' he shouted, over his shoulder, as he continued on his way to Makeup.

'Hallelujah,' muttered Derek. 'A suit I'll be able to steam without gassing myself. Let's leave all the other stinky suits hanging in the cupboard,' he said nastily, putting down the needle he had been threading. He wandered up to Mike's dressing room.

It was always such a mess. It was no wonder Mike hadn't noticed that one of his mobile-phone bills had gone missing ...

'Oh, Keera,' said Mike, pasting on a smile like a pair of lips on a Mr Potato Head; 'I've sent you an email about a mate of mine. He's a copper at Scotland Yard. May be quite useful meeting up with him. Awards ceremonies, corporates, that sort of thing. Anyway, I've sent you all the details. I'll leave it up to you. He's apparently very good-looking, according to women I know. If that makes any difference,' he added as he swiped a baby-wipe over his face.

He knew that his alleged mate had nothing whatsoever to do with corporate events, but hoped that would be enough bait to tempt her into phoning him.

Keera's supreme self-confidence had taken a mild knock that morning. She had heard the suppressed laughter in the gallery down her earpiece during the throws to the weather, and realized they were laughing at her. But she had won the man, hadn't she, in a fair contest? On the other hand, Dee didn't seem that bothered. Was it a prize worth having, if your rival didn't really want it? It was rather taxing.

She massaged moisturizer into her clean skin, gazing at herself in frank admiration. 'Vanda, can I borrow some of your makeup, please?' she asked, and put on a light foundation, a ray of blusher and a hyphen of eyeliner, then went to the morning meeting.

There was a hush as she walked into the room. Simon looked up from his notes. 'Keera, hi. Well done today. A difficult situation.' And he continued the meeting.

As everyone filed out half an hour later, he asked her if she could stay behind. She sat down again, saw herself crossing her ankles in Princess Diana fashion, and checked her manicured hands as they lay in her lap.

'Do you still want to go ahead with this William Baron strand?' he asked, his bony hands playing with a biro. 'I can totally understand if you don't want to – under the circumstances.'

Keera looked out at the sky for a moment, as if to focus. In reality, she was giving Simon her favourite profile. As if she hadn't already considered the question, she thought. Did he think she was a moron?

'I don't know,' she said, after appearing to cast about for an answer. 'I mean, obviously it's not very nice for Dee if he comes in. But she seemed all right with it this morning – unless she was putting on a stiff upper lip, as they say. What did she say about it when you asked her?'

He seemed faintly surprised by the question. 'I haven't,' he said. 'You're the one who's going to be doing the strand. It's not her call. Is it?'

'I suppose not,' considered Keera, turning her face slightly more into the sun for maximum flattering lighting. 'I think ...' she mused '... I think I would still like to do it. I think our viewers could really benefit from William's experience. I know that, as a lifestyle guru, he could be said not to have organized this part of his life very well, but when the heart is involved ...' She tailed off. Then she started again: 'And, of course, what he advocates is making plans in all areas of your life, and trying to stop being chaotic.' She thought for a moment. 'Funnily enough, Dee is exactly the sort of person who could benefit – she's all over the shop, isn't she?' She chose a little silvery laugh from her anthology of humorous responses.

It sounded more Cruella de Vil than Tinkerbell, but Simon wasn't complaining. And he hated Dalmatians. He smiled back. 'Naughty,' he said appreciatively. 'I must say, I think it'll go down very well with the viewers. I know we're talking about your personal life here, but it will give an added frisson. If you don't mind that?' He left the question hanging.

Keera snatched it out of the air, breathed it in, and let it out in a soft 'No ...'

The weather broke in a proper Thomas Hardy *Return of the Native* way, just as Katie had wanted. The thunder was loud enough to make her look out of the window to check whether or not Battersea Power Station had taken off. Sheet lightning gave it a dramatic backdrop. She loved her flat on a day like today. It was like having front-row seats at a rock concert put on by the rock god. She wandered over to her CD collection and selected Janáček. That was what was needed. A lot of trumpety sounds and cymbals.

An hour later, the sky had been thoroughly washed and the sun came out to dry it properly.

Katie nipped down to check on her post. Bills. Bills. Bills. 'More bills than a flock of falcons,' she mumbled to herself, as she went up the stairs. 'If that's what a collection of falcons is. An unkindness of ravens. A murder of crows. A parliament of owls. A nuisance of cats. Yes, it's a sign of madness,' she said, 'talking to yourself. Oh, and there are hairs on the palms of my hands. And I'm talking to them. And here I am on the stairs, looking through my post and talking. But if I'm mad, I wouldn't know it. So the very fact that I think I am … How can there be so many bills?'

She opened a few as she climbed the steps. Council tax. Darn. She should have paid it when she was working. Water. Gas. Electricity. Is this a conspiracy? Two phone bills. As she let herself back into the flat, she opened the rest.

A few were on direct debit, the others involved having to get out her cheque book. While she was at it, she grabbed her last bank statement and a calculator. She was going through her savings in a spectacular fashion. Living is too bloody expensive, she thought. It's not as though I've *done* anything expensive.

Dinners. Few bottles of wine here and there. Obviously last Thursday night. But that was a one-off. Nothing spent in Yorkshire, apart from the Oddbins trip. Train. But that was cheap. She went through her bank statement with a fine-toothcomb. Maybe I've had my identity stolen. I may have been cloned. I may not be me. There is only one way to check. If I can eat a whole tub of Marks & Spencer trifle, I am still me.

She went out to the King's Road. While she was securing trifle, she bought a bottle of pink champagne. And a pair of black patent shoes.

'Bloody stupid,' she tutted, as she got back to the flat and put them on. 'What I should have done is Sellotaped over another black pair.' But they did look gorgeous, she thought, as she admired her feet walking backwards and forwards from the sofa.

She got back to the statement. She needed to cancel those charity things until she could afford them again. And as for the three clubs, she could cancel membership of two without much hardship. One was miles away. The other was full of trendy young people who made her feel old. Only way to appear young and thin, stand next to old fat people. The more she fiddled with the figures, the more she realized she was going to have to do some work. And not just a column in a magazine. That was merely a finger in the dike. She had a nasty mortgage habit. And unless she wanted to end up in a squat, she was going to have to do something fairly swiftly.

She phoned her agent.

The production company for the dating game *All Mine At Nine* hadn't got back to him. 'Looks like it might have been offered to someone else, and they're waiting for a response from them. So shall we remain optimistic on that one? You've got the magazine column, and they'll be happy with the profile you're getting at the moment. Unless this woman decides to press charges.'

'It's unlikely they'll do me, though, isn't it?' asked Katie, slightly holding her breath.

'Unlikely. The Crown Prosecution Service would get involved, and they'd have to prove malicious intent if they were going to do you for actual bodily harm. It was an accident. The witnesses would have to say it was deliberate. Fingers crossed it will go away. You're proving one of my most entertaining clients,' he said, 'if to be entertaining is to be constantly in a state of alert waiting for the next instalment.'

'Britain needs more lerts.'

'Sorry. Didn't get that.'

'State of a lert? Britain needs more lerts?'

'Ah. Right. So, where was I? Yes. Nothing else has come in. Shame you didn't get that programme Mike's doing with Saskia Miller.'

'Yes, I know. He told me he pushed as much as he could, but you know how the BBC likes its own home-grown presenters. And actually, with hindsight, perhaps it would have looked a bit odd with two people hosting it who are – or were – better known for breakfast television. Can you try to get me some corporate stuff, though? I'm down to my last bottle of Cristal, and the servants are threatening to leave,' she said, in a Penelope Keith kind of way.

'You know that even if I did – and don't assume I'm not hustling on your behalf – the readies wouldn't come through for months. If you really are strapped, I could lob you a grand or so to tide you over, but I'm afraid there's nowt much out there at the moment. I've suggested you as holiday relief for virtually everyone apart from *Postman Pat*.'

'You *know* I could stand in for Pat.'

'You know you couldn't handle that much mail.'

'You forget,' she said tartly, 'to whom you are talking. I can handle vast amounts of male.'

CHAPTER TWENTY

It was time for the annual 'blue sky thinking' weekend at the Wolf Days production company. They had been pitching for a number of commissions. Adam Williams and Nick Midhurst, the joint managing directors, were very keen on a new late-night slot, which was available on Channel 4, after its long-running arts show had been forced out by the new bosses at the channel.

There was also an afternoon series going for UK Living, and a health strand for Channel 5, after the success of a series on horrible diseases. Every year the two men took their gang of workers away for team building – alias a piss-up. Before setting up the production company, they had both worked at the BBC, and hated the lack of fun they'd had during their working week.

'All work and no play makes for a deathbed speech devoid of anything but a list of accomplishments,' said Adam, in his inaugural speech. 'Which is why we've set up Wolf Days. We want it to be a great place to work, where creativity isn't stifled by umpteen layers of bureaucracy, where the show isn't run by accountants, where you put in the hours and work your arses off, only to be told that someone else is going to get the glory – or that it's being shelved because we've had our quota of home-decorating shows. Wolf Days is going to get out there, win the commissions,' he said, 'and deliver. On time. On budget. And occasionally on edge. But always with a large dollop of enjoyment.'

At that point, there were precisely ten people in the company.

Adam had come up with the idea and Nick had brought the name, after a night out scavenging for girls.

One of Adam's exes had described them dismissively as the Matt Damon and Ben Affleck of the production world. In her mind, that meant shallow. And although it was intended as a criticism, they took it in extremely good part. She was an art critic Adam had met at a BAFTA party, as beautiful and as cold as an ice sculpture; for a short while, they had called their company Good Will Hunting.

Their good looks had done them no harm in securing commissions from female bosses at some of the television companies. The company had now swollen to forty, and what had started as a thank-you had turned into a blue sky thinking weekend. A chance to brainstorm away from the office. This year it was in Wales. Adam and Nick had booked a beautiful hotel on the banks of a lake. There was to be canoeing, sailing, cycling and clay-pigeon shooting during the morning, then working all afternoon. In the evening there was to be a slap-up meal with no alcohol ('Sorry, want you all sharp and looking pretty in the morning,' said Nick), and an early start on Saturday, followed by more of the same.

'I want at least a hundred suggestions by the time we come back on Sunday night,' Adam told the staff, as he unveiled the details.

There was a murmur.

'All right, at least ten good ones, then,' he amended, smiling.

There was a sigh from the women. Not because of the revised estimate, but because he was so damned attractive, particularly when he smiled.

'And,' as Gemma confessed to her fellow production assistant, 'he has the most gorgeous voice. And bottom. And torso. And crotch.' She giggled.

'Do you think it's the way his jeans are cut?' asked her friend Rose, seriously. 'Or do you think that, basically, it's *enormous*?'

'Hmm,' mused Gemma. 'Difficult to say. Sometimes it's all testicles and no penis, don't you find?'

'And sometimes it's like there's a posing pouch attached to the front of the jeans, and nothing inside,' insisted Rose. 'You know how Nick seems to have less. And I can't believe it's because he *does* have less.'

'What do I have less of?' asked Nick, coming up behind them on his way out of the building for a meeting.

Rose blushed. 'Less, er, less, er . . .'

'Lesser what?'

'Lesser spotted woodpeckers near where you live. You live near Crowborough, don't you? Do you get woodpeckers?' she burbled.

He stopped. 'Didn't have you down for a bird-watcher, Rose,' he said.

'Oh, yes. Only just started, though,' she explained.

Gemma smiled broadly behind her friend. 'Now you're going to have to start bringing in binoculars and talking twitchers,' she said, as he left. 'I thought I was going to die when he came up behind us like that. You don't think he heard, do you?'

'Doubt it,' said Rose. 'But, God, wouldn't you just die if he kissed you? Talk about twitching.'

'You're terrible, Muriel,' said Gemma, in a bad Australian accent.

'But really,' said Rose. 'And I wouldn't mind rummaging around in Adam's nest, either.'

There was silence then as they tried to get their desks cleared before the trip that started at the weekend.

Nick had been on his way to a meeting about the late-night show on Channel 4. He wanted more information on exactly what the commissioning editors were after.

He felt he could probably write their demands himself – the same words would keep on cropping up – edgy, fun, sexy, appealing to the seventeen-to-twenty-fives – but he wanted to get it from the horse's mouth in case they were barking up the wrong tree. To mix a metaphor.

Talking of which, Rose a bird-watcher? He laughed. Wondered what they'd really been talking about, then put it out of his mind as he headed into the coffee shop.

Back at the office, Adam was thumbing idly through the news-papers. He wondered whether it was worth trying to poach the press officer from *Hello Britain!* There was rarely a day when there wasn't a story in one paper or another. Now it was about a man he'd vaguely heard of called William Baron. Apparently he'd been knobbing two of the presenters, and been given a lifestyle strand. He'd keep an eye on that one. If he was good, he might be suitable for the UK Living programme.

He was looking forward to the weekend away. He was tired after a series of shouting matches with his girlfriend, who was angling to move in. He didn't want her messing up his routine. He liked his towels nicely folded, his fridge nicely organized, his washbasin unsullied by makeup, and his CDs put back in their boxes. She may look like Scarlett Johansson, he thought, but she's as messy as a Jackson Pollock painting. Had it come to the end of the road? he wondered. Was it the awful but inevitable move-in-or-split-up moment? He'd get a bit of perspective in Wales, where there was erratic phone reception. And where one of the conditions was that mobile phones were switched off during the day.

By Friday, Katie was worried about her financial situation. Reluctantly, she borrowed five thousand pounds from Jim, and phoned to investigate remortgaging the flat. She really could have done without it, though. The repayments would be higher, and she could see that things might spiral out of control. She had grown up with the idea that you didn't borrow money. Ever. Even having a mortgage felt like a gross betrayal. Like Eve not only biting the apple but actually snogging the snake in the Garden of Eden.

She looked through the newspaper. Yet another story about William Baron and his wretched lifestyle strand at *Hello Britain!* 'That rat fink,' she said. She couldn't believe the man-management skills at *Hello Britain!* 'How bloody insensitive to give him a series. Poor Dee. She's well out of it with that idiot. But, really, they need their heads examined.' Although she could see that it would be essential viewing – and, shamefacedly, had to acknowledge she would be tuning in to watch it herself. Nothing wrong with being a hypocrite as long as you know you are. For something to do, she wandered over to her dictionary and looked up 'hypocrite': 'A person who pretends to be what he is not.'

Well, that's all right then, because she knew she was. So she wasn't. Which would make her a what? A 'hypogeal', she read. 'Occurring or living below the surface of the ground.' No, she thought, I'm not one of those. Although I know a number of people who are. Or who should be.

She flicked on: 'Catachresis. The incorrect use of words, as in luxuriant for luxurious.'

Excellent. She was definitely guilty of that. She had once said she was feeling inclement, when she meant tearful. Or did that count? Was it only if they sounded similar? 'Disinterested' and 'uninterested', for example? She looked up 'disinterested': 'Freedom from bias or involvement.'

Right. 'Uninterested': 'Indifferent. Unconcerned.'

Bingo! As she'd thought, one meaning unbiased, the other meaning uninterested.

She looked at her watch. Ten minutes well wasted.

She went to the mirror, took out the eyebrow tweezers and got rid of a few stragglers. Then checked on her bikini line. Got rid of a few stragglers. Tweezered out a grey hair. Then tweezered out another from her head. Looked at her watch. It was amazing how little time some things took.

She phoned Andi at Greybeard TV. 'Do you want me to come and act in anything?' she asked.

'It's come to that, has it?'

'It sort of has,' explained Katie.

Andi had been in touch throughout her trials and tribulations, cheering Katie up with one particular text after her night in the cells: 'You looked ridiculous. Wouldn't have recognized you but for the knickers.' Andi promised to keep her ear pinned firmly to the ground. 'But, you know, these days actors get paid bugger-all unless they're out of the soaps. So even if you were to do a cameo role – say, falling out of a nightclub with a man who's not your boyfriend – you're talking in hundreds, not thousands. Tops. Oh, by the way, did you read today what's happened to your ex-snog?'

'What – Bob?'

'No. Is he your ex? Thought you were still with him. Please remember to fax me your movements in future so I don't put my foot in it. I meant the married man, Mr Krishnan O'Flaherty or whatever his name was.'

'I have no idea what's happened to him and no great interest in it,' said Katie, irascibly. 'I've got to the stage where I've decided I like my men as I like my coffee. Ground up and in the freezer.' And then she added, 'And I don't know whether or not Bob's an ex. But I have a strong feeling he may be.'

'Well, that's sad. He sounded lovely,' said Andi. 'And to get back to Mr Ravi Murphy. Even though you don't want to know, I'm going to tell you. His wife has apparently left him and taken their child to live in Zambia. Or Zanzibar. Or Zimbabwe. Somewhere beginning with a Z. It was the final straw, she said. Constant philanderer. So you've done them a favour.'

'I fail to see how that's done them a favour. Child with no dad around. Single mother.'

'Yes, but happier mother. And philandering ex-husband off the scene, so that new and non-philandering man can be introduced to give the daughter a sensible and proper back-ground.'

'God, what a mess,' said Katie. 'I'll never order another Cosmopolitan in my life. Not that I can afford one anyway. Whatever I drink will have no alcohol, no mixer and possibly no ice, no lemon, or glass. Just a straw. Do you want to go out for a drink of water from a tap somewhere tonight?'

'Tempting,' drawled Andi. 'However, I do have a couple of toenails to rip out by the roots. And I was thinking of watching a line of paint dry afterwards.'

Katie laughed.

She trailed round the flat. She checked the fridge. Two olives, suspiciously shiny. She ate one. It was off. She crunched a vitamin tablet to get rid of the taste.

Why did she never buy any useful food? It was always designed to be eaten within two days of opening (like anything went back in the fridge) or had to be cooked.

She squeezed a whitehead in the bathroom mirror, applied nail-varnish remover and a dob of toothpaste. Squeezed an in-growing hair on her leg. Put nail-varnish remover and toothpaste on it. Accidentally tried to squeeze a mole, which made her feel faint. Put nail-varnish remover on it and a bit of toothpaste. Filed her nails. Looked up another word in the dictionary. There were four entries for 'bob', followed by 'Bob's your uncle: everything is or will turn out all right'. (Nineteenth century: perhaps from pet form of Robert.)

Which it won't.

She felt an ache somewhere in the region of the heart.

Perhaps I'm so hungry I have low blood sugar, she thought.

There's no way I'd be getting this maudlin if it wasn't for that.

She picked up her mobile. Her hand hovered over the keys. She dialled her brother. 'Ben Fisher. If it's urgent, call me on ...' He rattled off his bleeper number. 'Otherwise do the usual stuff after the flatline.'

'Ben. I've said sorry about the, erm, Bob thing, but I'm feeling a bit hungry. And I'm trying to conserve my money. And there's nothing in the cupboard. Can you please bring the poor dog a bone? Or take it out to dinner?'

She pottered round the flat again and rearranged the towels.

She was considering descaling the kettle when Jim phoned. 'I've organized meetings with every twenty-four-hour news station, including Al-Jazeera. I'm not necessarily advising it,' he said, 'because they'll be wanting contracts of a sizeable length.'

'I like a sizeable length,' said Katie, trying her best to be her normal self.

'Oh, behave,' he said, all Austin Powers. 'We're talking two years minimum, locked in. Which would mean you're off terrestrial for all that time. You would get big viewership, but mostly in places you haven't heard of.'

'Try me,' she said.

'Spain.'

'You're right. Never heard of it. Is it near New Zealand?'

'Being serious for *uno momento*,' he continued, 'there would definitely be openings, but the money you'd be offered is likely to be pretty bad, particularly if they smell desperation. But it'll keep the wolf from the door. And you might as well keep your oar in – give you a reason to get dressed in the morning.'

When Ben eventually called her back, she had dozed off in front of the television and appeared to be watching a programme with half-naked women talking about their breasts. 'What time is it?' she asked groggily.

'Late. I've been on shift until now. I'm whacked. And I'm still pissed off with you. If you're hungry tomorrow, though, I'll cease hostilities long enough to feed you. I'm going to a comedy club with Oliver.'

'Oliver the proctologist?'

'Yes. He's thinking of supplementing his income by writing and performing on the comedy circuit.'

'But he's not funny,' she said, confused.

'Neither are you, but some people think you are. You don't think he's funny because he's clever, and you always reason he's having a go at you. Look, I'm too knackered to talk. Fancy it or not?'

The comedy club smelled of mushrooms and feet. The walls were red and damp to the touch. But it was cool after the hot day outside. Ben and Katie had eaten an enormous amount of empanadas, tortillas and guacamole, and were sitting in their seats releasing quiet, garlicky burps when Dee rushed in.

'Phew! Not last, I'm glad to see,' she panted, taking off her jacket over her handbag and having to put it back on again.

'You are, actually,' said Katie. 'Oliver had a late shout. An urgent bottom, as it were. Could it be described as dis-arse-trous?'

'That's rubbish,' tutted Ben.

'Arse-k and you shall be given?' she essayed.

'Just give it up with the bad puns,' her brother advised.

'I keep telling her, too,' sighed Dee, 'but I think it's seeped into the fabric of her being. Like mildew on damp clothes. Talking of which, it does smell musty down here.' She sniffed.

'Reminiscent of your flat,' suggested Katie, 'where I once found a three-year-old cheese sandwich stuck underneath an ornament, as I recall.'

'It was cheese fondue. And it was not three years old.' Dee frowned.

'It was definitely a toddler,' said Katie. 'It was well beyond the crawling stage.'

Ben laughed. 'You two should do a stage show,' he said. 'Tweedledee and Tweedledumb.'

'Hey, you.' Katie dug him in the ribs with a pointy finger. 'Less of the dumb, if you don't mind.'

'Dumb is absolutely the right and proper word. To be used about girls who make it so that it's impossible for their family to speak to an old family friend. Poor Mum was hoping to go and do more painting round at the Old Coach House. But, oh, no, Katie goes and puts her sticky paws all over everything, and we're having to pussyfoot about the place.'

Katie's mouth went down at the corners. 'Can we not talk about this, please?' she begged. 'I've said I'm sorry. OK, so I've cocked up. *And* I really did like him. But if he can't cope with a little extra-curricular snoggage, it's just as well it's over now. Because while there's drink in the world, and an opportunity to drink it, I will over-indulge at some stage, and either have to be stuck on to a wall by the mouth or kiss someone. Because that's what I want to do when I've had a few. And it's a damn sight better than some people who want to fight when they're drunk. Or have your actual full-blown sex when they're drunk. So can we please, *please*, stop talking about it?'

There was a pause.

'Nil by mouth from now on, eh?' queried Ben, pursing his lips.

There was another pause.

'Fancy a drink?' asked Dee.

'Five pints of whisky for me, please,' said Katie.

'Yurk. I'll be kissed by my own sister,' said Ben, making a face like a snail on a slug pellet.

'It's all right,' said Dee. 'She can kiss me. I could do with a kiss. Do you really want something to drink, though? I'll go and get the beers in. Or water, if you'd prefer, Katie.'

'Oh yes. I love going out and having a nice glass of water. Excellent stuff. No. Can I have a beer, please? Whatever they've got.'

'And me,' said Ben.

Dee wandered off.

Ben sat thoughtfully for a moment, listening to the buzz. The show wasn't starting for another ten minutes. Oliver still had time to make it. 'You know, I don't think it's a bad idea. Tweedledee and Tweedledumb. Even if I do say so myself. It could be like *The Vagina Monologues*, with fewer vaginas. Or more, if you preferred. You could tour the provinces. Sell mugs and T-shirts. Pick up as many men as you like. Live out of a suitcase. Eat crisps.'

'Tsk, it was all going so well until then. I couldn't cope with the crisps. Too crunchy by half. Could I do chocolate instead?' asked Katie.

Adam and Nick were having a quick post-meeting meeting, pre-dinner. The weekend had been constructive so far, with some genuinely creative ideas coming out.

The brief had been: 'Let your imagination run riot. It doesn't matter whether it's impossible. What programme would you like to watch, and who would you like to present it?'

There had obviously been a lot of George Clooney suggestions from the girls and Angelina Jolie from the boys. But then they had settled.

'I'm quite keen on developing Gemma's idea of a programme where you look seriously at the ageing process and what can be done now to help,' said Adam. 'All the medical stuff right from the conventional to the unconventional – like injecting sheep foetuses or whatever. All the blood and gore, lots of computer graphics. It might be a bit too expensive for us, unless we get a guaranteed big budget. But I think it's got legs.' He wandered over to the window to check whether the pretty waitress was still windsurfing on the lake in the very skimpy bathing suit.

'I think it has a fine pair of legs, judging by the short skirt it was wearing at lunch,' said Nick, coming to stand by him. 'But Naomi has a fine pair too.'

'I'm thinking we might be over,' said Adam.

'I thought it was about to end in marriage,' said Nick.

'That's what she thinks,' admitted Adam. 'But I'm not sure I could cope with the mess.'

'For fuck's sake, that's a ridiculous reason to end it. Six months ago you could barely make it through the meeting for *Disgusting Diseases* without rushing off to jump on her.'

'I know. I think I've run out of sperm,' said Adam.

Nick smiled.

Adam took a swig from his bottle of water. 'She's such a mess and so disorganized that nothing's ever easy. We can't find anything. She's always forgotten to do something. It's a palaver,' he said.

'A posh man's jumper, a palaver,' said Nick.

'Ha. Like a crèche. A car crèche.'

'Or sex. Sex of potatoes.'

'Enough. As I was saying, Gemma's idea on ageing is very good. And Sol's trying to work on space for the science slot. Although it might be impossible to achieve. One giant leap too far for the money. But great idea.'

They continued talking as they descended the staircase and went into the leather-chaired library for pre-dinner elderflower cordial and gingerade.

CHAPTER TWENTY-ONE

There was a snidey piece in the *Mirror* on Monday about Keera and William Baron. 'Where There's a Will, There's a Wa-hey' was the headline. But Keera couldn't have cared less about gossip columnists. Only one thing was worse than being talked about, and that was *not* being talked about. She liked being in the papers.

Plus, her agent had been on to *GQ* and they'd told him the magazine was out this week. She'd get *loads* of publicity. Of that she had absolutely no doubt. She also didn't care that her cavalier attitude towards Dee's cavalier had cost her a few friends at *Hello Britain!*

'You lose some to win some, Sheila,' she had told her mother at the weekend. She had been taught to call her parents by their first names from about the same age as she was being taught how to dress her Barbie. 'There will always be those who are lost by the wayside as you make your way to the top of the mountain.'

'Do be careful, though,' her mother had said, putting a doily on a plate. They had talked about her magazine cover ('How very exciting, Keera') and her new man ('How exciting, Keera') and at the end of the phone call her mother had cheered her on her way.

And she had then got on to her friend Pat, who worked at the Co-op. 'She's going out with a very nice young man, apparently,' said Sheila. 'He's in the papers today. Very handsome. Something to do with coaches.'

So when Keera went in on Monday morning, and found that some people were a fraction offhand with her, she put it behind her.

What was that thing people said? Revenge was a dish best eaten cold? No, not that one. The best form of revenge is victory? Not that it was revenge, exactly. Maybe there wasn't a quote about it. What she *meant* was that she would show them who was going places, and who wasn't, so yah, boo, sucks to you. Kent was still being sweet to her, and that was useful because the email that had gone round recently, threatening instant dismissal to anyone found speaking/leaking to the papers without permission, had given her a moment of mild fright.

But she had thought it over and decided there was no way anyone could connect the stories to her. She had used Kent's email (he had given her his password when she had first needed to use the computer in the newsroom), and any phone calls were from her publicity agent.

She might give it a break for a while, though.

As she was coming off air, the press officer was opening the big bundle of magazines delivered every week. He flipped through his advance copy of *GQ*, and was shocked. He didn't like Keera. He *had* liked her, but then he had overheard her telling The Boss that he made her flesh creep. He couldn't believe she'd got this photo shoot past those at the top. It was obscene.

He read the article.

The woman's deranged, he thought. Calling herself a serious journalist. Laughable. If she's a serious journalist, I'm a sweaty heterosexual. He peered closely at the photograph. For God's sake, you could almost see what she had for lunch in one photograph. No wonder the panther looked horrified.

Disgusting.

Blah-blah-blah, he read ... War correspondent. Pah. Blah-blah-blah ... Don't make me laugh. Like you did a searing interview with *anything* that had more cells than an amoeba.

Blah-blah – what? That's revolting.

He closed the magazine, and took it up to the managing director's office. 'Is the MD in?' he asked the secretary, who was de-leafing a wilting rubber plant.

'Go right in. I don't think he's busy.' She nodded.

The press officer placed the magazine squarely in front of the MD.

* * *

Who did a double-take. What an extraordinary photograph. He felt a slight stirring as he gazed at the stunning picture of his main presenter draped round a panther wearing nothing but a smile.

'I know,' said the press officer. 'Outrageous, isn't it? Did she run it past you?'

'No, she didn't. But, as you know, it's really not my shout. However ... obviously she should have spoken to you about it. I'm assuming she didn't.'

'No, she did not. I would've told her it was inappropriate,' he said. 'Plus, I would've sat in on the interview and made sure she didn't bring the station into disrepute.'

'Has she? What has she said?'

'That she likes to stand naked in front of the open windows in her flat.'

'Perhaps unwise, but not a sacking offence, I would have thought,' said the MD, slowly.

'And that she, erm ... has a pleasant time in the bath while thinking of The Boss.'

'Oh dear,' said the MD. 'Although I'm not sure that's a sacking offence either.' He tried to stifle a smile.

'OK. How about that she used to shoplift?'

'Again, unwise, but we all have things in our past that we're perhaps not proud of.'

'She sounds proud of it.'

'Tell you what, leave the magazine with me, and I'll discuss the matter with The Boss.'

The MD poured himself a cup of coffee, and sat down to read the article.

Typical *GQ*. They'd gone heavy on the sex angle, and had obviously managed to get Keera to say rather a lot that she perhaps hadn't intended. He could see the writer leading her on, and her being unable to back down, each step drawing her further into the fly trap.

He sighed. He supposed she needed to be taught a lesson, if only to stop her being a silly girl.

He liked her naked ambition. Come to think of it, he liked her naked. He took another look. Yes. Sleek and beautiful, with her big blue eyes and silky dark hair. He also thought she was good for the show. She made him laugh out loud, occasionally. Not necessarily *with* her. But how much did that matter in the great scheme of things?

And she was a good foil for the cynical Mike.

He dialled The Boss's number.

Keera could barely contain herself. She had gone straight from work to do a spot of shopping – or, more specifically, to see the magazine in the shops. She gazed at it on the rack in WH Smith's with barely concealed excitement. She moved slightly away from it so she wouldn't block other people's view. And also so that she could watch them looking at it. She was as excited as a python in a rat lab.

That is *me* on the front cover of that magazine, she thought. Me. Me. Keera Keethley from Nottingham.

From Nottingham to Notting Hill.

From Nottingham to the front cover of *GQ*.

I'm so famous they put me on the front cover.

I'm unstoppable.

She bought half of the copies on the stand, then went to another newsagent to see what was happening there.

She sauntered home, swishing her hair. She could hardly wait to look through the photographs and read the interview.

She slipped off her shoes and sat cross-legged on her large beige sofa and spent a happy half an hour reading all about herself and perusing the photographs. One of her sultry looks had gone slightly wrong, she thought. She'd have to do more work on that one before she tried it again. But, on the whole, she was pleased with the result.

She wondered how much the papers would do on it the next day. She hugged herself, stretched like a beautiful cat, then got up and padded to the fridge for a celebratory tomato juice.

Mike had caught sight of the magazine on his way to lunch with the producers of his new show and was repulsed. Silly tart, bringing *Hello Britain!* down with her antics. What did she think she was doing? So much for her I'm-a-serious-journalist line. You didn't see the women from *Newsnight* doing things like that. He had a good mind to call his agent, tell him to get on to *Cosmopolitan* and ask if they'd like a nude picture of him. Hopefully they'd say yes. Then he could turn them down and mention that was what he'd done, show what real journalists did with invitations to get their kit off. And tell the newspapers, too.

At Wolf Days, the glossy magazines had been delivered and were being looked through for inspiration for new programmes. Gemma was leafing through *Heat*. 'Hey, Rose, do you think this skirt would suit me?'

Rose was engrossed in an article about Kerry Katona. She raised her head. 'No. It makes her look fat. And she's a model.'

Another producer went past, and stopped to peer over Gemma's shoulder. 'Nice shoes. Where are they from? Hmmm. Fifty quid. I might go and get a pair this lunchtime.'

Rose looked up. 'You didn't mention the shoes,' she said accusingly.

'That's because they're not good for those of us with cankles,' replied Gemma.

'You haven't got cankles.'

'Yes, I have. I know they're not, strictly speaking, cankles as in my calves hanging over my ankles. But they are cankle-ish. And not only are those round-toed shoes but they have a sort of ankle-strap thingy as well. Guaranteed to make your feet look wide and huge. Like a – like an enormous pair of marrows. And, anyway, you have enough shoes.'

'Enough shoes? Are you mad? Enough air. Yes. Enough food. Yes. Enough money. Debatable. Enough shoes? Never. Ever.'

'Never enough shoes?' asked Adam, who was late in after an early altercation with Naomi involving marriage and babies.

'Never,' said Rose, firmly. 'In fact, I can't believe there isn't a whole series – a whole *series* of series – devoted to shoes. I may write up a treatment right this instant,' she added, to make it look as if they really were doing some work. Not that Adam was like that. He believed that if you gave people a bit of leeway they'd come up with the goods.

He grabbed *GQ* from the pile of magazines that hadn't yet been snaffled and stared quite hard at the front cover. Very nice. Gorgeous body. And what a healthy-looking television presenter, too. He turned to the article. As he read, an idea formulated. He sauntered into Nick's office to toss it around.

Nick thought the idea not only had legs but perhaps an entire corporeal surrounding.

They called Gemma in and told her to write up a proposal for the Channel 5 slot they were pitching for.

Summer was proving a glorious addendum to the beautiful spring that had bathed the country in sunlight since April. Keera couldn't decide whether to take a copy of *GQ* or whether she could safely assume it was already in the office. She had spent hours on Monday afternoon, trying on various outfits for the next day. In the end, she had settled for tight white trousers, a black and white stripy V-neck top, black patent sandals and a white handbag with the black and white cover of *GQ* poking out of it. She stood in front of the mirror before she left. Yes. Elegant. Understated. She smiled at herself, then struck the sultry pose. Hmm. It really did need something. She pouted.

She looked good pouting. She'd practise sultry later. Now she needed to get to work and shine, shine, shine.

'Good morning,' she said graciously to the driver of her Mercedes as she stepped in.

'Good morning, Miss,' he said. 'The usual on the radio?'

'Yes, please,' she said, and he tuned in to Heart FM.

Keera turned on the car light, and started reading through her briefs. It was the usual mix – a wallow in the main news of the day and a few frivolous items, plus a showbiz or two.

She noticed that, despite her conversation the afternoon before, she hadn't got the big interview of the day. No doubt Mike's handiwork. She might need to have another word with The Boss. Not today, though. Wrong outfit for that. Oh, good. She was doing the item about men and trunks. Should they ever wear budgie smugglers? She had strong views on that. Absolutely not, unless the man's body was as fit as a weightlifter's snatch. No, that wasn't the right expression. Anyway, she thought William Baron would look good in them. He certainly looked good *out* of them. She smiled. Their relationship was going rather well. She'd been relieved when he'd told her that he'd never done the evil deed with Dee. It would have made the situation at work just that bit more difficult.

As it was, her entry into the newsroom was not greeted with the required fanfare of trumpets and laying down of cloaks.

The input editor nodded, and Richard, the news producer, said good morning rather distractedly. He was having a terrible time. One of the freelancers had just produced a VT that was almost unusable. And the other had gone AWOL. He now had two VTs that needed to be done, and he hadn't finished writing up the programme.

'There are some gaps in the show,' he said, swivelling his chair to speak to Keera, 'but generally it's all there. Let me know if there's anything confusing.'

'Will do,' she said, and logged on to the computer. 'Anything in the papers I need to know about?' she asked innocently.

'Don't think so,' replied Richard, equally innocently. They had been talking about it since the papers came in, and had a sweepstake on how long it would be before she mentioned it. He couldn't jeopardize his position. He was on two minutes and forty seconds from her entry at the newsroom door, and the clock was ticking. They were up to one minute thirty.

Keera wandered over to the newspapers and started flicking through them as she waited for her computer to boot up.

Bingo. Page three of the *Sun*. Along with the page three 'stunna' Nikki ('I think Arsenal will win the FA Cup this season'). She paused. Why had no one said anything about it?

She glanced up. Everyone was staring at her. She opened her mouth. Richard checked his watch. Two minutes thirty-five seconds. He'd won. He smiled.

Keera saw what he was doing, and felt confused. What was going on? She shut her mouth. Another ten seconds had gone.

The input editor looked surreptitiously at her watch. Excellent. If she won, she could take a taxi home instead of getting the tube.

Keera saw the movement. Something was up, but she couldn't put her finger on it. She took the *Sun* and went back to her desk. The input editor seemed disappointed. But a reporter on a computer at the end of the office perked up.

Keera couldn't hold off any longer.

'Erm,' she said, and stopped. A VT editor, who had been hovering, checked the big clock at the far end of the newsroom. Bingo. He'd won. Fifteen quid would come in very useful at the pub after his shift.

Keera had no idea what the hell was happening, but she had a vague feeling it was to do with her. And she wasn't going to fall into their trap. She read the piece. It was very complimentary. Talked about her cracking figure, the fact that thousands of men lusted after her, and here she was, finally giving them what they wanted. The headline was 'Morning Glory'.

She couldn't help herself. 'Anyone seen the *Sun* this morning?' she asked.

Keith, the cameraman who had been insouciantly flicking through a copy of *Lens and Microphone Nonsense for Spods*, adjusted his watch, looked smug and demanded the envelope. Richard handed it over. 'Don't spend it all at once,' he said sourly, and went back to his computer.

'What's all that about?' asked Keera, suspiciously.

'Nothing,' he replied. 'Anything a problem so far?'

'No. I've only just got into the programme.'

An hour later, she finished, and went to her emails. There was an ominous one from The Boss, asking her to see him. She bit her bottom lip. It could only be about two things. The worst-case scenario was that she'd been fingered for the leaks. It was unlikely, but she had her alibis ready. The second was the *GQ* cover: she hadn't exactly told him the full extent of the photo shoot. And she had perhaps gone rather further than she ought to have done during the interview. She honestly didn't remember saying half of it. But on the other hand she was sure there had been a number of racy questions, to which she had assented. The interviewer had been handsome and rather flirty, he had gone so gradually into the smutty talk that she hadn't noticed until it was too far along. Not that she regretted it in any way. Her publicity agent had told her that she'd have to 'do the business' or she wouldn't get the cover. It was as simple as that. But with hindsight she should have kept the fantasies out of it.

Hey, what was the worst that could happen? She would say sorry, get her knuckles rapped, and keep her head down for a bit.

She wished she'd worn a short skirt and a low top. Too late for that. She comforted herself that no one had ever been sacked from *Hello Britain!*, apart from Katie, and that was because she was too old and talked rubbish.

However, she went down to Makeup with the edge taken off her swagger. As she left, the noise quotient went up as three people brought out their copies of *GQ* for more of a fingering.

* * *

Bob had spent the weekend considering his options. He lay in bed watching television, in the absence of anything constructive to do. He had been listening to Radio 4's *Today* programme but had got bored as it went from one political interview to the next. He had quite enjoyed a very long-winded question from James Naughtie, which had elicited a one word response from the Chancellor. But that wasn't enough to keep him tuned in. He had turned the radio off and clicked on the television.

He had to confess that Keera Keethley was an exceptionally pretty girl. A bit thick, but nothing wrong with that. He flicked on to the BBC. Still dull. A report about a lack of youth centres. He used to love the youth centre, hanging out with his mates, an occasional game of pool. Snogging Teresa April round the back of the building, the first fumblings before he finally had his way with her. God, she was good. It had been months before he discovered that the love bites on her thighs were not self-inflicted, as she had claimed. They had come courtesy of Dave Marsh, a boxer from Leeds. He had been visiting his aunt, and copped off with Teresa – who, apparently, always put out. Bob had been so in love with Teresa April, but there was something offputting about a nymphomaniac. Did kissing everyone when you were drunk constitute nymphomania?

He reached for his mobile as Keera's lacy bra made a brief appearance on *Hello Britain!*

'Good morning, Harry. And how are we this fine Tuesday?'

'A bit hung-over. I've been given a rather nice commission, and we were celebrating. I think the port was off.'

'It so often is, I find.' Bob smiled. 'Are you still going to Kerry next weekend?'

'Certainly am. Are you going to come?'

'If I can get a flight, I will. Who would I be sharing with?'

'Choice of three at the moment. Me, Joe or Kevin.'

'Kevin? You have to be joking. He snores like a walrus. And Joe wheezes. But, then, you sleep-walk and scare the life out of me. It's a difficult decision. Do I have to make it now?'

'Nope. It's two hundred quid per person for hotel and activities. It doesn't matter whether you do all of them or none. Same deal. Saves all that nonsense about "Well, I only did half an hour's fishing and you did loads of golf." And it encourages us to get out of bed, no matter how rough we're feeling. There are nine of us at the moment, and we're all on the seven-thirty a.m. flight out of Stansted, if you can get on it.'

'I'll fire up the computer and see what I can do. Anything I need to bring?'

'Pepto-Bismol. Nurofen. Big pot of Vaseline?'

'Obviously,' said Bob, watching Mike sneer at something Keera had just said. 'It goes without saying. I'll speak to you later. 'Bye.'

Keera came off air feeling discomfited. She phoned her agent. 'This magazine article,' she began … 'They can't sack me, can they?'

'Of course not. It's brilliant publicity for them,' he said. 'Why?'

'Oh, something Mike said to me. But that's all right. I've got to go and see The Boss about it. At least, I assume that's what he wants to talk to me about.'

Dee, overhearing the conversation, hoped – vainly, as it turned out – that Keera would be ignominiously sacked, and that Katie would be triumphantly reinstated. Instead, Keera's prophecy came true. She was given the smallest of knuckle raps, barely bruising the skin, and promised not to do anything else without going through the press office. She kept her fingers crossed behind her back as she said that. It would be at least two months before the profile piece for *Cosmopolitan* came out. Time enough for her to play the finky-diddle with the men who held her future in their hands.

In a building not a million miles away from *Hello Britain!*, Gemma was putting the finishing touches to the programme proposal suggested by Adam. It was called: *Dare to Bare*. It was about stripping celebrities and was, tentatively, a three-part series. Her suggestion – and she thought this was genius – was that it would be hosted by a presenter or presenters who would take off more clothes each week. The last programme could be presented entirely in the nude, with strategically placed items, *à la Calendar Girls*. Or *The Simpsons, the Movie*.

After 'Presenter' she had put two names: Keera Keethley and Veronica Flade, a Rubensesque celebrity who had done a plastic-surgery series for them, and whom she knew Nick secretly fancied.

Could go either way, she smiled to herself, as she handed it to Adam.

CHAPTER TWENTY-TWO

Kerry was going to be the equivalent of the Gumball Rally for livers. All ten men were up for a weekend of debauchery, four in particular. Bob was nursing wounded pride and determined to get as hammered as possible as quickly as possible.

Harry was on a pink ticket from Sophie, and was determined to recapture life as a single man.

Kevin had just sold his bathroom business and was determined to celebrate.

Joe had been sacked from his job in the airline industry and was on a mission to forget. He wasn't so much determined as programmed to self-destruct by Sunday.

They were sharing two rooms, which they planned to see as little as humanly possible.

By the time they got off the plane, they had already had a few sharpeners, a few chasers and a couple for the road.

It was a handsome group that checked into the hotel. As the receptionist handed over to her night-shift replacement, she commented, 'There's something for everyone there. Shame I've got the in-laws down for the weekend.'

Harry, as team leader, reminded them that it was an early round of golf the next day. 'I could only get an eight o'clock game. They've got a stag party in.'

'How very unoriginal,' said Bob. 'Fancy having a stag party in Kerry. Who on earth would do anything so prosaic?'

'Bloody good fun, wasn't it?' smiled Harry. 'Anyway, I'm going for a quick walk. I've got leg-ache from sitting down so long. And it'll give me an appetite for the oysters and Guinness I'm planning on having in … ooh …' he consulted his watch '… two minutes. No. In all seriousness I'm walking down to the lake to see if I can spot the large trout I'm catching tomorrow afternoon, then going up the hill to see if I can get a signal.' He waved his mobile. 'See yez all later,' he said, in cod-Oirish.

Bob went with him. For ten minutes, they swung along companionably, not saying much.

'How's things?' asked Harry, eventually.

'Cool,' said Bob. 'Feeling better already.' He was actually thinking how lovely it would have been if it was Katie, not Harry, walking with him to the lake, the low sun throwing out its last dregs of gold and bestowing a satin sheen on the water. Right, he thought. This is pointless. She obviously doesn't care as much for me as I do for her. It's better this way. God, I'm sounding like shit dialogue in a crap rom-com film. I won't think about her again. I need to think about the hospice garden. Every time I think about Katie I'll think about the garden. Oh,

God. I can't stop thinking about her. This is hopeless. He groaned.

'What?' asked Harry.

'Sorry. Nothing. I may have left my nasal tweezers at home.'

Harry laughed. 'Yeah. Right. Obviously the first thing you put in your bag when you're going away for a weekend with your mates, followed by your best underpants, and your big book of knots.'

'Damn. Knew I'd forgotten something else. I've brought a gross of condoms and no book. What *can* I have been thinking?'

They continued the walk, and Bob tried to stay in the moment.

That evening, there were oysters, pies, chips and boiled potatoes.

Bob did a thoroughly good job of forgetting Katie for at least ten minutes at a time, due to the many pints of Guinness he consumed. 'Have you noticed,' he asked, in the last coherent sentence he spoke before slumping sideways, 'that everything we're eating and drinking is brown?'

'And the point is?' asked Kevin, checking whether he had any more money in his pockets. 'What we should be discussing is where we're going to find women.'

'You won't find them in there, unless they're very small ones,' said Joe, burping lightly.

'Why should you never shag a stupid dwarf?' asked Matt, a wiry actor who mostly did adverts for cheap sweets.

'Because it's not big. And it's not clever.'

'I had a small one, once,' said Harry. 'She was so tiny I called her Rumpelstiltskin.'

'Don't you mean Thumbelina?'

'Thumpelina? Was she a punch-bag?'

'Who?'

'Your little one.'

'Who are you saying's got a little one?'

And the evening wore on.

At one in the morning they started singing 'Danny Boy'. Nobody could remember any words beyond the pipes calling. Despite their early start the next morning, it was three before most of them made their way to their rooms, with much shushing and many admonitions to be quiet. And trouser-coughing. And belching.

Only one person didn't make it to breakfast.

'He thinks he ate a dodgy oyster,' said his roommate, to general guffawing.

Bob got to the third hole before pronouncing that golf was idiotic. 'What *is* the aim of this?' he asked. 'It's a game for people who've had their frontal lobes replaced with dingleberries from a sheep's bottom. I will meet you at the nineteenth hole, where I'll be testing pints and checking that the salty snacks are up to snuff.'

He stomped back up the hill. At the top, he turned. It was what the Irish called a soft day. He was in the lightest of clouds, which cast a translucent glow over the golf course. It muffled the sounds and moistened his face.

The nineteenth hole was a bit cold, and it was possibly too early to be having the hair of the dog, so Bob ordered coffee and took a newspaper from the table. He was just reading an article about the upcoming Puck Fair Festival in nearby Killorglin, when an attractive woman with dyed bright red hair, cut into a sharp bob, came in and ordered a pint of Murphy's.

He looked at his watch.

She saw him do so, and raised her eyebrows. 'Yes, I know.' She smiled. 'It is a bit early. But I'm a late arrival and the rest of my group appear to be nursing hangovers. I thought I'd try to catch up.'

Her voice was low, husky, a bit posh.

'Oh, I wasn't criticizing,' he said, taking in her outfit of black trousers, vest and a pair of boots so high they almost doubled her height. 'Bit overdressed for golf, though, perhaps?'

'Ha. Yes. I decided I'd do nothing but stand around decoratively for a couple of days, since the only options were this or fishing. And I'm not that keen on either. One involves standing around endlessly waiting for something to happen. And the other . . .'

'. . . involves standing around endlessly waiting for something to happen,' he finished.

'Exactly,' she said.

She looked at him sitting there with his paper and his coffee. And she liked what she saw. Handsome. Tousled blond hair. Good age. No wedding ring. 'Can I join you?' she asked.

'Please do,' he said, gesturing to the chair alongside him. 'I was only reading this until my mates finish their round of golf, which should be in – what? – about ...' he peered at his watch again '... three weeks.'

She laughed. 'Yes, it does seem to take for ever, doesn't it? I would have gone for a walk, but I appear to have forgotten to bring anything even remotely waterproof, seeing as I checked the weather and it's supposed to be sunny.'

'It's early still. You may get your walk later. I'm assuming you brought some other item of footwear – or were you planning on hiking up a mountain in those?' he asked.

She wriggled her toes in her boots. 'I bought them the other day,' she confided. 'Spent rather a lot of money on them, and thought they'd be lonely sitting at home on their own. They requested a weekend away. Very unsuitable, obviously, but I'm a marine biologist, so I spend most of my days up to my ears in rubber. And not in a sexy way,' she added, as she caught his smile. 'I'm here on a stag weekend. Yes. I know. Eighteen boys and me. I think the groom wanted to make sure nothing too terrible happened. I'm a friend of his wife and, apparently, I know more filthy jokes than anyone else in the world. And I can generally hold my drink. Having said that, because I'm a woman I'm allowed to have halves without being patronized. Everyone else came yesterday, and I flew over on the stupidly early plane this morning. Hence the lack of hangover, and the decision to have a pint of Murphy's. There's nothing quite like it.'

'Funnily enough, I'm over here with a bunch of guys who came over for a stag weekend years ago. There are ten of us. Where are you going tonight?'

'So you can avoid it?'

'Not necessarily. We can offer you support and encouragement.'

'Right. You mean drinking games, and activities that involve so much alcohol your swim bladders go. You can't help but feel sorry for the poor locals.'

'I think they invented most of them,' he responded.

He addressed himself to his coffee for a moment, then looked up into the deepest blue eyes he thought he had ever seen. She really was quite gorgeous.

'By the way, I'm Bob – Bob Hewlett.'

'Clare McMurray,' she said solemnly.

'Our stag weekend involved a sheep,' he said conversationally.

'Ah. Couldn't afford the stripper?'

'She was better-looking. One of the party was going to bring something called Barbara the inflatable love sheep. Another of the boys decided it lacked a certain finesse and bought a sheep from a local farmer. It accompanied us to dinner. Wore a nice bow-tie for the evening.'

'I see. A male sheep, then? Interesting. Did it have its hoofs buffed?'

'Naturally. To a high shine. And a blow-dry.'

'As long as that was all,' she said severely.

By the time the golfers started to arrive, Clare and Bob had been flirting for a couple of hours and had agreed to meet up later.

'Aye aye aye,' remarked Kevin, coming over with his Bloody Mary. 'I wondered why you cut short the game. Particularly when you were doing so well.'

'Yeah, right,' said Bob. 'Two balls in the thicket is enough for anyone. Don't you agree, Clare?'

'Abso-bloody-lutely.' She gave a firm nod. 'Two of your balls in the thicket and, frankly, you're scuppered.'

Introductions were made as a mixture of friends from both sides trickled into the bar, some trickling more than others, having rescued their balls from the water feature. Others were steaming gently as the sun had finally appeared.

By the time they were ready to peel off for an afternoon's fishing, there was general agreement that at some later stage a rendezvous would be essayed.

'Cracking bird,' said Harry to Bob, as they were leaving.

'Yes. Very nice. Fun. All of a sudden I'm rather looking forward to this evening.'

'Thanks,' said Harry, sarcastically.

'Oh, you know what I mean,' said Bob. 'It's good to have something decorative to look at as we while away the hours.'

'By the end of this evening, I was rather assuming we'd be seeing nothing but the bottoms of our glasses. But I agree. Always as well to make sure they look good *before* you get the beer goggles on. Don't want to wake up with a pig-scarer. Like that one – do you remember, when we were at uni? – when I chewed half my arm off to get away in case I woke her up? I couldn't believe she hadn't squashed me flat during the night. Enormous hairy feet and legs like a carthorse's.'

'Are you sure she was human?'

'Now I come to think about it, perhaps not. And she did wear a cloak. And, oh yes, she slept in a coffin. Are you coming fishing?'

'Yup.'

'And I bet you want to borrow my nasal tweezers, eh?'

'Of course. Do you want to borrow my big book of knots?'

'Why should I? I know them all. Sophie and I practise every night. The winter evenings fly by. And talk of the devil ...' said Harry, answering his mobile phone. 'Hi honey. How are you coping without me?' He listened as Sophie brought him up to date with news. 'Aaaah ...' he said, nodding at Bob. 'Is she? ... Well, I'll tell him, but we're rather tied up this evening so I think it's unlikely ... Yes, I am with him ... Speak to you later ... Love you. 'Bye.'

'What?'

'Apparently your true love is on the telly at eleven o'clock tonight. There's just been a promo on, saying she's a guest on some chat-show. Going to be talking about being dumped by breakfast television, etc., etc. You think she'll mention you?'

'Pah,' said Bob. 'Unlikely.'

Did he want to watch her? No. No. Thrice no. Unless he happened to be in bed by eleven. Which was always a distinct possibility. Suddenly he felt quite tired. But what was the point? No, he wouldn't give her the satisfaction.

Adam had had a massive row with Naomi. She was so late getting home that they'd missed the opera. 'If I'd known you weren't going to be back in time, I'd have gone on my own and sold the other bloody ticket,' he said belligerently.

'Well, why didn't you?' she'd countered, opening the fridge and taking out a packaged soya-bean salad.

'Because I'd have preferred to go with you. But your phone kept clicking on to voicemail so I kept waiting for you, hoping you were on your way, when instead, you were just pissing about. So we've wasted two tickets.'

'We could get there for the second half.'

'Second half? It's not like a bloody football match. And anyway,' he said, looking at the clock, 'we've probably missed that too. And you now appear to be having dinner. You've succeeded in completely ruining my evening. Thank you. Thank you *very* much.'

'It's not as though you can't afford an occasional opera ticket,' she responded, chewing frantically at a small piece of rocket.

'Actually, it's not about the money, as you well know. It's about your – your – your chaos. Your cavalier attitude towards time-keeping. Towards things. Towards me, now I come to think of it.'

He walked through to the sitting room, sat down on the sofa, then stood up again. He looked through to the kitchen. She was stunning. She was wearing the smallest dress he had seen outside Baby Gap. But ... but ... 'This isn't going to work,' he said brutally.

She inhaled a snow pea. 'What?'

'Us. I'm sorry, Naomi. It isn't.'

The ensuing row had gone on for hours. They had both been in tears. They had then had the best sex. And resumed the row after she had wiped her damp mascara on the white duvet. 'Not even the *corner* of the duvet,' he had shouted, after she demanded he stop tutting.

Eventually she had stuffed a random selection of clothes into a holdall and slammed out of the house 'to sleep on the street'.

Adam went back to the bed. Almost ripped off the dirty duvet cover. Threw the sheets and towels into the washing-machine. Opened a bottle of wine and tossed back half of the contents before recalling that he hated Fleurie and opening a bottle of Barolo. He finished that, then the Fleurie, and sat slumped in front of the television, unable to decide whether he would be happier if it was definitely over or happier if it wasn't.

On the plus side, no more mess.

On the minus, no more Naomi.

No more mess. Sounded like the name of a kitchen roll. 'Buy Nomoremess – does what it says on the packet.'

He flicked through the channels. Was *Scrubs* on every single night? He stopped to watch Katie Fisher talking about *Hello Britain!* She was looking fit. Shiny auburn hair. Shiny green eyes. He turned off the lamp. That was better. He looked closer.

Weird. There was a gap in the lashes of her right eye. He really should have bought a smaller screen: it was kind of offputting having a person's head twice as big as your own. Like how he imagined lab rats felt when the scientists were observing them. Only without the experiments.

Katie was animatedly telling a story, trying to make sure they got their money's worth. She was a last-minute booking because a tennis player had tested positive for cocaine and pulled out at the eleventh hour. '... I was always a bit late on to the set,' she was saying, 'but on this particular occasion I tripped over a cable, lost my shoe, twisted my ankle, then tried to hobble forward as the titles were going on. And Mike was co-hosting from Washington. So the camera cut up, and there was the sofa. No presenters. I looked like a right idiot, shuffling on, wincing. But that was – *is* – the lovely thing about *Hello Britain!* Not that it's encouraged *per se*, but that it's accepted it's very early in the morning and things happen, which are funny.'

Adam was finding her mouth rather fascinating.

Then a rather large celebrity came in to talk about his new travel show on BBC2. He told of how he had been sunbathing naked on his balcony in Spain before the first day's filming. Unfortunately he had locked himself out, and had had to take refuge under his sun-lounger. He had been there for five hours until the crew had returned. Various bits of him had burned to a crisp.

Adam went to open a bottle of Chablis and a bag of roasted onion and Cheddar crisps. He lay on the sofa, and some time between a programme about transvestites in Brazil, and a foreign film featuring much running about by a woman with plaits, he dropped off.

A few hours later, with a crick in his neck, he stretched, went back to the now beautifully clean bed and slipped between immaculate sheets where he had a dream about being a secret agent with a deadly thumb.

In a pub in a small town in Kerry, the stag-nighters and the former stag-nighters were starting on the shorts. The rounds were getting bigger. The bills were getting larger. The singing was unpleasant.

Bob the Builder had never been ruder, and if he had really had all the attributes assigned him, he would have been working in a strip joint in the gay section of Soho.

Clare McMurray had excelled herself with the harmonizing, and was snuggling up to Bob. Not that he was complaining. She stretched up to his ear, warm breath making his neck tingle, and asked why he wasn't married.

'Divorced.'

'And nobody since?'

'What do you take me for? But not married again. No.'

'Will you marry again?'

'Not if I can help it.'

'Why not?'

'What's the point?'

'Children?'

'Scroungers.'

'Don't be silly.'

'All they do is eat, poo and demand new clothes, until they're eighteen when they demand a car and a house.'

'You're just being provocative,' she said.

'A long word for this time of night and after so many drinks. Are you sure you're not pouring yours on to the carpet?'

She looked at it. 'You're right. I don't think you'd notice if I had been.'

'Anyway, as for being provocative, you must confess I do have a point. When they're little, they run around carrying their excrement with them. They grow up and say they hate you, despite all the effort you've put in. Then they have children and demand you look after them, just when you've taken down all the gates and finally got your DVD player working again. Dogs, on the other hand ...'

'I don't know,' whispered Clare, leaving warmth by his earlobes. 'I hear they're constantly on the phone booking massages at poodle parlours.'

Bob smiled and pulled back to look at her.

Her deep blue eyes smiled at him. He held her closer and moved forwards until his lips were touching hers. She didn't resist. Then, with a number of interested onlookers, he kissed her. It was a kiss that went on for quite some time.

And was repeated.

And repeated.

Until Clare excused herself to go to the loo.

She looked drunkenly in the mirror, closing one eye to see better. Whoops, my girl, she thought. She ran her hands through her hair, which had begun to give itself a centre parting, and splashed cold water over her face. Dried it with a hand towel. Washed her hands. Went to the loo. Washed her hands again. Dried them on her trousers. Bent over to wash the splash marks off her shoes. Almost fell over. Stood up. Noticed her hair had gone into a definite centre parting. Put water on it, and rubbed it with a hand towel. Left.

Bob, who had suffered an intense ragging, was relieved to see her and immediately made room for her to snuggle up to him.

'Mmm. Missed you,' he said. 'Why is your hair wet?'

'Needed a refresher.'

'Ah. Failed its A level, did it?'

'Yes,' she said, and gave him a searing kiss that resulted in a rush of blood to a part of his anatomy not unadjacent to her thigh. 'Is that a gun in your pocket ...?' she asked, as she came up for air.

'Or my inhaler,' he answered, with a frown.

That was the last coherent conversation they had, as the early-morning haze rose round the bar. A miasma of Guinness and pheromones. Vodka and body heat. Lust and peanuts.

CHAPTER TWENTY-THREE

On Monday there was perturbation at Wolf Days. They had been given the commission for the late-night chat-show on Channel 4, and everything was ready for the launch in two weeks' time. Only the presenter had pulled out: he had been told that his three BBC jobs would be in jeopardy if he insisted on doing it.

'I'm so sorry,' he had explained to Adam, 'but if the show isn't recommissioned after the first series my family will be out on the streets within a month. It's not as if my agent hadn't already run this past my bosses, but they've suddenly cut up rough about me having every Friday off for eight weeks.'

'Is there anything I can do?' asked Adam.

'Honestly? No. They've made it abundantly clear. And I daren't risk it. I can't apologize enough. I was so looking forward to a trip to Dorset every Friday, too. I am so, so sorry.'

Adam put the phone down. Damn. He'd had a shit weekend and now he was having a shit Monday. 'Nick,' he called down the corridor, 'we have a problem.' He sat back on his black-leather chair and doodled on his pad.

This thing was turning into a nightmare. It had seemed like such a good idea, using Nick's country house as a studio, with a lighting rig in the sitting room, and an OB shed in the garden. But they'd had to slash costs, down to £150,000 per show, and operate with a skeleton crew of twenty. Gemma and Rose had been drafted in to act as greeters/runners/floor managers, and everyone else was doing two jobs. 'And now we need a host.'

They sat gazing out of the window as a large black cloud moved centre stage in the sky and hovered like a bad omen.

'By the way, is everything at the house done?' asked Adam.

'Mmm. Rig's up. Shed appears to be almost finished. Looking forward to seeing how my accountant gets the mortgage payments through the system.'

The rain started.

'What a relief. That's the garden watered for another week,' said Nick.

Adam was watching the water trickling down the window. 'How about Katie Fisher?' he asked suddenly. 'She's available. She's a good interviewer. I saw her the other night, looking rather attractive for an old bird ...'

'And she'll be grateful,' finished Nick, 'and therefore cheap. Bingo. Brilliant idea, my man. We probably need to offer up a few more names, too, just in case.'

'We'll get Rose to pick some randomly from Spotlight Presenters,' said Adam, 'because I think Channel 4 will absolutely go for Katie Fisher. And while we're talking of *Hello Britain!* presenters, it was inspired of Gemma to suggest Keera for *Dare to Bare*. Guaranteed audience ratings ... if she can be persuaded to do it!'

When Jim Break took the phone call on Tuesday, he was thrilled and relieved. He'd get his five grand back – and he was genuinely pleased for Kate. He didn't think she'd turn down the offer, and he was right.

Katie was filling in a questionnaire to see whether she was clever enough to join Mensa and eating custard from a tin. When the phone rang she had one eye on an edition of *Friends* she'd seen before.

She put down the custard and threw the unfinished questionnaire (she was stuck on question two) on to the floor. 'I'm now leaping round the sitting room like a capering deer,' she said, in answer to the question as to whether she was interested. 'How brilliant. How wonderful. Thank you, *Hello Britain!*, for sacking me. Thank you, Wolf Days. Thank you, Channel 4. How much are they offering, incidentally? Should I stop capering?'

'It's not the biggest of offers. I'll try to get more, but I've a feeling they're not going to budge. They know you haven't got much else at the moment. And it does start in a fortnight. With your permission, I won't push too hard. You want the job, your own show, and it'll probably be lovely going down to Dorset on a Friday morning, or Thursday night. I'd suggest we do a reasonable deal now. And we can always get unreasonable if it goes into a second series.'

'Thank you. Thank you. Thank you. Thank you to whoever suggested me. Do we know how it happened? Do we care how it happened?'

'I think you should stop capering now. It sounds exhausting. You'll knock something over if you're not careful. Can you get to a meeting tomorrow, assuming we get the money side sorted?'

'Let me look through my packed programme of events,' said Katie, consulting an imaginary diary. 'Oh dear. Tomorrow I'm getting up and staring at the wall all day. What a shame I can't fit in a meeting.'

'Right. Do you mind if I give them your mobile number and you can deal with it from now on?'

'Yes, yes, oh, yessity, yes, I think you should and, yes, I can.'

'Now don't go celebrating in the Fisher Fashion, will you?' he admonished.

'Which means?'

'Which means don't go getting legless and ending up in a police cell.'

'How unkind. You shag one sheep ...'

'I'm sorry. I don't get that one. Is it one of your bad puns?'

'No, it's the joke about the bloke who's in the pub looking depressed. Other bloke comes in and says, "Why are you looking so miserable?" And the first bloke says, 'You know, all my life I've worked hard. I actually built the school you can see from this pub. But do they call me Jack the builder? No. I carved the clock on the church tower. But do they call me Jack the clock-carver? No, they don't. You shag *one* sheep ..."

'Hah,' he barked. 'If only you *had* stuck to *one* drink'. I'm going to get straight on to this. I'll give them your number so you can get your meeting organized. But, hopefully, I'll have glad tidings on the cash side by the end of play today.'

The negotiations were surprisingly swift, and at five p.m., a press release was winging its way to the nationals, revealing the new presenter of *Start the Weekend*. Katie phoned her parents.

'Well done,' said her dad. 'I knew it would all come good in the end. Here, speak to your mother. I'm at a crucial stage with the béchamel sauce.'

'What's for dinner?'

'Your mother will tell you. I really do have to go or it'll be all lumpy. Here she is.'

'Hello, Katie. I hear congratulations are in order.'

'I just wanted to say thanks to you both for putting up with me when I was going a bit, erm – a bit mad. I know it drove *you* mad. But I've learned my lesson on the drinking front. And on the photographer front too.'

'And the lesson is, always smile as you're falling over?' asked her mother acerbically.

'Of course. Will you come down to Dorset for the first show? You don't have to, but it would be really nice if you did. They're not having an audience as such because it's being filmed in a house –'

'A house?' interrupted her mother. 'They could have used ours. Your dad could have provided a steady stream of canapés.'

'Great idea, Mum,' laughed Katie. 'I'll suggest it if they do another. What's for dinner?'

'He told me, but I've forgotten,' whispered her mother. 'Don't make me ask again.'

'Fine. Well, will you come down?'

'I'll check with the chef, but I'm almost sure we could do that. A week this Saturday?'

'This Friday. I'm going down on Thursday to get the layout and see what's up. Actually, I'm suddenly feeling nervous.'

'You'll be fine. As long as you stay sober.'

'Mum,' said Katie, annoyed, 'I'm not permanently plastered. It was a phase I was going through because I didn't have a job. Let's not argue. Can you just check with Dad and try to come down? I know it's a schlep, but you could take the train to London and come with me in my car.'

'Have you bought one?'

'No. I'd have told you if I had. The car they send for me. It'll be a nice one. Dad can talk torque with the driver, while we open bottles of champagne in the back.'

'Katie!' said her mother, scandalized.

'I was joking,' said Katie, with a smile.

There was a gap, while they both responded to a shout from the kitchen.

'It's curdled, apparently,' said her mother.

'You don't want that on a Tuesday, do you? Erm ... have you seen anything of Bob?'

'Funnily enough, yes. Your dad saw him at the pub last night with Harry. They'd been away for the weekend somewhere in Ireland.'

'How did he seem?' asked Katie, mentally kicking herself for asking the question.

'Same as usual. He's a lovely man,' said her mother, deliberately.

'I know. And I can hear the criticism implied in that statement, Mum.'

'Oh, do stop taking a huff. But he is. He looked the same as he always does. He was wearing a blue shirt, if that helps. And he told me to come round and paint whenever I wanted. So I assume he's not holding a grudge.'

'Good,' said Katie, deciding that it literally hurt to talk about him. Or maybe she had indigestion.

'I'll talk to your father about that Saturday ...'

'Friday.'

'Friday. I've written it down. Is Ben coming too?'

'I haven't asked him yet, but I will. And I'm going to see if Dee can make it. You'll be a select group. Witnessing what may be my final ever appearance on British television.'

'Oh, stop it. It's like riding a bike. You'll be fine. Oh dear. Hercules has licked the steak. That dog. We should swap him for a hamster.'

'Remember what happened to the hamster ...'

'Who would have thought it could make such a mess of the skirting-board, eh?'

'Actually, I've just had a thought. If you come with me on Thursday, you'll have to overnight in Dorset. But whatever, I could definitely sort you a car. For free,' she hastened to add, knowing how careful her parents were on the money front. 'So it's up to you. 'Bye, Mum. Say 'bye to Dad for me. Hope dinner hasn't been ruined.'

Katie went out to the King's Road, sat in her favourite café with a slice of pecan pie and a pot of tea, and texted all her friends.

Dee was the first to phone back. 'Well done. Such good news. I'm so jealous. There's part of me that's so jealous I can barely speak. But bloody well done. And one in the eye to *Hello Britain!* Can I come and watch it go out?'

'I was going to ask you. Do you fancy it?'

'Is your brother coming down?'

'I'm about to ring him. Why?'

'Can he bring that nice proctologist down?'

'Oh, yes?' said Katie.

'Yes,' replied Dee. 'I did think he was rather, rather ...'

'So you *did* get it together that night at the comedy place?'

'No, we didn't get it together, as you so horribly put it. But we did have a moment. And I thought I might help the moment along. If possible. And you said he was single – and so am I, now that William Baron has been taken by that piece of work.'

'You wouldn't have wanted him. I watched him on the lifestyle strand. If he was chocolate, he'd eat himself. He and Keera are well suited. They can either get lost in their own vacuous thoughts or stare into each other's eyes and admire their reflections.'

'Changing the topic slightly. I hesitate to ask. But ... Bob?'

'Nothing. I assume it's over. I know it was my fault. But it wasn't *totally* my fault, I don't think. I know I should have told him earlier, but we were having such a good time and I didn't want to ruin it with a "discussion". It wasn't as though I'd shagged the other man. It's not the first time anyone's been caught out doing something they shouldn't after a few drinks, is it? And I bet he's done worse.'

'Men do tend to take the high ground on that, though.'

'Yeah. As I say, like they're all angels.'

'Anyway ... you could always text him about the show.'

'And say what? "I know you think I'm an unreliable drunken slapper ... Come to Dorset"?'

'I don't know, but I'm sure you could think of some way of putting it where it sounded all right. Sort of placatory and ...'

'Come-hitherish?'

'Yes. Placatory and come-hitherish.'

'At this instant, I cannot imagine any combination of words that would conjure that up. If they *do* occur to me, then maybe. If Ben could speak to him ... But he says he wants nothing to do with it.' She pulled out an eyelash, stuck it on the side of the table and admired its length.

'I've got to go,' said Dee. 'Ask Ben if he can bring Oliver, and maybe we can all go together.'

'OK. 'Bye.'

While she had been talking, the phone had beeped in a flotilla of nice texts. Mike had sent her one. There may have been a whiff of miff behind it – but that was the way with all presenters. Even if they were happy about someone getting a new job, there was always an element of 'It should have been me.' But, for now, Katie basked in the warmth of her return to the spotlight.

When Katie met Adam, it was lust at first sight. She was bang on time, which earned her major Brownie points, and was wearing a long black fitted dress, flat silver sandals, and a little grey cardigan. Her long auburn hair was newly washed, and she had put on just enough makeup to look as if she wasn't wearing any.

He wasn't to know that inside she was full of trepidation. She was wearing the black dress because it was the only thing that would stretch to fit her new ample curves. She couldn't believe how much weight you could put on if you mostly wore tracksuit bottoms and mostly ate out of tins.

But as she smiled at him and shook his hand, Adam only noticed that she oozed sex appeal, and decided he would definitely be very hands-on with this project. He offered her a cup of coffee, and left her in his office while he went to gather the relevant troops.

When they were assembled, and introductions had been made, he sketched in the outline of the show. 'It's one hour – so forty-seven minutes' actual time. Eight shows, as I think you know, going out from, erm, well, to be honest, Nick's house.'

Nick nodded at her. 'One of my many spare homes,' he joked.

'Yes,' Adam went on 'We've got an OB shed in the garden, and a lighting rig that will go up on Thursdays. It would be helpful if you could be there that evening, so we can check that it's all OK?' He raised his eyebrows.

'No problem,' said Katie, green eyes gazing straight at him.

'There'll be four cameras. Three in the "studio", as it were, one of which is roaming. I'm assuming you like open talkback?'

'Yup.'

'Never knew a breakfast-telly presenter who didn't. We'll be doing a tease some time between eight and ten p.m., then we're on air at eleven. Any questions so far?'

'Yes. Will there be any audience?'

'We weren't planning on it. Why?'

'Oh, just friends and family threatening to make an appearance.'

Adam looked at Nick enquiringly.

'I wouldn't have thought it was a problem,' said Nick. 'It might be quite nice to have an occasional camera pan past a collection of people. *À la Big Breakfast* when it started. We could try it on the first show, and continue it if we like the look of it.'

He wrote it down on his notepad.

'As for the guests, well, Gemma can take you through those who are confirmed. We're going to do a maximum of five pages research per guest. We want it to be loose chat, rather than going over the old stuff. So the research will be there for back-up more than anything else. How does that sound?'

'Fab.'

'And I'm sure every chat-show worth its salt tries to avoid the plugging element, but we're going to do it as obliquely as possible. Oh, and we're also going to have a couple of VTs, which are really short – say, two minutes max – which are going to be about anything from a man with a strange job, such as – Rose?'

'Such as a bloke who trims badger hair for shaving brushes.'

'Right. So from the man or woman with a strange job to the quickest way to put a duvet cover on.'

'There can't be that many options, can there?' asked Katie, aghast. 'Don't you open buttons, shove it in, and shake hard?'

'You'd have *thought* so,' replied Adam, mock serious, 'but you'd be wrong. Anyway, during the VT we'd get one guest off and another one in so that we go into each break promising more of the guest you've been talking to *and* teasing up the next one.'

Katie was in her element. She nodded, commented, flirted and charmed everyone. None more so than Nick, who generally went for very slim girls but was suddenly as keen as Adam to get very involved with this project.

As the meeting concluded, Adam asked her a final time if she had any more questions. 'Yes. I was wondering – that is, if it hasn't been organized already – if I could have any input on the guests. It's just that I'd quite like to get Mike in, at some stage. Mike Dyson, from *Hello Britain!* He's been very supportive, and I know he's got a new show starting.'

When she hadn't got the job co-hosting the new show with him, she'd felt as if she'd been hit with a pillowcase full of bricks. But now she could afford to be generous. He'd tried to get her the gig *and* he'd been locked in meetings with the bosses at *Hello Britain!* to try to stop them sacking her. She'd like to repay the favour by having him on her new show.

Nick, who was now convinced that she was flirting *only* with him, and would have granted her first dibs on his prized collection of Dinky toys, was hardly going to deny her this. 'You know,' he said, pondering, 'I rather like the idea of having him on the first programme. You can have a go at your former employer … if you want to, obviously. And he can defend it. Make for a spirited interview. What do you think, Adam?'

Hours later, as Katie was heading to a wine bar for a drink with Andi, Mike's alleged mate at the Vice Squad was putting together a collection of people to be investigated during a clamp-down on prostitution in an area of north London that was becoming known for its abuse of illegal immigrants. A number of Chinese and Nepali girls had recently been freed from a brothel. And a number of high-profile people appeared to have visited the area. The detective had had no response to repeated requests for a meeting with Keera. He resigned himself to the fact that Mike no longer thought he was important. His cursor was blinking ... he did a right-hand click on the mouse.

CHAPTER TWENTY-FOUR

The day before the first programme, Katie headed down to Dorset. That morning, the mail had contained an official-looking envelope. She'd opened it after bracing herself with a strong cup of tea and a prayer to the goddess of small things. A letter from the Crown Prosecution Service saying that she would not be facing a court appearance. Skipping round the kitchen, she sent a text to everyone on her phone, including (accidentally) the woman who waxed her legs and a hotel in Paris.

Katie was excited and scared in equal measure, with a dash of indigestion and a *soupçon* of desperation for a bracing snifter of whisky.

Do something that frightens you every day, she thought. Was that something she had seen on an advert? Or a poem. That would make her sound more intelligent. She wouldn't mention it to anyone today just in case it was a naff ad. And how could you keep finding things to frighten you every day?

Surely there would come a point when you were too exhausted from being scared to be scared any more. It must have been an advert. No one sensible would tell you to be scared every day. It was too horrible to contemplate. Even a week of it – and not counting hideous things like facing a gang with flick-knives and guns. First day, sky-diving without lipstick. Second day, potholing in a lemon boiler suit. Third day, wrestling a grizzly bear immediately after a manicure. Fourth day ... would have to be walking over Niagara Falls on a tightrope in your favourite Gina shoes. Fifth day? Going to the bottom of the Philippine Trench in a submarine without access to a mobile phone. Sixth day ... base jumping off the Empire State Building with mismatched earrings. Sunday, live television before you've lost weight.

'Could you turn up the radio a bit, please?' she asked the driver. Anything to stop her brain running round in her skull, trying to upset her equilibrium. Equi-librium. Isn't Librium what you take when you're schizophrenic? Oh, no, that's lithium. Oh *no*. Don't tell me my brain's going to do this tomorrow. Please don't, she begged it. But her brain was on the Big One at Blackpool Pleasure Beach. It was refusing to stop even though she wanted to get off. It swooped round the corner and plunged down into a rambling concatenation that made her so hot and dizzy she had to ask the driver to pull into a service station so that she could have a walkabout.

'Sorry,' she said, as she got back into the car. 'Ridiculous at my age to still be getting car sick. Can I sit in the front, please?'

For the rest of the trip she talked to the driver about his history degree and whether history could ever be entirely accurate, what with one person's truth being inconsistent with another's.

Nick and Adam were at the house to greet her. They were being uncharacteristically quiet on the subject of Katie Fisher. Nick had expressed an interest in rather crude terms. Adam had felt a resentful surge of jealousy – stupid when he considered that his relationship with Naomi was fresh in its grave.

They had confined themselves to a conversation about the colours she should wear that would go best with the set, and the last-minute technical stuff. It looked a bit of a mess at the moment, with cables all over the shop, and men with tool-belts, but they had been assured it would be fine for the run-through, scheduled for six o'clock.

Katie uncurled herself from her snail-like position in the front of the car and smiled up at Adam as he came forward.

Nick scowled slightly.

'Problems?' enquired Katie.

'No,' said Nick, shaking his head.

'Oh ... I thought – but – so – erm, everything ready?'

'We're on schedule,' said Adam, leading the way into the building. 'Welcome to Nick's home.'

'Hey, I can do my own introductions,' laughed Nick. 'Mind your feet, there are cables everywhere. This is where you're going to be doing the best late-night show on television,' he said, with a flourish, as he opened the door to the sitting room.

It was beautiful. A vast white and bleached-wood space, with double doors to one side, and french windows on to a sweeping lawn on the other.

'My goodness. Did you win the lottery?' exclaimed Katie.

Nick smiled smugly. 'I was lucky with the property market. Flukily bought and sold homes at the right time. The rest of it was down to a lot of hard work. Obviously.'

'Obviously,' said Katie, gravely, walking over to the hessian-coloured suede sofa. She could never resist a furry fabric. She bent over to stroke it – and two sets of eyes flew to her peachy bottom.

Adam was thinking of a DVD he had watched recently.

Nick was thinking thoughts that would have done an eleven-year-old boy proud.

'Very nice,' said Katie, turning – and echoing their thoughts.

'You'd be sitting there,' Nick pointed, 'with your guests on your right. They would be waiting over there in our "green room"' – he waved at the double doors. 'It's a sort of den/snug area, call it what you will. It means they can talk and chink glasses, et cetera, without being heard too much. Hopefully they won't be heard at all, but even if something does filter through it shouldn't be a problem. Now. Your friends and family. We were thinking they could park themselves around here,' he said, gesturing towards a small collection of chairs and a table in front of an enormous painting of an ant's head.

'We could reconfigure it, of course,' added Adam, walking over to the table, 'so that the chairs are more angled towards you. And there are some fluffy lambskin carpets upstairs that we could drag down for the more limber to sit on – and to muffle the sound of scraping chairs. We were maybe thinking that if we need them to, they could be doing something like playing cards or whatever so that they're not just staring into the camera. Or at you. Or whatever.'

'You mean, like they're really uninterested in what's going on?' asked Katie.

'Hmm. Sends the wrong signal, you think? We were a bit tired when we came up with that. We'll work on it. Maybe have one of them bring you a cup of tea as we go into the break. And as we come out of the break, taking the cup and saucer away. You do have a cup and saucer, not just a mug rack, Nick?'

'Mug rack,' said Nick, scathingly. 'You're so eighties. Yes, as it happens, I have some bone-china cups and saucers which my mother bought me for my first wedding.'

'How many others have there been?' asked Katie, interestedly.

'I don't know why I said first. I meant my only wedding. Once wedded.' Then he added quickly, 'And once de-wedded. And nothing serious since.'

Adam looked at him quizzically.

'Anyway, the point is,' Nick said, 'that we can have them featured or not. It'll also depend on whether they *want* to be in shot, of course.'

'I'll tell my dad to wear his pink dress, then,' said Katie.

'If he *wants* to be seen in shot,' Adam reiterated.

'Yes, of course. It's his favourite.' She noticed them exchange-ing a glance. 'He doesn't *really* wear a dress.' She smiled.

'What a shame,' said Nick, with an edge of relief. 'Now, you won't want to be given a whole lot of names you're going to forget by tomorrow, but I know the director would love to meet you,' he said. 'Have you ever worked with Nat Walters? He's fantastic on live programmes, very cool under pressure, and a soothing voice in the ear when all around is collapsing.'

Katie was taken through to the garden.

'Welcome to the OB shed,' he said, opening the door to a larger version of a Wendy house. A bear of a man was talking to a younger man wearing the regulation jeans and T-shirt, and pressing the buttons on the mixing desk.

'Can I introduce Katie to you?' asked Nick. 'Katie, this is the director, Nat, and Rob, the TD.'

The technical director smiled at her. Katie hadn't felt so ex-cited since her first day at *Hello Britain!* She hoped she wouldn't be as rubbish as she had been then. She had forced herself to watch the tape at the end of her first week. In her pink jacket she had resembled an overfed salmon. She had lurched from one link to the next, like a rabbit in the headlights. Thank goodness the regime at the time had been generous and understanding.

She was taken round the house, and told what was going to go where, and the back-up plans for the inevitable hitches.

'What do you think?' asked Nick.

'Brilliant,' said Katie, enthusiastically. 'Hopefully, it'll be a ratings winner and we can all go and buy houses like this. Eh, Adam?'

He put his hand on the small of her back to guide her to the banisters, and neither was displeased with the contact. Although Nick was.

'We've booked a local restaurant where they do particularly fine fish, if you fancy that?' Adam said. 'We thought we'd take Nat, Gemma and the head cameraman, Darryl. If that's all right with you?'

Katie thought for a minute. 'Well, I was planning on going to an all-night sprat-counting contest in Poole but hey, what the hell? There'll be others. Lead on, Macduff.'

On Friday morning, Bob woke up and, for a minute, forgot that he had been thinking about something when he went to bed that had made it quite difficult to sleep. Then he remembered.

He flicked on *Hello Britain!* as a bit of distraction. A grey politician was droning on about taxes. He wasn't in the mood. He turned to the BBC. A grey man in a grey suit droning on about taxis. He pressed the programme button and went through about twenty channels before landing on Challenge. He watched a man with an unfeasibly large head ask questions of four celebrities he wouldn't have recognized even with their names written across their chests. He answered some of the questions out loud. Two hours later, he was on the verge of watching a programme on one of the terrestrial channels, featuring people shouting at each other about who had slept with whose mother. It really was time he got up. He pressed the off button and lay there for half an hour staring at the ceiling and thinking.

His drunken evening with Clare had made him feel essentially grubby. He'd had too much Guinness to do anything. Their morning parting had been slightly embarrassing, as they'd rushed to apologize for their behaviour.

'I don't normally do this sort of thing,' they'd both said, almost simultaneously.

They'd swapped numbers, but both felt it was unlikely they'd see each other again.

He turned the television off and sent a text.

In Dorset, Katie lay in her hotel bedroom watching *Hello Britain!* She wasn't surprised that the ratings were so high. It was very entertaining. Now that she had her own show, she was forced to admit that Keera had a certain naïve charm. Her questions were truly appalling, and some of the guests were completely discomfited. And although she knew Mike found her a trial, it was fun seeing his expressions, and wondering how he was going to extricate the programme from the madness.

Mike had sent her a sweet message, saying he was looking forward to coming on the show. 'Break a leg, and all that.'

Secretly, he was furious. Ever since the moment when he had silently slid the knife into Katie's career, he had found it difficult to appear normal with her. He had taken as many precautions as possible to ensure that she would never find out about his act of betrayal. But there was always the outside chance …

And he felt he had done it for the best possible motives. He'd thought she was getting too big for her boots and trying to dominate the show in a way that undermined the natural order. Men were designed to be top dog. He needed a new partner. And silly little Keera had been the obvious solution.

A quiet drink with the editor, and the plot was hatched. He had started a whispering campaign and there'd been orchestrated phone calls, emails and letters sent to the right people. No one – he felt relatively secure in this – no one could have known that there even *was* a plot and that he was in the thick of it.

But could he, in all honesty, sit opposite Katie Fisher, knowing himself the architect of her downfall … and pretend?

And, what was worse, pretend to be thrilled that she had a new, possibly more high-profile job?

He had phoned his agent before he agreed to the request.

His agent had been confused: 'Why would you *not* want to do her programme? It'll be great for you because it's late night. It'll get good ratings because viewers will tune in in their millions to see how the fallen heroine manages to extricate herself from the ashes. And you can promote your new show. I repeat, why would you say no?'

'I hate to sound like a prima donna,' he said, without a hint of irony, 'but don't you think it'll look like I haven't done as well as she has?'

'It's up to you,' said his agent, 'but I think it would do you a lot of good to be seen on it. And Wolf Days are a good production company. It would be as well to get in with them. And it's a different audience, which is no bad thing. You'll have a laugh.'

'Ha-bloody-ha.'

'Don't do it, then.'

'How much are they paying?'

'Above average. A grand. You get a car there and back – obviously. And they're offering a hotel room if you want to stay.'

Mike thought of Sandra. Last night they had gone to yet another charity do. Her red dress was so tight and low it was like he was seeing a clothed X-ray. The diamond necklace he had bought her early on in their relationship, when he had found her boyish figure exciting, hung straight down with no flesh to hinder it. 'Fine. Tell them I'll do it – and I *will* stay overnight.'

Katie had spoken to him as soon as she had found out he was coming down. 'Thank you *so* much, Mike. It'll be great. We can catch up on the goss. And we're all going out afterwards to celebrate – or commiserate. I'm sure you can join us. If you fancy it,' she added anxiously.

'That would be great,' he answered, digging a fingernail into his palm.

The other two guests were an actress from a major American drama series about to be shown every night on Channel 4, and the male author of one of the bestsellers of the year, who was reputed to be a serious goat.

Katie had written out a staggering number of questions, which she whittled down to ten for each guest. Adam and Nick had stressed that they wanted the interviews to be fun. 'We don't want them confrontational. If they don't want to talk about a certain subject, let's keep off it. Unless it's the elephant in the room. In which case mention the elephant on your way to another area of the room, as it were. We're hoping for more on the lighter side. Someone telling us about their collection of cat furballs, rather than how much therapy or coke they've had. Most of the people we've got lined up will be fine. We haven't got any weirdos that we can see. Talking of which, if anyone's had obvious facial surgery, let's not get bogged down in whether they have or haven't. Obviously, if they appear to be speaking out of their hips, not their lips, you'll have to say something.'

'Even if *they* can't.' Nick laughed.

Adam continued, 'Rose and Gemma are good producers. They'll check on minefields, topics to be avoided, et cetera.'

Katie was feeling so positive she hoped she'd only need her questions as back-up.

Mike got into his car, having packed an overnight case with a couple of alternative outfits for the show – and a couple of alternative outfits for his possible late-night entertainment – and set off down the M3. He inserted a CD of Abba hits and was singing away in what he felt was a pleasing baritone, when he realized that the police car behind him with its blue lights flashing, was actually stopping *him*.

He pulled over, annoyed. He'd only been doing 80 mph. This was *definitely* going to be a rant on his radio show.

The demonization of the motorist.

Some yobbo gets injured burgling a house and gets away with it because the homeowner hasn't thought to provide a trampoline under the bedroom window. But a motorist gets penalized at every turn.

He got out of the car and waited as the policeman approached him.

Mike smiled at him. 'Good evening, officer,' he said, ingratiatingly. 'I hope this is just to ask me for my autograph.'

In Dorset, the morning flew by, with checks for sound, lighting, wardrobe and constant phone interruptions from Katie's friends and relations.

Dee was thrilled that Ben was bringing Oliver, and was gushing all over the phone.

Ben was annoyed that he was to be a gooseberry.

Her mother and father were driving themselves and having disputes about the best way to get to Dorset.

And then she got a text from Bob: 'Good luck for tonight. I'll be thinking of you. Bobx'

Katie read the message near the garden OB shed and smiled.

Did that mean ...?

Could she hope ...?

Should she reply ...?

Who should she phone for advice ...?

She checked her watch. Noon. Yes, she had time.

Not Dee. Rubbish on the boyfriend front.

Not Ben. He would tell her off again.

She phoned Andi.

Fifteen minutes later, with a hot ear, she considered the two suggested options. She jotted a few words on a spare piece of paper.

Apology.

Lovely to see you.

Miss you ?????

She phoned Bob.

Just when she was sure it was going to voicemail, he picked up.

'Hello, it's Katie,' she said shyly.

'Yes. I know. How are you feeling?'

'Excited. Trepidatious. How are you?'

'Fine.'

'Erm . . . you know, I'm sorry, truly sorry, about that thing.'

'Ah,' he said. 'That thing. Yes. But is this a conversation you want to be having with your show hanging over you, metaphorically speaking?'

'Possibly not. Are you busy tonight?' she blurted out.

'Going to the cinema.'

'Oh, right. And then watching the show?' she asked hesitantly.

'Possibly.'

'I was going to ask if you wanted to come down. But it's a bit stupid, really,' she rushed on. 'I mean, it's in Dorset and you're in Yorkshire. Which almost couldn't be further. But you could make a weekend of it? Although it's a bit late now. And I would have asked you earlier if I'd known you were speaking to me again. And I am *so* sorry. So very sorry …' A lump rose in her throat. To hear his voice was making her feel weepy.

'As you say, it's a long way,' he said. 'I'll speak to you after the show. I've got to go now. I've got to sort everything out before my friend arrives.'

'Harry?'

'No, not Harry.'

She heard herself ask the next question, even though she knew the answer might hurt like hell. 'Male friend?'

'No. Girl.'

There was the sound of thick air.

'Good luck for tonight,' he said. ''Bye.'

His girlfriend. She felt as if all the air had been sucked out of her lungs.

His girlfriend.

Of course he had a girlfriend.

He was gorgeous.

Why wouldn't he have a girlfriend?

But, oh, no … a girl who was going to be wrapped round his golden loins. She sat looking out of the window with glassy eyes. Why had she rung him? Why? How bloody ridiculous. On the day of the first show. How to do a programme when you're dying inside, by Katie Fisher.

Adam came in to find her gazing morosely into the middle distance. 'Do you fancy anything to eat?' he asked, then looked closer. 'Are you all right?'

'Yes. Yes,' she replied hurriedly, sniffing . 'Phone call I should-n't have made.' She took a punt on his being understanding. 'Ex-boyfriend.'

Adam was relieved. Ex-boyfriend. That was good. She hadn't been very forthcoming when he'd probed that subject earlier. An ex was good. 'We could go for a walk to the pub, if you want? There are sandwiches and snacks here for the crew. But if you want a breath of fresh air . . .'

They strolled along the street, Adam thinking lascivious thoughts, Katie thinking that it was odd how even in the depths of lost love (was it love? or thwarted lust?) she could still have enough energy to find Adam sexy and keep thinking acciden-tally about him naked.

The pub was exactly as a country pub should be. Low beams. Gleaming wood bar with a selection of local ales and cider on tap. She thought about the outfit she was wearing for the programme. It wouldn't do to look too bloated. 'I'll have a pint of Badger, please,' she said.

After half an hour of serious flirting with Adam, she felt much better. If not in high spirits, then a seventeen per cent fortified wine.

* * *

From then on, they were tearing up the pea patch. A sense of controlled panic gripped them as time rushed on. And at seven o'clock, as a lull had stepped gently through the doors, an enormous hiatus burst in with muddy feet.

Or, rather, Gemma rushed in, shouting, 'Mike Dyson's been arrested. His agent phoned. What are we going to do for a guest? Where's Rose?'

'Rose! Rose!' she shouted, running out into the garden.

'Been arrested for what?' asked Katie, appalled.

'Something to do with kerb-crawling, sex things. Don't know yet,' Gemma flung over her shoulder.

A meeting was hastily convened as the details emerged. Mike had apparently been arrested in his car as he travelled to Dorset. What they didn't know yet was that he had foolishly put some of his kit in the boot in case the opportunity arose to do a little late-night perusing. And that the police were, at that very instant, viewing a collection of gimp masks, whips, handcuffs, restrainers and condoms. And that Mike was contemplating the end of his career.

Katie couldn't believe it. That Mike had murdered someone, maybe, but sex? No! She'd always thought he was incredibly straight. If anything she'd sometimes thought he wasn't interested in sex at all.

Nick's house was turning into an Escher etching, with people rushing up and down stairs as the hour drew nearer for the broadcast. Gemma and Rose were on their mobiles, trying to get a stand-in. They kept looking at their watches in a hunted manner.

'How come the hands go round so bleeding fast when there's no time?' asked Rose, of no one in particular.

Katie had already given them several home and mobile numbers to ring but it was Friday evening. And they were in Dorset.

'I knew there was a reason why people didn't do this sort of thing from their own homes,' said Adam, stomping upstairs to find Nat.

Everyone who wasn't running was on their mobile phone, trying to get a stand-in guest.

Gemma and Rose were co-ordinating.

Nick found Katie as she was going over her notes to tell her about their contingency plan. 'We've got some standby VTs. We'll probably have to use one and expand the other interviews. Maybe even ask viewers for comments and read out any good ones. We'll busk it, if that's OK with you?'

'Very *Hello Britain!*,' she responded. 'Nothing I like better than being on the hoof.'

He smiled at her, his eyes crinkling attractively at the edges. He really was a very handsome man, she thought. He and Adam were like the princes in the fairy stories she had been obsessed with as a child. Was one an evil prince, who, if chosen, would turn into a frog on the wedding night?

What *was* she on? She gave herself a mental shake, rattle and roll.

Half an hour later Ben arrived in a huff, with Dee and Oliver in the first throes of fizzing physicality. 'I can't believe it,' he told

Katie, giving her a hug. 'They've talked non-stop all the way from London. God save me from the early days of anyone else's tedious nascent romance.'

'You've loved every minute of it,' joshed Oliver, holding Dee's hand.

'Yeah. It's been the most scintillating evening he's ever had,' said Dee.

'You look very good,' Katie told her brother, plucking at his shirt. 'Is that a Paul Smith blouse I see before me?'

'Maybe. How's it going?'

'Weeeell ...' she said, and told him the news. 'We're going to try to watch it on the ten o'clock, if we're sorted by then. It's a bit chaotic at the moment.' She showed them the green room, and got them beers.

Her parents were next to turn up, swiftly followed by Kathy and Carina.

Katie raised her voice over the hubbub. 'Can I leave you all here while I go and get changed? And don't wreck anything. This is Nick's house, and he's rather attractive. I know that's got nothing to do with the price of fish. But don't. And, Dad, no looking at the books. And, now I come to think of it, hands off Nick *and* Adam, Kathy. They're both mine.'

And she left the room, blushing slightly as she passed Nick and Adam, who were having a conversation on the stairs. Had they heard? How much did she care? She smiled as she disappeared into the bedroom she had been assigned as a dressing room.

Twenty minutes later she was dressed, and the makeup artist was doing her face, as the newscaster on television revealed the details of Operation X, the Met's crackdown on prostitution, brothels and illegal immigrants. 'Mike won't like that picture of him,' she commented, as a photo of *Hello Britain!*'s main presenter flashed up, showing him with what looked like a squint.

'They always choose the horrible ones for those stories,' said the makeup artist, dabbing face powder under Katie's eyes.

Adam came in as she was fixing her hair. 'Gemma's managed to get a comedian to replace Mike. He's filming a series down here in Bournemouth. We were supposed to have him on the show in a few weeks when he's finished, but he's agreed to get on a fast bike. He'll be on last so he has time to sit down, chill out and get rid of his helmet head. Gemma'll brief you in a minute. But he's a dream to interview. Wind him up and let him go. Very entertaining. See you in a minute for the tease. You all right?'

'Spiffing.'

Bob's view of life, love, the universe and everything had been changed by his weekend in Kerry.

On the flight home, he had had a long conversation with Harry. Harry was a more forgiving animal than Bob. He thought that women should be forgiven everything except running off with your best mate. 'And it means they have to forgive us all our sins. I do enjoy having the upper hand, don't you? I know you think kissing's tantamount to a betrayal, but women don't see it that way. You and me, we take it as a green light to having sex. I once kissed a woman for months before she confessed she didn't fancy me enough to have sex with me. I found it incomprehensible. But there you are …'

'And, of course, I no longer have the upper hand, anyway,' said Bob. 'Even claiming that I am technically single. I have virtually done exactly the same thing as Katie. Does that make me as bad as her? Or less bad?'

'Questions only you can answer,' replied Harry. 'I think I may have to have a beer.'

After Katie had phoned Bob, he had got straight on to Sophie. 'Sorry, I don't think I can be your escort this evening,' he said. 'I have an appointment in Dorset.'

Sophie was thrilled. 'Harry and I'll get the address of the place, and all the roads you need to take. And maps. And things. Do you need any food?'

'No, thanks. I'll manage,' he said, then spent an inordinate amount of time trying on all his T-shirts and shirts, so he was barely ready when Harry, Sophie and Elizabeth arrived with a selection of photocopied maps and a hair product that Sophie guaranteed would get rid of helmet hair and make him smell lovely.

'And will it guarantee I get the girl?' he asked, smiling at her. She sighed.

'What?' asked Harry and Bob, simultaneously.

'It's *sooooo* romantic,' she said, in a girly voice. 'It's like *An Officer and a Gentleman*.'

'With a landscape gardener instead,' said Bob, pulling on his biker boots. 'And let's face it, *A Gardener and a Gentleman* sounds more like *Being There*.'

'Well,' said Harry, rescuing Elizabeth from Caligula the cat's food bowl, 'you've got bags of time to work on your impenetrable pronouncements.'

Bob and Sophie looked impressed.

'Not a sentence you want to be saying after a bottle of whisky,' said Bob, doing a final check. 'Can I trust you to feed the cat tomorrow and Sunday if, by any chance, I should not be here?'

Elizabeth answered for them. 'Of courth we will,' she said, pulling Caligula towards her by his tail as his claws clung vainly to his basket.

Bob had broken a number of speed limits to get to Dorset. He had made it just as Katie went on air.

Gemma had seen him roar up, and had thought, for a moment, he was Mike's stand-in, the comedian.

When he took off his helmet, she suddenly wished she'd done a better job on her own hair and makeup.

He had introduced himself, then been taken to a bedroom to get rid of his motorbike kit, and swiftly apply Sophie's magic hair wax.

He nodded in the mirror. 'Well done, Sophie,' he said, making a final check of his teeth.

Gemma came to find him. 'Are you all right?' she asked.

'Fine. Can I stay up here and watch the show go out on this enormous television?' he asked, nodding at the vast screen opposite the bed.

'Probably. I'll go and check if it would interfere with the broadcast – but I'm sure it'll be OK, as long as you keep the volume down. Do you not want to sit with everyone else to watch it go out?'

'Do you mind if I don't? I want to be a surprise.'

Gemma thought he was so gorgeous he could do whatever the hell he liked. She wouldn't stop him. Bloody shame he was taken, as she said to Rose when she went into the OB shed to ask about the television in the bedroom being on.

The show was a triumph.

Katie had been witty and engaging – as had her guests.

Nick and Adam couldn't have been happier as the closing credits rolled, and the director thanked everyone.

Katie stood up from the sofa, unclipped her microphone and took out her earpiece.

Adam and Nick were there immediately – doing their best not to betray their burgeoning interest in their star.

'Well done,' said Adam, giving her a big hug.

'Ditto,' smiled Nick, giving her a slightly overlong hug with one hand pressed into the small of her back.

Katie didn't miss the signals.

Life was suddenly full of possibilities.

She turned to thank everyone, and then saw Bob. He smiled at her, and she melted. 'Hello,' she said. 'I thought you were going to the cinema with your girlfriend.'

'My friend who's a girl,' he said, his blue eyes gazing solemnly into her sparkling green ones. 'You look beautiful.'

'You're not so bad yourself.'

'How was the show?'

'Fine.'

'How do you feel?'

She looked at him steadily. 'I feel a lot better now you're here,' she said, and turned to speak briefly to the two men who had helped save her from a life of meaningless questionnaires and tins of rice pudding.

She'd be sorting out the sleeping arrangements later.